EVENTUALLY EVERYTHING CONNECTS.
-CHARLES EAMES

ISBN: 978-1-956764-06-2

Cover Design by The Pretty Little Design Co.

Editing by Fairest Reviews and Editing Service

Proofreading by Rumi Khan

For those who believe in fate.

PROLOGUE

FOURTEEN YEARS OLD

From the moment I was born, I was destined to be alone. Found behind a dumpster in an alley at the backside of a bar. My birth mom left me there only hours after having me. From what I've heard, the owner of the bar found me wrapped in a dingy towel covered in blood, with my umbilical cord still intact.

I was told I didn't even cry. Just looked up at the bearded fella and stared at him as if I knew my battle against the world had begun. At least, that's what I took from the story.

I was a loner through and through. Didn't care to please anyone. Never tried.

Until I met her.

Isabella, or Bella as we all call her. She's the only reason I ever smile unless I'm getting kicks for screwing with someone. That can be pretty fun. More so than not, my smiles are accredited to her.

She's my best friend, my only friend. The only one I need or even want.

Which is exactly why I need to repay her for all the smiles she's given me. Tomorrow we're getting adopted together and our lives are about to begin. Public schools, dances, sports—we're doing it all—together.

Layla, one of the foster girls here, pops her head in the door of my bedroom as I slip on my hoodie. "Where ya going?"

I grab my coat off my bed pole and throw it on. "Gotta take care of something. Cover for me if the old hag comes looking for me?" I give her a pat on the back and leave my room before she even has a chance to respond.

Looking right then left, I make sure the coast is clear before jogging down the staircase and out the front door. The sun hasn't risen, but the streetlamps give enough light for me to see where I'm going.

There's about a foot of snow and my sneakers sink right into it, filling my socks with the cold shit. I don't stop hurdling over the mounds until my back is pressed against the siding of the Beckhams' house. They should all be at evening mass, but regardless, I hold my breath to make sure I don't hear anyone walking around inside.

When I'm sure it's safe to enter, I go to pull open the door beside me to the garage, but it's locked.

A locked door isn't stopping me from getting inside. I round the house and try to push up the living room window. It sticks from the ice building around it, but eventually budges and slides up.

I punch out the screen, fling my legs over the frame and climb in, poking my head out to look around the yard. Coast is still clear.

Once I'm inside, I stomp my feet on the clean white carpet to get the excess snow off, not caring that I left footprints on my way. It'll snow more and cover them up—I hope.

The house smells like fresh baked banana bread. I draw in a deep breath letting the scent linger. The Beckhams' house always smells like sweet treats and home. Anyone would kill to have what Trent and Lucy have. A mom and a dad who love you. Separate bedrooms, and television whenever you want it.

I've only been in this house a couple times, and it was never because I was invited. One night when the family was on vacation, I came here after Mrs. Webster, my foster parent, had gone to bed, and I ate all the Beckhams' snacks and watched three episodes of *Dexter*.

The next night, I brought Bella with me, and she played dress-up in Lucy's closet.

That's how I know which one I need to get. I'll never forget the sparkle in her eyes when she put on that pink dress. It's like she escaped to another world in just those few short minutes. Staring at herself in the mirror and pretending that this was her life. She was happy, and I swore I'd do anything to make that smile permanent.

I find myself grinning at the memory as I go into Lucy's bedroom. Trent's little sister really does have it all. Probably even more than Trent. She's spoiled, and I wish I could say she wasn't a brat, but she definitely is. Bella doesn't see that side of her, though. All she sees is everything she wants that Lucy has—mainly the family and love.

Shuffling through all the dresses, I find the pink one and pluck it off the hanger. When I hear footsteps coming from somewhere in the house, I immediately ball it up and stuff it under my coat then zip it up.

I'm not sure who it could be, but I need to get the hell out of here before I'm caught. The last thing I need is for a member of this family to contact Mrs. Webster and tell her I broke into their house—again.

With my head poked out the door, I listen intently, looking both ways. When I don't see or hear anything, I head back the way I came.

As soon as I reach the staircase, I realize I'm screwed. Though, I'm actually sort of relieved it's not Mr. or Mrs. Beckham.

"Well, well, well. What do we have here?" Trent asks, alongside Mark.

"Look, guys," I begin my descent down the stairs, brushing this off like it's no big deal, "just forget you ever saw me and I'll owe you both one."

Trent shares a look with Mark. "Oh yeah? One what? From what I hear, you might be getting outta that orphanage soon. Not that I believe anyone would want a loser like you."

"It's not an orphanage," I spit out defensively. I hate when anyone calls it that. It makes feeling like an orphan all the more real. I reach the bottom of the stairs, standing beside them. "I'll tell ya what. Twenty years from now when you losers need an alibi, give me a call. I've got you covered." I push past them, hoping they'll let this go.

Mark grabs ahold of my arm, ruffling my jacket. "What'd ya got under there?" His eyes wear his surprise. "Are you stealing something from the Beckhams?"

"No!" I huff. "It's just...none of your damn business." I jerk away from him.

Trent crosses his arms over his chest, puffing it out like some sort of superhero who has all the power. "Tell us what it is and maybe, just maybe, we'll let you live to see another day."

I don't dare tell them what it is. They'll ridicule me to no end. Call me pussy-whipped. Claim I'm in love with the girl, but it's also my best shot. "It's just something for Bella. She needed it."

Trent, being the asshole that he is, begins laughing. "What? Did she start her period or something?"

Fucking moron.

Mark just stands by idly, allowing Trent to do all the bashing. Mark is a follower, through and through.

"No. Gross," I snarl. "Don't worry about what it is."

They share another look, and Mark nods in agreement. "All right. We can let this go, but like you said, you owe us one."

I don't even say another word. I just haul ass out while I've got the chance. I'm not sure if I can trust those guys, but right now, I have no choice. I've gotta go wake Bella up before our future parents arrive. I swear, the girl would sleep all day if she could.

Once I'm back at the house, it's like I never left: still quiet, and Mrs. Webster is nowhere to be seen.

I go straight to the attic and pull the dress out of my jacket and stuff it in the box where I keep all my prized possessions—not that I have many. There are a couple things I'd like to keep with me no matter where I go. I shuffle through a few of my belongings. One in particular—a picture of all the neighborhood kids at the annual block party the Beckhams have. I could cut everyone else out and not miss them one bit. I keep it because it's the only picture I have of Bella and me.

"Callum!" I hear Mrs. Webster shout. The tone in her voice is enough to alert me that she's not happy. Not that she is often, but she sounds pretty fired up.

I close the box back up and kick it under the old armoire closet, unsure how long I was staring into the black hole of memories.

I slip off my jacket and toss it aside. It lands among some dirty books, and I head out of the room. Don't want to keep the queen waiting. God knows she already hates me enough.

I'm tucking my shirt in when I spot her walking out of my room. She closes the door with a loud thud and strolls toward where I stand at the opposite end of the hall.

"You just couldn't help yourself, could you?" Her jaw clenches, and she reaches out, grabbing my ear and pulling. "Breaking into the Beckhams' house and stealing. Don't you know this behavior will keep you here until you're eighteen years old?"

"Son of a bitch!" I spit out, immediately regretting my choice of words.

Mrs. Webster drags me to my room, by the ear, and opens the door then shoves me inside. "You've just lost your chance at getting a family today. Do not exit this room until you're called for breakfast."

"Wait. No!" I shout as the door slams shut.

Disregarding my punishment, I open it back up. "Mrs. Webster, I didn't steal anything." It's a lie, but it was only a dress. Who cares about a measly old dress?

"That's not what Trent Beckham says. Claims you stole money from Mr. Beckham's safe. Don't try to deny it, Callum. I saw the picture as proof that you were in that house minutes ago."

She stomps off in a fit of rage and I'm almost thankful because I don't like dealing with the old hag when she's acting like a royal bitch.

One thing is for certain, if I lose my place in this adoption, those boys will live to regret what they did to me. It's like I've always said, "Trust is priceless, but once you lose it, you are useless."

CHAPTER ONE

Bella

My nerves are officially shot. I'm holding the weight of a thousand bricks on my chest, and my heels feel like they are on the verge of snapping in half. It would be just my luck. They break and send me crashing down on the stage before I can even perform.

I grip the banister beside me, squeezing it so tight that the braided embellishment imprints on my skin.

I'm not sure if I'm losing my mind in the process of trying to find Cal, but I've noticed things lately. Or a person, rather. One man in particular that I'm almost positive has been following me since I arrived in the city this morning. The first time I saw him was when I checked in to my hotel. He stood back idly watching me over his phone. If he was trying to be inconspicuous, he failed.

The second time was when I arrived here at the hall. He was walking casually with his head held low, failing to be discreet once again.

It doesn't scare me, though; I'm almost positive Cal has sent him, or them, if there are more.

And now, I've managed to spot him in the crowd. Out of

hundreds of people, there he is. Same guy with the same *Men in Black* suit. Slicked-back, black hair and dark eyes.

I'll know who he is soon enough.

There are so many people out there. At least two hundred, all expecting me to perform like it's the most natural thing in the world.

I pinch my eyes shut, thinking that maybe if I do it long enough, the entire crowd will be gone when I open them.

Nope. Still there.

It's been years since I've played the piano for an audience—well, aside from the time Cal requested I play for him nude. But it was only him and, oddly enough, I felt at ease.

This is by far the largest audience I've ever faced and I'm not exactly thrilled to perform. Playing the piano is a passion I have behind closed doors. During high school, I dabbled in some musicals, but it wasn't the same as playing from my heart. I'm not sure that I'll be able to give this crowd what they want.

Nonetheless, I'm here. The only reason because I know damn well Cal sent my audition tape of *Our Song* to Carnegie Hall. It wasn't actually an audition. In fact, he must've recorded me playing for him during my stay at Cori Cove. There is no other way that anyone would know about this piece, unless it came from him.

Now I'm standing behind this cracked door, ready to make my way across the stage, wearing a teal gown similar to the one I wore that night I played for Cal. My caramel-colored hair in tiny little ringlets bounce off my shoulders as I take my first ungraceful step. Palms sweating, thighs sticking together, and breath being held as everyone watches me.

There are rows of people. Some on the ground level, some on the second floor, and more on the upper tier. The lighting dims over the crowd, and all that's left is a white beam following me as I make my way to the piano.

Another step. And another.

God, please don't let me fall.

My heels clack against the hardwood floor, the echo reverberating through my entire body.

Everyone begins clapping, and it's during that melancholic sound that I'm offered a sense of peace. A smile tugs at my lips, and before I know it, I'm at the piano. I place one hand on the hood and tuck the other around my waist as I bow before them.

The clapping subsides and I take a seat at the stool, sliding it in until my elbows are bent at a ninety-degree angle. My trembling fingers hover over the keys and I fill my lungs before beginning.

As soon as the first note fills the empty space around me on the stage, Cal enters my mind.

That first smile when I saw him at the top of the stairs at The Webster House. It was a cheesy grin and I knew at that moment that boy was nothing but trouble. Once my social worker left and I witnessed him filling his pockets with snacks, when he didn't think anyone was watching, I knew I wanted to be part of that mischief.

My heart cries for him. My soul bleeds for him. Each night apart has been an agony worse than the years we spent apart the first time I left him. There are times I cry myself to sleep, wishing I'd never known him at all, because then I wouldn't know what missing him feels like.

In a fluid motion, I hit the chorus. Pounding away at the keys, pouring my heart into the piece I wrote for him.

When I wrote it, it was meant to radiate positive energy. Now when I play, it's heartbreaking. I see two soulmates living a life where they are unwanted by others. Brought together during hard times and torn apart just to test the depths of their love. Only to be reunited and tested again because life is cruel like that. So very cruel.

It's like the crowd has disappeared, and it's just me. Back at The Webster House. An eleven-year-old orphan, gyrating my fingers across the keys as I search for myself in each note I hit.

Tears prick the corners of my eyes. It's impossible not to get emotional. Something this deep is meant to make you feel. As much as I don't want to, it's necessary to convey the passion as I play.

Near the end of the song, my heart gallops in my chest in anticipation of the crowd's reaction.

Seconds later, I end it on the final note and rest my hands in my lap. My eyes close briefly before I slide the stool back. To my surprise, the crowd erupts in a burst of applause. A smile grows on my face. I'm not sure if I'm humbled or surprised.

I feel empowered. Overjoyed and proud. Really fucking proud. I did it. I am the reason for the chants and whistles.

I take a bow, and as I come up, I skim the crowd. I'm not sure anything could bring me down from this high. What's even better is that I can feel him watching me. He's here. I just know it.

Now, I have to find him.

I'm heading back to the door of the sound room where I entered the stage from, but my movements stop before I reach it. I'm frozen in place—stunned at the familiar face before me.

"Byron?" I mutter, feeling the prominent crease in my forehead. Why is he here?

Once my head unfogs slightly, I continue to cross the stage in his direction. "What…what are you doing here? Did Cal send you?"

Byron places a hand on the small of my back, motioning

me inside the room. "That was amazing, Bella. Even better than the recording I heard."

"Cut the bullshit, Byron. What's going on? Where's Cal?"

"Cal?" He laughs. "What makes you think Cal is here?"

My heart sinks into my stomach, deeply and painfully. "You mean, he's not? Then—"

"Cal's gone, Bella. On the verge of being presumed dead. Why the hell would you think he was here?"

My brows perk, and a moment of hope washes through me. I'm confident Byron will feel the same way, once he hears what I'm about to say. "No. He's here somewhere. He's not dead, Byron."

His puzzled look leads me to believe he's skeptical, so I continue, "Cal is the only one who knew about that song. He had to have recorded me playing it for him during my stay at Cori Cove. He's the one who sent the tape. He's alive."

"Great performance, Isabella," Paul, the booking manager, says. "Your unease was for nothing." He smiles kindly, and while I know I should thank him for everything—the pep talk an hour ago, the opportunity—all I can focus on is Cal.

"Thank you, Paul. It was a pleasure to have had this opportunity." I grab Byron by the arm and pull him away, probably a little too rudely, so we're able to talk in private.

Once we're away from all the backstage people, I look up at him. "Please Byron, tell me you don't really think he's dead? How can you?" I wave my arms around. "I'm here because he brought me here."

It's the only reason I came. Sure, playing at this place is a dream, but I would have likely torn up the invitation and never given it a second thought had it not been for the song chosen.

Byron scrunches his shoulders, his expression loaded with sorrow that I have the urge to smack away as I scream that he's wrong! "Sorry, Bella. No one has seen or heard from

Callum since he went missing. If he were alive, I have no doubt that you'd be the first to know. He loved you."

Tears prick the corners of my eyes, but I ward them off. "Then who would have..." I take a few steps back, bumping into some control panels. "It was you, wasn't it? You sent the audition?"

"It was a beautiful piece. I thought you deserved recognition for your talent."

No! "No! It couldn't have been. How...how did you get it? Why would you..."

I can't even speak, unable to form a coherent sentence. For the last week, I've had hope. Celebrating the holidays, knowing I was going to see Cal soon.

My legs feel weak. There's a chair to my left, so I grab it and pull it over, then sit down.

"I went back to Cori Cove to search for answers as to where Callum might be. While I was going through some of his belongings—"

My eyes snap to him. "You went through his things?"

"I'm his attorney, Bella, and also his friend. Yes, I went through his things...to try and help him. I found a recorder and hit Play. It was the same song I heard playing the night I escorted you to the ballroom to meet him."

"And you just took it upon yourself to interfere with my life and send in *my* recording?"

"Well," Byron chuckles unnervingly, "if we're being technical here, it was Callum's, which, in turn, makes it mine, considering I am the rightful beneficiary of his estate."

Chewing on my bottom lip, I glower at him. His stance over me feels domineering, and I'm not in the mood for it. "Well, Byron," I emphasize as I stand up, "you being the beneficiary to his estate does not mean you get to control me or my life. In fact, no one does. Not even Callum. So thanks for setting all this up. But it's over now and you can go home."

Disappointed doesn't even begin to explain how I feel. I'm gutted. Downright heartbroken.

It was him all this time. It was never Cal.

Spinning on my heels, I begin unstrapping the left one as I walk, yanking it off my foot. Then the other, until I'm padding barefoot to the dressing room.

Fortunately, Byron doesn't follow me in, so I close the door and chuck my shoes in a corner, having no interest in bringing those damn things home with me. I can't believe I ever wanted to own all the dresses and shoes in the world. I had princess dreams as a child, but as I get older, dreams fade and reality slaps you in the face.

As I'm getting dressed, there's a knock at the door. I quickly finish by stepping into a pair of gray sweats and throwing on a black crewneck sweatshirt, then step into my, already laced-up, tennis shoes.

It's probably Byron. I can't imagine he brought me all this way just so I could play a song and leave. I don't like the guy much. Not only did Cal warn me before he went missing that Byron was up to no good, I'm also pretty sure he was only Cal's friend for his money. I shouldn't speculate, because I don't know much about their working relationship or friendship, but I took notice of the small things he did to piss Cal off.

"One moment, please," I holler as I roll up my dress and stuff it into a duffle bag.

With my bag and purse flung over my shoulder, I open the door, and sure enough, there he is. One arm pressed to the frame, a smirk on his face.

"I'm sorry," he says with remorse in his tone. "We got off on the wrong foot. Can we start again?"

"There's nothing to start, or finish, Byron. Please move. I have a warm bed at a nice hotel waiting for me." When he just stands there, gawking, I tip my head to his arm. "Do you mind?"

"Oh, right." He drops his arm and steps aside.

I go out and begin down the hall as he walks at my side, so I say, "I know he's alive. You can believe whatever you want, but he's out there, and I will find him."

"I've got no doubt that you will." I catch his glance in my peripheral. "Assuming he is alive and all."

My palms press to the exit door and I step into the darkness of the parking lot. Snow falls softly to the ground but melts before accumulating. It's cold here in New York City, but it's no different from home in Rhode Island.

I click the remote start on my car, but something stops me from walking. None of this makes any sense to me. I look at him, shivering under the lamppost as people pass by in the parking lot. "Why did you come here, Byron?"

Byron stuffs his hands in the pocket of his black trench coat, snow sprinkling on his sandy blond hair. "Came to watch you play."

"But why? We're not friends. Hell, we barely even know one another. Why would you go through all this trouble?"

"I made him a promise, Bella. A promise to make sure you are happy and safe, if anything should ever happen to him. I'm a man of my word, so here I am."

"Cal was never confirmed dead. A body wasn't found. As far as legalities go, he's still alive. Meaning, you're furloughed from your promise to him. I can take care of myself." I keep walking to my car, and of course, he's still here.

All I want is to go back to my hotel, get a good night's sleep, and go home tomorrow and continue my quest to find Cal. I don't give a damn what Byron or anyone says, he's alive. I can feel it. Cal and I are soulmates, and I'd know if he were gone.

"One drink," Byron says as I pull open my car door.

"Excuse me?"

"It's New Year's Day. Have a drink with me. We can talk about your theories on where he might be. I can't shake the feeling that someone put a hit on him. Especially after that body was pulled from the bay and the identity was never shared."

"It wasn't him," I spit out on impulse. I just know it wasn't.

This might be a good chance to find out if Byron has been searching for Cal. It is New Year's Day and there's no harm in one drink. Even if Cal's warning is true—that Byron can't be trusted—it's a public place. He can't hurt me.

I toss my bag inside, keeping my purse on my shoulder, then close my door. "One drink."

CHAPTER TWO

Bella

WE END up in a hole-in-the-wall bar about a block from the hall. Driving in the city is a bitch and I have no intention of doing so when I don't have to, so we walked. A very awkward, quiet walk. Now that we're inside, I almost think I'd prefer that over the blaring music and loud chatter of the drunks.

It is a holiday, so I should have expected it. This isn't my scene, though. Not anymore. I prefer to live under the radar in my own little bubble. For a while, I floated outside of it, and it was freeing and eye-opening, but in the end, I crawled back in with a broken heart. Now I never want to leave it again. *It* being home. My hometown, my family. Should've never left in the first place. If I could go back and live my life with just the childhood memories of Cal, instead of adding the ones we made during my stay at Cori Cove, I would. Maybe then it wouldn't hurt so badly.

Byron manages to find us a small, empty, round table at the back of the bar. It's covered in a sticky liquid and bread-crumbs, so I avoid touching anything but the chair.

Byron places a hand over mine, and I take a step back,

letting it fall to his side. "I'll get the waitress to clean this up and get us some drinks at the bar." He must've noticed my turned-up nose at the grotesque table. "What'll you be having?"

"Dry martini, please." I sit down and take my phone out of the front pocket of my purse and begin scrolling through it like I actually have anything to read.

A few minutes later, Byron returns, and I put my phone away and take my drink from him. The first sip feels nice. I relish in the burn as it slides down my throat, already relieving some of my stress.

With a draft beer in hand, Byron sits down across from me. He takes a sip, then licks the foam from his lips. "So, Bella. Tell me what makes you think Callum is alive."

"No, Byron. How about you tell me why you think he's not?"

"Easy. If he were, he'd have come for you. Callum spent most of his life pining over you. Exacting his revenge and planning your," he points a sharp finger," future. There's no way he'd just let you go after everything he did to get you back."

"Or maybe this was part of his plan all along. Capture me, keep me long enough to make me fall in love with him, then push me away. It's actually a solid act of revenge, if you ask me." I take another drink as the words I just said replay in my mind. I never even thought of that until now. Talking about it has me considering different scenarios and what I just said is very possible. I tip my glass back, taking down half the contents.

No. He wouldn't do that. Would he?

"Doubtful. Callum doesn't play games like that. He wanted you, therefore, if he's alive, he will be coming for you. Watch and see."

My brows rise. "I guess I will." I finish off my drink,

already thirsty for another. My fingers dig into the bottom of the glass and I pull out the toothpick and take the olive off with my teeth.

Byron searches the crowded space. "Where the hell is that waitress?"

"I don't know, but when you find her, tell her I need another one of these." I hold up my glass, then set it on the table, already feeling a little woozy from drinking it so quickly.

Byron finishes off his beer in one big gulp. "The service here is fucking ridiculous. I'll be right back."

I nod, bored and ready to drink away my sorrows before passing out in my hotel bed.

Once again, I pull my phone out and look at nothing as I wait for him to return.

A guy passes by the table, gives me a double take while I resume doing nothing on my phone. When I glance up, I see that he's standing right in front of me. I'm not really in the mood for small talk, but I'm also not a total bitch, so I say, "Hi."

He leans forward, hands pressing into the goo on the table. I don't even tell him because he's going to figure it out in two seconds when I shoot him down and send him on his way. "Sorry, I just had to ask why a pretty girl like you is sitting here all by herself?"

"Actually, I'm not alone."

"Hmm," the guy looks around, "I don't see anyone coming for you. Maybe you should let me buy you a drink."

I avoid eye contact and look down at my phone in my hand. "I'm good. Thanks."

"Oh, come on. No one should be alone on New Year's."

Getting frustrated, I shut my phone off and drop it into my purse. "Listen, asshole, I told you I'm here with someone, so if you wouldn't mind backing up and leaving me alone, I'd appreciate it."

"Wow. Someone's a feisty thing. I happen to like feistiness."

I reach into my purse, clenching my pepper spray, ready to use it if need be. "Get lost, creep."

His lip tugs up in a cocky grin and he leans in, invading my personal space. I crane my neck at the repulsive smell of ash and stale beer rolling out of his wretched mouth. When he wraps an arm around my neck, I lift my arms up between us; I'm able to shove him back and he stumbles into a table, knocking down another guy's drink.

"You bitch!" he howls. He comes charging toward me, but I'm ready for him. Another guy comes into view and tries to pull him back while shouting profanities, but I cock my fist back and lay it right on his nose. Except, it's not him. I accidentally punch the guy trying to help. The familiarity throws me off guard. I've seen him before. "I'm...I'm so sorry," I say. Blood streams down his face, and I give my hand a shake, working out the kink in my knuckles.

Byron comes out of nowhere, grabbing me by the hand and pulling me away. "Come on," he says, "let's get out of here before you get your ass arrested."

"That poor guy. He was trying to help and I punched him by accident." I look over my shoulder, realizing it's the same guy who's been watching me.

"He'll be fine. Pick up your pace." Byron begins walking faster, as if he really believes I'll get arrested.

Once we're away from the crowd, he lets go and holds the door open for me. The cool, fresh air hits my face, and I take a deep breath before I burst out laughing. "I can't believe I just did that." I'm still shaking my hand. There's a bite of pain, but my adrenaline is pumping.

"Damn, girl. That was quite the punch. Maybe you should take up boxing."

"Yeah. Maybe it would help to alleviate some of this stress." I look over my shoulder, though we are already halfway back to the performance hall. "Who was that guy?"

Byron glances over his shoulder. "What guy?"

"The one I hit. I've seen him before."

He shrugs his shoulders, without a clue as to what I'm talking about. "No idea."

We walk down the snow-dusted sidewalk, passing by the same stores we did only thirty minutes ago. Though, they look different—blurry almost. I find myself staggering, and Byron places an arm around my waist. "You okay?" he asks.

I look down at the space between us, hoping he drops his hand before I have to move it for him. When I look back up and he catches the scowl on my face, he lets go.

"Hey. If he is out there, we'll get him back. Don't worry."

Just hearing him say that offers me a sense of calm. Byron was so skeptical at the hall and I was sure he was going to try and convince me that Cal is dead. Now, my hope is slowly returning.

"He is. And we will."

We reach my car and I struggle to get my keys out of my purse. My head feels like it's spinning, and I can't focus my eyes. "Sorry the night was cut short, but I really should get back to my hotel. I'm not feeling so good."

"You okay? Maybe you should let me drive your car to your hotel. I took an Uber anyway."

I grab my stomach, suddenly feeling nauseous. My head feels like it holds the weight of a bowling ball and it's a struggle to balance it on my neck. "Umm. Yeah. That might be a good idea. I'm at The Veranda. Up on Seventh Street."

"Really?" he says, surprised. "That's where I'm staying. How bizarre." His hands fly up. "It's fate."

Fate. It's the word Callum used when we reunited. He said it was fate, but I soon learned it was orchestrated.

Much like then, I highly doubt fate has anything to do with this encounter with Byron or the fact that he's staying at the same hotel I am.

I've been so closed off the past few weeks, and it was nice to get out after my performance. Even if it was just for a half hour that ended with swollen knuckles.

"Penny for your thoughts?" Byron says from the driver's seat.

My fingertips dig into my temples, massaging them and trying to alleviate this strange feeling in my head. "Save your penny. I wanna know about you and Cal. How did this whole working relationship turn into a friendship?"

Byron glances at me, one hand on the steering wheel and the other in his lap. "Well, let's see. I worked for the former Mr. Ellis as his attorney. He and I put our heads together and came up with some ideas that would really make Ellis Empire stand out against our competitors."

I look over at him and notice the cheeky grin on his face. My eyes sway from him to the road. "Wait. Are you talking about the sex club? Were you part of that addition to the hotels?"

Byron shrugs sheepishly. "I might've had a thing or two to do with it. The club was already established at one of Ellis Empire's biggest resorts in Europe. It was doing exceptionally well, so Vincent and I decided to expand to the U.S. resorts. We had a partnership that continued even after his death. Only now, that partnership is with Callum." I nod, listening intently and watching the road as he continues, "Callum was never a big fan of the clubs. Thought the resorts would do fine without them. I beg to differ. We draw in men from all over the world who have an insatiable need for..."

"Sex," I spit out. "You can say it. I'm not a child, Byron. I know exactly what happens in those clubs."

"Oh yeah? Callum filled you in, did he?"

"He didn't have to. I snuck down there one night and saw it with my own two eyes. Actually, I saw you." I look over at him, expecting him to look humiliated, but instead, he smirks.

"Did you like what you saw?"

"What?" I gasp, picking my jaw up from my lap. Is he serious right now?

"It's a simple question. Did you like what you saw?"

"No! Absolutely not. I was...disgusted." It's partially a lie. I was intrigued. Okay, I was highly turned on, but not by Byron. I find him to be a good-looking guy, but he's also somewhat of a creep to me.

Byron chuckles. "It's nothing to be ashamed of if you did like watching. You'd be surprised at how many people enjoy that sort of thing."

There is no way in hell I'm admitting to Byron, of all people, that part of me did enjoy watching. We're way off topic here, though. "Back to our original conversation. Yes, I know all about the clubs."

"Right. So the clubs are part of my partnership with Callum."

"And the fact that you know he killed Mr. Ellis?" I look to my left and notice the stunned look on Byron's face.

"Wow. Is there anything he didn't tell you?"

Byron pulls into an empty parking space, and suddenly I'm feeling worse. Barely able to keep my eyes open, they slowly close as my head sways back and forth.

Byron reaches over and grips my chin, forcing me to look at him. I don't even have the strength to ask what he's doing.

"You know, Bella, too much knowledge can get a pretty girl like you in trouble."

My heart drops into my stomach, pulse racing as Byron's expression shifts to one of mischief. The look on his face is formidable. "What?" I managed to choke out.

His hand reaches out like a claw, fingers spread wide as he grabs me by the throat. I squirm, trying to free myself from his clutches, but he only tightens his hold as his fingertips dig into the thin flesh of my neck.

I'm not able to do a damn thing to stop him. I feel so weak. I'm so tired. So helpless.

"By...Byron," I sputter as he chokes the life out of me.

This is it.

This is how I die.

CHAPTER THREE

CUFFED. Tied. Shackled. My entire body is bound to this bed. Sprawled out like an X, with each bedpost holding one of my limbs.

This has to be a nightmare.

I close my eyes, only to open them again, finding myself in the same position, wearing the same clothes I put on when I left the hall last night.

My head lifts, trying to get a look at my surroundings.

I've been here before.

I'm in the basement on Cori Cove. The island where it all began. And Byron brought me here. But why?

"Help! Somebody, help me!" The words scratch at my throat like a sharp razor blade.

I'm thirsty. So damn thirsty. My entire neck feels swollen and these thick metal cuffs are digging into my wrists. I wriggle, trying to loosen something, anything, but it's no use. He did this with the intention of keeping me in place.

I rest my head back, tears sliding down my cheeks and falling onto the red satin pillowcase.

I'm at The Grotto, but this time, I'm not watching anyone.

I have no doubt someone is watching me, and that someone is most definitely Byron. There's a camera on the ceiling pointed directly at me.

"I hate you." I clench my teeth and hiss the words knowing he hears me. "When I get off this bed, I will kill you."

My body jolts when a door opens then closes. Footsteps drudge in my direction, coming closer and closer as my heart beats faster and faster with each step.

Byron comes into view, wearing different clothes than when I last saw him. He's got on a pair of gray slacks and a white dress shirt. He adjusts the buttons on one of the sleeves and rolls it up, then does the same to the other. "Good morning, Bella. Welcome back to Cori Cove."

"You tricked me, you son of a bitch." I was feeling sick last night. Far too woozy for one drink. "You drugged me, didn't you?" He drugged me, then choked me out to finish me off so I was lifeless for the trip here.

"In my defense, you made it quite easy. After Callum lured you here the first time, I figured you'd be a little more vigilant. You ate right out of my hand, though." Byron presses his hands to the mattress between my widespread legs. "Maybe you're just hungrier than I thought you were." He moves one hand up, then the other, crawling up the open space.

"Byron," I say his name as a warning. "What are you doing?" I pull my hands, trying like hell to free them, even though I know I'm stuck. "Stop!" I'm not sure what he has planned, but that devilish smirk on his face says it can't be anything good.

How could I have been so trusting? I talked to him like he was an old friend, even though I knew something felt off. You'd think I would have learned my lesson after Cal coaxed me here two months ago and wouldn't let me leave.

Cal could be here. He could be tied up, too. Or worse, he could be part of this.

No. He wouldn't allow this to happen. There is no way in hell he's working with Byron this time. If Cal is here, then he's likely restrained the same way I am.

I glower at him as his face lingers over mine. "Where is he?"

The deceiving, sweet scent of cinnamon rolls off his vile tongue. "Who?"

"Don't play dumb with me. I know you did something to him. It all makes sense now. This was never about a partnership. You want Cal's money and the only way to get it is to kill him. Something tells me you didn't because, otherwise, you wouldn't have me here."

"You know what I don't like about you, Bella?" He enunciates my name in a way that sends chills down my sweaty spine. "You're too perceptive. You have all these pieces scattered all over and you observe each one until you find out where it fits."

Byron sits up, straightens his back, and digs a knee into my crotch. I make a mental note to shatter that kneecap once I'm free from this bed. "However, this time, you're wrong and all your little pieces are floating in the bay with your boyfriend's dead corpse."

His words are like a knife to the heart. More tears fall, but I don't stop thrashing, trying to get one of my limbs free. I grit my teeth, glaring at him. "You won't get away with this."

"Oh, I will. I always get what I want, sweet Bella." He presses a disgusting kiss to my forehead and slides down the bed the same way he came up.

"Why are you doing this?"

Byron pulls out his phone and begins tapping into it as he speaks. "Because I deserve it. All of this should be mine. It almost was. I got rid of the one person standing in my way.

Now I have the final piece to my own little puzzle," he smiles cruelly, "you."

My eyes pinch shut, pushing out more tears. "Did you... kill Peter?" It hurts to even say the words. I'm still not over Peter's death. I go to sleep at night, and I still see his cold, blue face. He didn't deserve to die, especially not like that.

I go to the sixth floor, to Peter's room, and when he doesn't answer, I use the key to go inside.

It's at this moment, the world stands still. My heart stops beating, the tears stop falling, and I hold my breath before screaming at the top of my lungs, "Nooooo!"

Still clutching the dress, I snap out of the state of shock I'm in and hurry over to Peter's lifeless body, lying in a puddle of blood on the floor.

Maybe it's not too late. Maybe I can save him.

"Oh, Peter," I choke out as I reach down and place my fingers on his cold wrist. It's no use. He has no pulse.

Peter is dead.

I sit there next to him, crying for minutes before I finally get up to try and call for help, then it hits me. Someone did this. Peter didn't die of natural causes. The puddle of blood is enough proof that he was murdered. Whoever did it could still be here.

I knew I should have fought harder to find out what happened to Peter. I never should have believed Byron when I saw him right after finding Peter's body. I'm not sure if it was because I was in shock, or because I was desperate for help. Regardless, I was a fool.

"And another piece fits," Byron says, all too cheery.

He's referencing my puzzle pieces that he claimed were scattered in the bay with Cal's body. It's an admission without saying the words. He did kill Peter.

There's a pang in my chest. But I use my heartache to fuel the fire inside me. It's another reason for me to torture this man and make him pay miserably.

I don't take Byron to be a complete idiot, but he seems to be ignoring one big possibility. "You know if Cal is alive, he could easily hire a new attorney and change his will."

It's actually ridiculous to me that Cal didn't do that a long time ago. We never really talked much about the will, but I do know that they can easily be changed.

"Ah, but you're wrong. Callum and I have a written contract that his will cannot be revoked. Therefore, I'd have to die before him for that to happen." His hands rest on his chest, head tilted to the side condescendingly. "And here I am. While he is...well, dead."

"You did something to him. I know you did."

"Enough of this senseless conversation," Byron continues, stuffing his phone in the front of his pants pocket. "We have company joining us and I'm going to need you to be a good girl."

"Company? Here on the island?"

"Here, as in, this club. I'm running a business, Bella. My business."

Is he insinuating that this hotel is up and running and there are guests? "What kind of business?" Byron disappears from view, so I shout. "What kind of business, Byron?"

He returns seconds later, and I immediately notice the collar-looking thing in his hand. "What is that?"

Coming closer, he never loses that sinister grin he's been wearing. He looks completely deranged. Like he's manic and lost his damn mind.

Fear washes over me, once again. Byron is a fucking psycho and he has access to do whatever he wants with me and to me.

"This will ensure that you don't get out of hand. I wouldn't want to have to hurt you, Bella."

I'm able to get a better view of the collar as he unfastens it. There's a black ball on the end with a...

He shoves the ball in my mouth so hard, it hits my top and bottom teeth. A mask-like shield presses to my face, covering my entire mouth. I try like hell to spit it out. Pressing my tongue forcibly against it, hoping it will budge, but he has the upper hand and fastens the clasp around my head, setting it in place.

My heart is beating so rapidly that it's rattling my rib cage. I'm suffocating. My entire body is filled with heat while feeling like I'm getting poked continuously with pins and needles. Anxiety is kicking into high gear because, no matter how hard I try, I can't get a grip on it.

I've never been so scared in my life. I think I'd rather die than face what Byron has in store for me.

Please. Please get me out of this, Cal.

Byron reaches into his pocket and pulls something out.

A needle.

He presses his index finger to the end, pushing up some of the liquid inside. It squirts out before he grabs my arm.

I flail through my restraints, crying out around the gag in my mouth.

It's no use, though. The needle pierces my skin, and he pushes down, watching me with menacing eyes as he pumps me full of whatever drug he's feeding me.

My arm goes limp. Hot and cold collide inside me. My thoughts shut down, and I just lie there, slowly drifting to sleep.

CHAPTER FOUR

I SEE A GIRL.

No. Two girls.

Maybe three. And a guy. He's big. Really muscular and tan with black stubble coating his sharp jawline. He's not wearing a shirt. My eyes skate down his body. He's not wearing anything.

I'm hardly fazed. Even the fact that there's a girl on her knees sucking his dick doesn't fully register. My mind and body are so relaxed that nothing seems out of the ordinary. Or maybe I'm just too high to care.

I'm too high to even care that I'm high.

She's a pretty girl. Long, blonde hair that dips below her perky breasts. Nipples puckered around her golden locks. Her mouth forms the perfect O around his cock. Sliding back and forth, taking him so far that I can see the bulge in her throat.

Does anyone even care that I'm lying here shackled without a voice?

No one seems to mind.

My heart gallops when the muscular guy's eyes land on

mine. He tips his head, smirks, then returns to fisting the girl's hair. His slow and steady movements quicken as he begins fucking her mouth so hard that she can barely keep up with his thrusts.

Why am I here? What is the point of all this?

Another girl joins. This one's a short brunette, wearing a black, leather bustier with chains on the front. She looks familiar. When she catches my gaze, she licks her bottom lip in a seductive manner, and I remember where I've seen her before. The waitress from the yacht. I think her name is Serena.

I'm not even sure she recognizes me. Our first encounter wasn't a pleasant one and Cal fired her that night. It seems Byron has rehired her, or he's just fucking her still. I watched them once. Watched him ram his dick in another girl while she feasted on Serena.

The image in my head is oddly satisfying.

Serena steps behind the blonde on her knees, gives her hair a jerk and pulls her mouth from the guy's cock. She leans forward and kisses her. Hard. So hard that the blonde loses her footing and drops back. Being the bitch that she is, Serena pushes her to the side and steps up to the muscular guy. Her hands shimmy down his arms, and she licks the side of his face. "I thought you were waiting for me," she says to him before getting a firm grip on his cock.

I'm deranged for enjoying this so much. It's like watching dramatic porn.

I close my eyes. This is too much of a distraction, and I need to think about how the hell I'm supposed to get out of this mess I'm in.

Where is Byron? And what the hell did he inject me with?

The three shadows in front of me become blurry, and I find myself fighting to keep my eyes open again.

I'm not sure how long I dozed off this time, but I'm

woken up when the mattress presses down at my side. My eyes open, and I blink a few times before I realize that it's Byron. I'm grateful to see that he's dressed, unlike the other people I see. There are at least six of them now. Two guys and four girls, not counting Byron.

Byron crawls toward me, straddling my lower half. My stomach clenches, and I gasp behind the ball in my mouth. I gurgle and choke, trying to get words out, but it's pointless.

"Time to get you up, pretty girl." He reaches over me and unclasps the cuff on my left arm. It falls weightlessly. If I had the strength, I'd try to fight him off with just my one free hand, but I'd fail miserably.

He undoes my other hand, then moves to my feet. He knows whatever he gave me has made me weak and incoherent enough to let him do whatever he wants to me. I can think logically, but my body fails to react the way I'd like it to.

"Come on, let her join in," I hear a guy say. "We won't hurt her...much." He chuckles, and it's unnerving.

"Not yet," Byron says as he scoops me in his arms like a baby. He carries me through The Grotto, passing everyone who is still chasing an orgasm even as a prisoner is being carried away with a gag in her mouth.

They must all work for Byron. At one time, they worked for Cal. Byron must've taken over Cal's place in the business. He must have inherited it all, just like he wanted.

But why does he need me?

"Time to get you cleaned up and ready for the ball, pretty girl."

We go out the door that leads to the main entrance, and I remember it all so clearly.

The backside of the castle that was once open is now closed with a pair of wooden double doors, ones that resemble the doors to a barn, only with gray-weathered wood instead of the common red barnwood.

A beam of light shines through, which tells me that it's either early morning or late afternoon. I must have been out all night.

Byron flips me over his shoulder and takes the elevator up. It stops on the eighth floor—the floor I stayed on.

He doesn't stop until we get to my old room. The memories hit me like a tidal wave. From that first day to the last night. So much happened in those short weeks, and while it was only a month ago, it feels like an eternity.

I'm dropped onto the bed like a sack of potatoes. Byron reaches around my head and unclasps the collar. I immediately spit out the ball in my mouth, then wipe the excess saliva from my face with the back of my hand. I'm half tempted to rub it all over his face, but I refrain.

My entire jaw aches. My teeth chatter from the constant pressure against them, and my tongue is just happy to be able to move around.

Byron goes into my closet, returning with a dress.

"Please, just let me go." I whimper through clipped breaths. I'm thirsty as hell, my heart feels weak, and I'm almost positive Byron injected me with some sort of sedative.

I slide down until I'm sitting on the end of the bed with my feet on the floor. I could try and run, but I wouldn't get far. I have to save my strength to use it at precisely the right time.

"This one should do." He holds up a red, satin gown.

My head lifts, slowly. Staggering breaths escape through my gritted teeth. "Fuck you."

Byron laughs in a mocking tone. "Eventually."

Fuck saving my strength. I should jump on this bastard

right now and dig my dirty nails into his perfectly-sculpted cheeks.

"Callum was obsessed with finding you, Bella. I've never seen a man so hell-bent on capturing a woman in my entire life—even as an attorney for psychos and stalkers. For years, he planned for you." Byron slouches down in front of me, slipping off my shoes. "The thing is, I'm not sure if he loved you more than he loved his empire. He planned on marrying and impregnating you just so that I could be taken off his will," he laughs. "Who fucking does that?"

Impregnating me? Cal mentioned marriage, but he never mentioned a baby.

Why am I even listening to this asshole?

My eyes roll, looking away from him. "Quit speaking of him in the past tense. *Loves* me." I raise my voice. "Not loved. Besides, you're lying. Cal had me take birth control just because he *didn't* want a baby."

That laugh again. I never imagined a simple sound could infuriate me so much. "Shows how gullible you are. Don't feel bad, I fell for his games, too. He swore he'd never get married or have kids, and I'm the dumbass who believed him while thinking my place in his will was secure." Byron begins pulling at the straps of the gown like a demented maniac. "That fucker doesn't give a damn about you. You're his escape clause—the future wife he never wanted. All he cared about was getting me out."

The threading of one of the straps comes undone, and he holds it up with an ominous grin. "Looks like we need to find you a new dress."

God, Cal. Please come save me from this lunatic. There is no saying what lengths Byron will go to at this point.

I'll deal with Cal's lies later. If there even are lies. I'm not sure why Byron would insinuate that I was gullible when it comes to taking birth control, but the guy talks in circles and I'm having a hard time believing anything he says right now.

Byron returns from the closet with another dress. This one is form-fitting and black velvet. "I've always liked black more than red. How about you?"

I just sit there, looking at him and waiting for his next volatile move.

He tosses the dress at me. "Put it on."

My eyes wander to the dress. Gaping at it like it's coated in anthrax.

"Now!" Byron snaps. "Or else I'll put it on you myself. I've been wanting to get under those clothes, ever since I watched Callum fuck you on that piano. "

"How do you know about that?"

"Because I was watching. I heard every moan, saw every kiss, and watched every thrust as he pounded your pussy that night. I won't lie and say I wasn't jealous that it was him getting all the action."

I stand up, grab the dress and throw it at him. "You're the one who recorded me playing, aren't you? You said it was Cal, but it was you."

A smirk parts his lips. "It was a beautiful song."

"How long have you had this planned out?"

He doesn't answer, just throws the dress at me again. "Put the fucking dress on, Bella. Don't make me take what I want because you want to behave like a stubborn little cunt."

His words should cut deep, but they don't. They only make my impending victory that much sweeter. Byron will not get away with this.

In the end, he will lose, even if I pretend.

"Fine," I snatch up the dress. "I'll put it on. *If* you promise me a dance." The thought makes my skin crawl, but I'm willing to do whatever it takes. It's time to repay Byron for knocking me out and holding me against my will. We'll see how he likes it.

Byron's eyes dance across my body, his mouth drawn up in a smile. "A dance?"

Gripping the ends of my sweatshirt, I lift up and peel it off, exposing my bra to him. I feel sick for what I'm about to do. "Mmmhmm. In the ballroom. Just like my dance with Cal. I've always loved dancing."

Cal used to say that without trust you are useless. If I gain Byron's trust, then maybe I'll be of use to him, maybe even sway his plans. At the very least, distract him when and if Cal arrives.

His eyes never leave my peeping cleavage. My fingers trail downward, painting the way to the cup of my bra. I bite the corner of my lip. "What do you say?" Bypassing my breasts, I keep going until I'm at the waistband of my pants. I push them down, stepping out one leg at a time until I'm standing there in nothing but my bra and panties, feeling more exposed than I ever have in my life.

"Umm. Yeah. I guess a dance wouldn't hurt."

Hook. Line. Sinker.

"Great. Now if you don't mind, I need to get changed."

Byron clears his throat. "I'll just..." His thumb shoots over his shoulder. "I'll just be outside the door. No funny business."

"Byron," "I chuckle, "I'm not Rapunzel. I can't escape from this tower. I'll be out in a minute. Promise."

"Wouldn't matter if you were. You should know by now, you can't escape the island." He heads for the door, but stops midway in the room. "And don't think I'm falling for your little reverse psychology tactic. I know you hate me. But one day, we will learn to tolerate one another."

Tolerate him? Never! I'm not sure why it's even necessary, but I'm beginning to feel like this is a permanent placement and not a temporary stay. Just like last time I was here. Only, this is different—I hate Byron with every fiber of my being, whereas Cal held a piece of my heart.

This could be harder than I thought. Byron isn't going to be an easy one to crack, but I have to gain his trust somehow. I still feel pretty out of it, but I'm coherent enough to make rational decisions. At least, I hope I am.

I just know Byron did something to Cal. Even if I don't believe he's dead, I know he was behind his disappearance.

Byron chews on his bottom lip, glaring at me, before he turns and leaves. The door closes behind him, and my smile instantly drops. I mutter under my breath, "Asshole."

CHAPTER FIVE

Bella

I STEP into the black gown and slide my arms beneath the thin spaghetti straps. Reaching back, I zip it up as far as I can reach, knowing that I'll need to ask for help to get it all the way up.

An eerie feeling washes over me. It wasn't long ago that I was in this room and Peter was waiting outside the door to zip me up. He was such a gentleman. This time, Byron is out there and the thought of his filthy fingers grazing my skin is as appealing as getting my fingers chopped off. For what it's worth, I prefer the latter.

In the closet, I pull down a pair of flat sandals and put them on. Screw heels. I'm done with them.

Without even bothering to look in the mirror, I walk to the door. It doesn't matter that my makeup from last night is probably smeared all over my face. My fingers rake through the matted mess of my hair, and I don't care about that either. I have zero interest in looking presentable for this asshole, so he can take it or leave it.

As he said he would be, Byron is waiting on the other side of the door. At first sight, I'd probably fall for a guy like him.

On the outside, he's so put together. On the inside, I'm pretty sure he's dead.

Byron's eyes rake over my body a few times before landing on mine. "You look lovely. Would have been nice if you'd run a brush through your hair, but this'll do."

Such a fucking asshole. I snarl before turning my frown into a smile. "Didn't want to keep you waiting." I turn around, giving him my back. "Would you mind?"

Byron's cold, calloused fingers scratch against my skin as he zips me up. Once he's finished, he ushers his arm out, and I hook mine around it, hesitantly. "I'm sure you're starving, though the sleeping medication may have curved your appetite."

"Sleeping medication?" I ask, playing dumb, though I assumed it was some sort of drug he injected me with.

"It's very safe. No need to worry. It was the same medicine used to comatose patients when they have an operation. The last thing I want to do is hurt you, Bella."

I blow out a sarcastic chuckle. "Right? So kidnapping me and bringing me to this island is for what...my protection?"

"If I remember right, Callum did the same thing, and by the time he left you, you were head over heels in love. Who's to say it can't happen again?"

We reach the elevator, and the doors open. As soon as we're inside, I slither out of his hold. "Cal and I have history. He was never a stranger, and he didn't kidnap or drug me."

"Oh, but he did lie to you. And if he were alive, he'd still be lying to you. There's so much you don't know. Don't fret, I'll fill you in eventually."

The elevator comes to a stop, and Byron offers his arm again, but I snuff my nose at him and walk on my own. I know exactly where the ballroom is and I don't need his assistance this time.

Last time he ushered me to Cal, I tripped and fell and

threw a shoe at him. If I had heels on this time, I might hammer it into his thick skull.

It won't be necessary, though. Somehow, I'm going to steal Byron's phone. There might not be any boats for me to escape on, but if I can reach Mark or Dad, they'll send for help. Until then, I just have to bide my time.

When I enter the ballroom, I'm taken aback by the changes. The piano is now in the far corner, and there's a large, white screen hanging on the back wall with a projector pointed at it.

"What's this?" I ask Byron when he enters behind me.

"Tonight's entertainment." Music begins playing and it's "Für Elise," just like my dance with Cal. "But first, we dance." Byron takes my hand and I follow his lead as we chassé across the dance floor.

Each step pools more nausea in my stomach until acid starts creeping up my throat, readying to spill out all over Byron's white shirt.

Every now and then I look up and see him peering down at me like I'm some prize he won at a fair, by cheating his way to the win.

He will not win. Not me. Not Cal's empire. In the end, I'll make damn sure that Byron has nothing. Even if Cal is never found, I will fight for what belongs to him.

I decide to break the silence with a simple question. "So, how'd you manage to take over if Cal isn't even presumed dead?"

Byron extends his arm with my hand in his and twirls me around before pulling me snug to his chest. "It's easy to take over when there is no one to stop you. Ellis Empire might not be legally mine...yet," he snickers, "but as far as all the staff go, I am in control now. Out with the old and in with the new. It's only a matter of time before his body is found and the estate is settled."

Byron missteps, causing me to step on his shoe, and I grumble under my breath. He's a terrible dancer.

The music comes to a stop and Byron takes a step back, still gripping my left hand in his. "You must be tired after the events of the last twenty-four hours. I have one more surprise before you can settle into your room with dinner. I expect you to get a good night's sleep, because we have a busy day tomorrow."

"Can't wait to see what my next surprise is." My words are laced with sarcasm, and I'm beginning to realize that even pretending with this guy is damn near impossible. "I'm feeling pretty thirsty, though. Would you mind getting us something to drink? Wine, perhaps?"

Byron's expression shifts unceremoniously to one of anger. His voice rises. "You can't wait two damn minutes, so I can show you my surprise?"

My eyes shoot wide at his outburst. He's completely unhinged. "Okay," I say quietly, "show me your surprise."

Byron's scowl turns into a beaming smile. Almost too excitedly, he pulls out his phone and begins tapping into it. A sinister glance at me and he walks over to the projector and grabs the remote.

The white screen fills immediately.

I gasp at the sight in front of me. My knees buckle, and I stumble, trying to catch my fall.

"What the hell is this?" I sputter, now looking at Byron who's on one knee with an open jewelry box held out. My voice rises to a scream. "What the fuck did you do to my brother?" Air gets lodged in my throat, and I feel like I'm slowly suffocating.

"Save him and marry me. It's the only way."

I walk steadfast toward Byron, who's still crouched in a proposal stance. My arm extends, and I slap the box out of his hand, sending it flying across the floor. "Marry you? Have you lost your damn mind?"

Byron stands up, grabs my shoulders, and grinds his molars. "Marry me or Mark dies."

I'm speechless. At a loss for words. My head is spinning so fast that I don't even know what is real anymore. This has to be a nightmare. I convulse in hysterics and my mind escapes me as my hands begin flailing at Byron. I smack him, punch him, knee him, all while screaming profanities and vile words of hate. I could kill him. I *am* going to kill him.

A swift slap across my face halts my movements. Byron grabs my wrists, restraining me. "Listen here, you fucking cunt. You will marry me or I'll kill your goddamn brother. In fact, I'll kill your entire family. Everything you love will be gone."

Tears fall recklessly down my cheeks while my already broken heart shatters into tiny pieces. "Why are you doing this? Why me?"

I don't understand any of this. Byron has Cal's fortune like he always wanted. He has it all. Why me?

"Because I lied to you. Callum did love you. More than anything in this world. His empire included. I vowed to myself long ago that I would take everything he loved and make it mine." His cold lips press to mine. I'm too stunned to move or care or react. "You included, Bella. Callum is gone and he's never coming back; I can promise you that. No one else wants you but me. You have nothing to lose."

My eyes find the screen once more. Mark is bound and gagged. His head hangs unconsciously with his chin pressed to his chest. I see blood. Lots of blood. He's really hurt and if I don't do what Byron wants, I don't doubt for a second that he will kill my brother.

My face falls into my hands, unable to look at Byron or that screen any longer. What is this life anymore? All I want is normalcy, but I don't even know what that is. I never have. An orphan at the age of four, who never knew what love truly was until I was eleven years old. All my life, I've searched for happiness as if I'd find it behind a closed door. Then I did. I found it when I wasn't even looking and it took me by storm. Then in the blink of an eye, it was gone. Just like everything that made me feel whole, as temporary as it is, it just vanished. *He* vanished.

"Okay," I finally say, my voice almost a whisper, "let him go and I'll marry you."

Byron squeezes my wrists harder, his blue eyes wide and full of anger. "Stop treating me like a fool. You will marry me, *then* I will let him go."

I clench my jaw, attempt to jerk my wrists away to no avail, and hiss, "And you stop treating me like a damn fool. How do I know you won't kill him anyway?"

"Your brother doesn't know who has him or why. He has not seen any of my men's faces; therefore, I can safely free him without implication."

I'm trying so hard to piece together the events of the last twenty-four hours and come to terms with my reality, but it all feels too unreal. Like a horror movie playing out before me.

When I don't respond, Byron tosses my wrists away and stops the livestream on the screen. "It's been a long day. Get some rest and we will talk tomorrow. Before the ceremony."

"Tomorrow?" I spit out in one breath. "You can't be serious."

"Oh, I am serious. This time tomorrow, you will be Mrs. Byron Davis."

My eyes pinch shut as tears still manage to find their way out. I open them abruptly. "Like hell I will."

I storm out of the room, my feet never stopping until I

make it to the elevator. I hit the button and take it up, then go straight to my room.

My door slams shut, and I curse Cal for never putting a lock on this door.

I'm hungry, exhausted, and feel like I'm on the verge of vomiting, but sleep is the last thing I plan to get. I have to devise a plan to either escape this island, or kill Byron.

One way or another, I'm saving Mark, and it will not be by me taking Byron's hand in marriage.

CHAPTER SIX

I've paced the length of this room at least a dozen times. I've even gone as far as throwing a leg over the banister on the balcony, thinking I'd attempt to escape even if it meant falling to my death. Death actually sounds more appealing than marrying that scumbag.

I don't have a clock, so I'm not sure on the time, but I'd say it's somewhere around midnight. For all I know, Byron could be a night owl. I'm also certain that there are eyes on me at all times, but I have to try something. I can't just sit in this room while Mark is being held prisoner and Cal is still missing.

Barefoot, in a pair of black, silk pajamas, I creep down the hall, glancing at all the cameras I pass by. I see them, but most importantly, they see me.

Screw it. I've got fight left in me and it's time to prove it.

I stroll down the hall, casually, as if I'm up for a midnight snack. Heading for the elevator, I pass by Cal's old room. My heart twinges, and I find myself backstepping. One hand reaches out, presses to the door, and my eyes close.

God, I miss him.

We spent so many years apart, and I really wasn't sure I'd ever see Cal again. Our reunification was not as sweet as I would have wanted it to be; in fact, it was torturous at best. But the more time we spent together, the louder his heart sang to mine. I wanted to fill that empty void inside him and repair all his broken pieces. In the end, I'm the one who paid the price. I paid with my heart shattering and now Byron expects me to pay him with my soul.

Fuck that.

I drop my hand from the door and continue to the elevator, but stop abruptly, when I hear footsteps coming down the hall. My heart jumps and, on impulse, I go back to Cal's door and take the risk of it being locked.

To my surprise, it opens. I go inside, closing the door quietly behind me.

With my breath held, I tiptoe over to the closet, hoping like hell I don't have to go inside. But when the bedroom door creaks open, I go in as fast as I can.

I don't let go of the handle as I close the closet door behind me. I grip it tightly, afraid that if I let go, it will latch and Byron will hear it.

I hear a switch flip, likely the light. "They're still here," Byron says, angrily. "I told you I want these fucking snakes gone or else I'll chop their damn heads off myself."

Oh my God, the snakes. I forgot all about them. I hope someone has been feeding them and giving them care. I don't even like snakes, but the thought of them being harmed while Cal's been missing breaks my heart.

"I don't give a shit who takes them. Call a fucking reptile shelter, for all I care."

There's a long beat of silence before I hear the shuffle of feet through the room.

My abdominal muscles pull in as I hold my breath. He comes closer. And Closer.

I'm a millisecond away from being caught and a sense of horror ripples through my bones.

My body jolts when Byron's phone begins ringing. I blow out a pent-up breath as the sound continues.

"It's about damn time you called back. How are our guests?"

Guests? As in hotel guests?

I can't imagine anyone else staying here. Especially since I have the freedom to roam. Byron knows I can't leave, but he wouldn't risk me alerting guests of my kidnapping.

No. It's only me and the staff that he's paying. He has to be talking about another hotel.

"Keep the brother bloody. I need her to see how far I go to get what I want. As for the other one, bring him to the brink of death, for all I care. Just make sure he's able to view the livestream of the wedding. I want him alive when I take everything he loves."

I gasp, clapping a hand over my mouth as the sounds continue to ride up my throat.

He has to be talking about Cal. He has him held captive somewhere with Mark and plans to livestream the wedding, just so he can watch before he kills them.

But the wedding is supposed to be tomorrow, or today, since it's past midnight. There's no way I can save them both. I only have one choice. I have to—

The door to the closet flies open, and I lose all train of thought.

I stumble back, tripping over a box and falling into the hanging suits.

"Aren't you just a sneaky little bitch?"

My hands move backward, attempting to crawl to get away from him. I reach back, touching the wall in search of the opening where the door to the basement is.

"Get out of the fucking closet, Bella."

I keep searching for the door, finally finding it, but I'm too late. Byron grabs my foot and begins pulling me. Slapping my hand around on the floor, I look for something to hold on to or to grab to use as a weapon against him, but all I find is a metal hanger.

Byron keeps pulling until I'm flat on my back and he's standing over me.

He crouches down, looking into my eyes with a heinous scowl. "Looks like we have to do this the hard way."

Gripping the hanger, I bring it up quickly, shoving the hook right into his eye. Well, at least that's what I tried to do. Instead, I missed and got the side of his face. Blood runs down his cheek, falling onto my chin.

"You're gonna pay for that. Oh, are you gonna pay."

Cold hands wrap around my throat, and it's a feeling I'm not foreign to. It was only yesterday Byron choked me from the driver's side of my car.

With his hands still around my neck, he lifts me up, and I press my hands against the floor to gain momentum as I'm pulled to a standing position.

I gasp, and fight, and try to get out of his clutches, but once again, I'm too weak.

Byron pulls me out of the closet and tosses me onto the floor of the bedroom. Coming out after me with thunderous steps, he begins unfastening his belt. I crawl backward again, trying to get away from him, while knowing that there is nowhere to run.

"You know," he begins, "I wanted to wait until we were married to consummate our wedding vows, but you've proven to be unworthy of my patience. Therefore, I should fuck you now. It's also never too soon to try for a baby, *baby*."

"No!" I screech. "Get away from me!"

He doesn't.

He comes closer and closer, his feet touching mine. Reaching down, he grabs me by the arm and pulls me up, then pushes me back until I'm lying on Cal's bed.

A lump lodges in my throat, and I swallow it down, tasting my tears on my tongue.

Fight, Bella.

Each movement he makes has me slithering farther up the bed until I hit the headboard. When there's nowhere else to go, Byron blankets my body with his. I snarl in disgust as he begins kissing my neck.

Crying and writhing beneath him, I try to fend him off, but it's no use. He's made it clear that he gets what he wants.

With my head turned to the side, I see a lamp on the end table.

Byron reaches down between us and cups my crotch while I reach my arm out to grab the lamp, but it's too far.

I reach farther, hoping he doesn't notice, and when he begins kissing my neck again, I know he doesn't.

Just a little...bit...farther.

In one swift motion, I pull the lamp, unplugging it and taking the cord along as I bash Byron over the head with it.

His body goes limp, and I shove him off me. Another shove sends him falling to the floor and I jump off the bed. Instead of leaving immediately, I grab the base of the lamp, go over to where he lies, and hit him in the head again to make sure he's knocked out cold.

I reach into Byron's pocket and take his phone.

Then I run like hell.

Tearing open the door, I go straight for the elevator in a panic. My pulse never slows as I tap the elevator button over and over and over again until the doors finally open. Once I'm inside and riding down to the main floor, I swipe the screen on Byron's phone. My hands shake uncontrollably, forcing me to grip it harder out of worry I'll drop it and never have the chance to pick it back up.

"No!"

Stupid fucking passcode.

Wait. There should be a way to call for help from the lock screen.

I try everything. Pressing buttons at the same time, swiping up and down. Nothing works.

I feel defeated as the elevator comes to a stop. I slam the phone down on the ground, ready to stomp on it, when I pause, my foot in midair.

I just have to wait for a call to come in. Once it does, I'll be able to answer and hang up right away, which will leave me on the home screen and able to call for help.

I'll just hide somewhere until that happens.

I go out the main doors and the light snowfall has turned heavy and blustery. A gust of wind has me hugging my chest as my bare feet sink into the accumulating fluff.

The cold snow doesn't even faze me as I make my way to the side of the castle, leaving a fresh trail of footprints. Fortunately, the snow is falling heavy enough that they should be hidden before the sun rises.

Without stopping, I keep going, until I'm hidden among untended bushes and weeds that have overgrown. Then I crouch down and I wait.

Someone will call soon. Hopefully long before frostbite takes hold.

CHAPTER SEVEN

WITH MY PHONE held out and a picture of Byron pulled up, I ask the nitwit for the umpteenth time, "You're sure this was him?"

"Yes, sir. That's definitely the guy she was with."

I continue to rummage through the hotel room, looking for something. Anything. "Fuck!" I shout, tossing the comforter to the floor. "Nothing. There's not a damn clue as to where she might've gone."

"Look. I'm sorry, Boss. After the girl broke my nose, I lost her."

I feel my jaw clench as I spin around and grab the imbecile I hired by the collar of his pretty-boy shirt. "You had one fucking job! One job and you screwed it up."

His cigar-infused breath hits my senses and I toss him back, allowing him to crash onto the bed.

"She's a feisty bitch. I'm telling ya—"

My fist meets his jaw, hoping I broke it to match his nose. "You ever call her that again and I'll shatter every bone in your goddamn face. You're fired. Now get the hell outta here." His eyes widen with surprise, and he just lies there propped up on his elbows. I point at the door. "Now!"

Crawling off the bed like the lowlife he is, he walks out with his tail between his legs. I slam the door shut behind him and immediately pull my phone out of the pocket of my pants to call my other, recently hired, man, hoping like hell he has more brain cells than this guy.

"Any word?"

"Nothing, sir. We've scoured every street she might've crossed, and there's not a single breadcrumb."

"I'm searching her car. Keep looking and call me the minute you find something."

I end the call and slam my phone down on the bed. "Dammit, Bella. Where the hell are you?"

I kept my distance for her protection. Watched from afar to make sure she was safe. I've had eyes on her ever since I gave Peter the orders to get her home. I didn't want to let her go. I can barely fucking breathe without her, but I had no choice.

Bella's life is more important than my own.

Byron took everything from me. Made my men believe I was dead and showed them that he was now in charge of Ellis Empire. The bastard is even spending my money already.

Fortunately, I had an offshore account and was able to tap into it to hire my own temporary crew. I've also made contact with Anders, my original head of security. The search for Bella is now underway. *Unfortunately,* these new guys are all amateur ass-kissers and I can't tell if they're keeping their eyes on my girl for the money or because she makes their dicks hard.

I snatch my phone off the bed and leave the room. It's been three hours since he lost her. Three fucking hours that she could have wandered to God knows where. Or worse, been taken.

I swear on everything worth a damn, if anyone touches a hair on her head, I will murder them in their sleep. Or maybe while they're awake, so I can look into their sorry eyes as I do it.

My thunderous steps take me down the hall, knocking into a housekeeper's cart and sending a tray of food to the floor, but I don't stop.

"Excuse you." The lady growls as I punch the down arrow for the elevator.

Once I'm in the main lobby, I stop at the front desk and slide the clerk my business card with a hundred-dollar bill beneath it. "If the guest in Room 280 returns, you call me immediately."

He picks up the card and money, taking a look at it before nodding. "Yeah. Sure thing, Mr. Ellis."

I tap the counter, then head out the revolving door into the parking lot.

There's a chill in the air that has me slipping on my black, leather gloves. The entire city is lit up in an array of red, green, and white lights. It's a miserable reminder that it's New Year's. I'll be thankful once this day is over and the holidays have passed.

Another one alone. It was supposed to be different this year. We should have been together—married, perhaps. Instead, my fortune and identity were stolen from me and I have to fight tooth and nail for what's mine, once again—her and my legacy.

Dragging my feet through the light blanket of snow covering the pavement, I go straight to her car. One good thing about the asshole I just hired is that he was able to attach a tracking device to her car. Little good it does when she leaves without it.

My eyes skim the parking lot before I take my elbow to the driver's side window, busting out the glass. A couple walking by hand in hand gives me an apprehensive look, before picking up their pace and walking off.

I reach in the open window to unlock the door, and dammit, it was never even locked. That's what I get for being presumptuous. I'll buy her a new window. Hell, when I find her and get my money back, I'll buy her a brand-new car.

With the door open, I lean inside and begin searching for anything—her phone, an airline ticket, her luggage. That's when I spot a bag. I pull it out and rifle through it. There's a dress and some makeup, but nothing helpful.

I toss the bag back inside and open the glove box. Nothing.

Damn.

Just as I go to stand up outside the car, something catches my eye on the driver's side floor.

Slouching down, with my gloves still on, I pick up an empty needle syringe. Upon closer inspection, I notice a smear of clear liquid trickling down the inside.

Dread washes over me. Gut-punching, rage-infusing dread.

I can feel it in my bones. He took her and it won't be long until he knows I've escaped. Once he does, there's no saying what he'll do.

He doesn't just want my empire.

He wants the only thing I love in this world.

Her.

Thirty-Six Hours Earlier

Blood pools in my mouth from the last blow, and I spit a mouthful on the man in front of me. I can already feel my eye swelling shut, and I'm almost positive I was knocked unconscious more than once. I'm not even sure how long I've been here or what day it is.

I knew he was coming for me.

Fuck! I should've been more prepared. Thought I had more time to get ahead of him while getting Bella to safety. She is safe, though. At least, she was the last time I talked to Peter. He had put her on a boat back to the main island, and she was going home. My only hope is that she never comes looking for me. I couldn't live knowing that she was hurt in a quest to save me.

It wasn't five minutes after I ended that last call with Peter that a bag was thrown over my head. I woke up in a cement block cell in a basement with my hands and feet tied up. At least the gag was removed, so I could spit at this guy a few times.

"Got anything more to say because this game of cat and mouse is pretty entertaining."

"Cat and mouse?" I chuckle sarcastically. "Who's hunting who? Seems I'm right where you want me. The question is, why?"

"That you are. Now, why don't you sit back and relax until you're needed."

My wrists lift, pressing against the metal cuffs they're restrained with, and I shout, "How the fuck am I supposed to relax?"

The asshole takes a sip of his crisp water from the bottle in his hand and screws the top back on with a shit-eating grin on his face. "Not my problem. I'm paid to watch you. Don't give a fuck if you're tense or relaxed."

"Paid, huh? By who? That fucker Byron Davis?"

He shrugs an unknowing shoulder. "Name doesn't ring a bell."

"Like hell it doesn't." I spit again, this time the blood splatters in a clot on the dirty cement floor. "How much is he paying you?"

"Not enough to deal with your chattering ass."

"Do you have any idea who I am? I'll double it. Hell, I'll fucking triple it."

"Don't know and really don't care. All I see is a bum who got himself in some deep shit with the wrong guy."

The only bum in this room is this jackass, and I'm almost posi-

tive he'd do just about anything for a buck. Obviously. He's here babysitting me.

"Give me a number. Whatever you want, it's yours."

"No amount of money you could pay me would be worth a bullet in my head. It's a hard pass but nice try. Now, if you'll excuse me, I'm gonna go fetch you a nice bologna sandwich so you don't wither away before my boss gets what he wants from you."

"Wait," I say, but he doesn't listen. Just tosses his empty bottle in the corner, on top of a pile of trash, then walks to the door. "Wait a damn minute," I shout louder. He clicks the lock on the metal door and leaves. "Fuck!"

My hands skew under the cuffs. I stretch my feet, trying to get something to snap or break that will free me.

He's a dead man. Byron and the assholes keeping me here. Once I'm out of this damn place, I will kill them all with my bare hands.

My chin tucks to my chest, and I close my eyes, still feeling the sting from the last punch.

A few minutes later, the guard returns, and my head slowly rises at the sound of the door opening. Sure enough, he's got a sandwich on a paper plate in one hand and a dirty glass of water in the other.

He comes closer, raising the sandwich pinched between his grubby fingers. "Open up."

"Get that thing out of my fucking face."

The sandwich flies across the room, hitting the cement wall and sliding down. "Fine. Starve, for all I care."

"Fifty thousand."

His brows hit his forehead, and it seems I've piqued his interest. "Come again."

"Fifty thousand in your account in minutes. You let me out of here and give me a head start, before alerting Mr. Davis that I've escaped."

"Mr. Davis, eh. Who?"

"Quit playing dumb with me."

The guy ponders for a minute, likely considering my offer.

"Sixty thousand," I say, upping the ante.

He turns away, pacing the floor while stroking his coarse, salt-and-pepper beard. "A buck fifty or no deal."

"Deal," I say in one breath. I'm surprised he's settling so quickly. I was prepared to go higher. "You let me out and I'll have it delivered on your doorstep tomorrow morning. But I need at least forty-eight hours before Mr. Davis knows a thing."

It'll take me some time to track Byron down and I need the element of surprise.

He laughs. "You think I'm fucking stupid." Grabbing his phone, he begins tapping on the screen. "A wire transfer before I let you go. And when I do, you walk out of this room and I'll give you thirty-six hours before I tell my boss you broke free."

"Fine. Gimme the damn phone."

He puts it in my restrained right hand, and I go into the browser to get to my online banking.

Seconds later, I'm cursing internally when I see that my password has changed.

I try another account.

Same fucking thing.

"That measly son of a bitch," I mutter. "Well, this might take a minute. Seems your boss is a fucking snake and a lousy thief."

I've got an offshore account with at least a half-mil in it. It was there for emergencies, and this is exactly that.

The guard gives me his bank info and the transfer is seconds away from being complete. Well, half of it. I'm not a complete fucking idiot.

All I have to do is hit Send.

"Now," I begin, gripping the phone in my hand. "To ensure your compliance, you get half now and half will be automatically deposited after thirty-six hours. You rat me out like the dirty crook you are and you're out 75K. Got it?"

"Look. A deal's a deal. You're good for thirty-six hours."

I scoff. "I highly doubt that."

He pulls out a key and doesn't hesitate to click the lock on the first cuff, freeing my right hand. I roll my wrist, working out the kinks, and breathe a slight sigh of relief. "And the other?"

"Make the transfer first."

I could probably manage to fight this guy with one hand. He'd come for his phone; I'd shatter it, then I'd shatter every bone in his face. He's not that big, just smells really fucking bad. I'm at more of a risk of throwing up than losing a fight to him.

I hit Send and the guard is seventy-five thousand dollars richer.

"Done," I tell him. "You fuck this up and not only will you lose the second half, I'll hunt you down and Byron Davis will be the least of your worries."

He uncuffs my other hand, then my ankles. It takes me a minute to stand up, but once I'm steady on my feet, I hand him his phone. Just as he reaches for it, I grab his head and ram my forehead against his. Stumbling back a few feet, he crashes into the door.

"That's for the fucking black eye. Thirty-six hours or I'll thank you for the bloody lip with a broken jaw."

I snatch the keys from his hand and toss his phone at him.

It takes me three tries to get the right one, but when I do, I leave the room and don't look back.

I'm not sure if there are other guards, but the place is pretty quiet, and I make no attempt to silence my steps.

As I'm making my way out, I notice a few more doors similar to the one I was behind. The possibility that Bella is behind one of them occurs to me, but it quickly diminishes when I remember that she's safe in Rhode Island.

I've got no idea where I am or how I'm leaving, but somehow, I'll find a way.

I have to get to Bella. Then I have to kill my fucking attorney.

CHAPTER EIGHT

BYRON'S PHONE DIED. There was a sliver of battery life left, and my continuous attempts at unlocking the screen must have drained it completely.

No one has come to look for me.

Not Byron, or his men.

I'm curled in a ball beneath the sloping branches of a tree with bare feet, wearing thin fabric. It's eerily quiet aside from the chatter of my teeth.

The temperatures are frigid, and the snow continues to blanket the tree that I'm using as a fort to hide out.

It's been two hours. Two long and treacherous hours, and I'm not sure I can make it much longer.

Byron knows I'm here. He has the safety net of my inability to escape, ensuring that I am somewhere on this island. It's only a matter of time before I'm found, and I'm wondering if I might as well face him before I die of hypothermia or lose any limbs from extreme frostbite.

Shifting my legs, I tuck my feet over them to keep them out of the snow. My fingers rub aggressively at my blue-colored toes, trying to warm them, but I can't even feel them anymore to know if it's helping.

My entire body shivers, and I can't take it any longer.

Leaving Byron's phone behind, I crawl out from under the tree and stand up. The moon shines brightly over the bay, offering me a source of light as I walk back toward the castle. I have to go inside and hide somewhere warm before I freeze to death.

Only, my plan is derailed when I go to open the main door and notice it's locked. Hugging my chest tightly, I go around the side and try another door. Then another. And another.

All the doors are locked.

I find myself at the back of the castle, where the new doors were installed, but no luck there either.

He locked me out.

Byron wants to marry me to hurt Cal but killing me might be the next best thing.

My back presses to the wooden door and I slide down. At least there is a lip on the roof that stops the snow from falling here. It's still cold as hell, but it's dry.

I close my eyes and wait. That's all I can do at this point.

"I FOUND her and she's alive."

That voice. It's so familiar.

"Bella. Bella, wake up."

My dry lips smack together. I dart my tongue out to wet them, feeling the rigid cracks and tasting a hint of metal.

"Come on. Let's get you inside."

Someone begins pulling me up until I'm standing, but it's a dream. No one is coming to save me.

I've only got myself.

The weight of my body leaves my feet, and I'm cradled like a baby.

"Shit. You're cold as ice."

It's a dream, Bella. Don't wake up. Just go with it.

I swallow, and it feels like razor blades sliding down my throat.

God, he's so warm—whoever *he* is. Pulling me tighter, I rest my head on his chest and smile.

If only he were real.

Warmth. I can feel it. There's no longer a cold breeze scratching at my skin. There's a fire. I smell wood burning and I can feel the heat of the blaze kiss my cheeks. It feels nice.

We sit down, me still in his arms. A warm blanket wraps around me with strong hands holding me tight. "Bella, wake up."

Don't do it. Don't wake up. You'll find yourself out in the snow again. Just enjoy the dream, even if it's not real, it's safe.

"Bella," he says again. My eyes open, and I immediately push myself off his lap.

"Trent?" I take a step back, making sure my eyes aren't deceiving me. "What the hell are you doing here?" The feeling returns to my feet, and it's a sharp, tingling pain. I sit down in the chair behind me as I try to wrap my head around Trent's arrival. I squeeze my toes, rubbing them and trying to get the blood flowing.

This has to be a dream. Or maybe even a nightmare. There is no way that Trent would be back on the island. He shouldn't even know I'm here.

"I came looking for you. Your parents said they haven't been able to reach you or Mark, and I was worried. She mentioned how you've been obsessed with finding Callum Ellis and I had to at least check this place. Why the hell were you out in the cold like that?" Trent jumps up, blanket in hand. "Did that bastard lock you out? I'll fucking kill him."

I spring up and grab him by the arm, attempting to pull him toward the door so we can leave, but his feet stay planted. "We have to go. Like right fucking now."

He doesn't move, just looks at me like I've lost my mind.

"Trent, I'm not kidding. We *have* to go!"

His arms extend and he sweeps the blanket out and wraps it around me. "You need to rest. Don't worry. I'll handle Callum. He'll never be able to hurt you again. I promise you, Bella."

My head shakes, and I try to speak, but the words don't come out.

"Just calm down—"

"No! Don't tell me to calm down, Trent. It's not Cal. It's Byron. His attorney. Or friend or whatever he is." I look over my shoulder, feeling like Byron is going to walk in here any minute. "He kidnapped me and we need to go right now." I pull him again, my hands shaking frantically, and the perplexed look on his face is unnerving. "Why aren't you listening to me?"

"You seem disoriented. Let me see if I can find someone to get you some water."

"I don't want water! I want to leave." I drop my hand from his bicep and hold it out. "Give me your phone."

"My phone? Why?"

"Have you not heard anything I'm saying to you? Give me your damn phone, Trent. We need to call for help."

He's acting weird. Looking at me like I'm a stranger who's lost her mind. Why is he just standing there staring at me like that?

"Phone!" I snap my fingers. "Now, dammit."

Trent reaches in his pocket, his eyes never leaving mine.

He retrieves his phone and places it in the palm of my hand. "Won't do any good. I have no service out here."

"But you were just talking to someone outside. I heard you," I choke out before my tears thaw and fall again. I drop down into the chair, still unable to control my shakes. Was it part of the dream? Was he really talking to someone on the phone?

Wait a damn minute!

My back straightens against the chair. "How did you get here? Do you have a boat waiting?"

"It's returning in one hour. But here's the thing, Bella..." His words trail off, eyes shooting behind me, wide and cautious.

I look behind me to see what stole his words, and my heart stills.

Jumping to my feet, I hurry to Trent's side, grabbing his arm and showing Byron that his game is over. Trent will never let him hurt me.

"Get away from me!" I screech at Byron.

Slow and steady steps bring us face to face. He looks at Trent, then me, with a spine-chilling grin.

I take notice of the huge gash on his forehead, blood trickling down from the wound and coating the left side of his face.

"It's over, Byron. We're leaving and there isn't anything you can do to stop us." I squeeze Trent's arm tighter, but he moves it, loosening my grip. I look up at him and notice he's staring down at me. The look on his face alarms every cell in my body.

"Trent," I say softly.

He moves his arm again and I completely lose my hold on him.

"Trent. What are you doing?" I look from him to Byron, and it's like four walls closing in on me, only it's two men.

"No." I shake my head. "Please tell me you're not on his side?"

I take a step back, tripping over the curled rug, but I manage to catch myself before backsliding into the fireplace.

Byron walks toward me, reaches out and grabs me firmly by the wrist, digging so deep I can feel my pulse pound against his fingertips.

"Money is a beautiful thing, Bella. And you should be thankful that my new employee found you out there or you'd have frozen to death." He shoves me until I fall back into the chair.

Employee?

"Sorry, Bella," Trent says with no empathy in his words. "When an old law school buddy reaches out and offers you a partnership at one of the biggest firms in the nation, you have to accept."

"Old law school buddy?" I mumble. How did I not see this? Mark and Trent went to law school together. That is, until Mark dropped out. That's how he got Mark. They all know each other and he lured him in with Trent's help. "Mark is your friend," I say to Trent. "How could you do this? Not just to me, but to him?"

My stomach churns. I grab it, feeling the rise of bile up my throat.

"What is a friend, anyways?" Trent continues, "Someone who takes his whore of a sister's side when she fucks her boss? Or how about a person who calls one time in the past eight weeks after you're brutally beaten to a near-death state? Mark's not my fucking friend." He comes toward me, crouches down to where I sit in the chair, and places his hands on my legs. "And neither are you."

CHAPTER NINE

A GUN, a phone, and list of every fucker who will pay for turning their backs on me. That's what I've accumulated since realizing Byron kidnapped Bella.

Now I'm on a call with my pilot, trying to fix the mess Byron has made. I can't even bring out one of my own jets because that asshole will be hot on my tail. "I don't give a flying fuck what he made everyone believe. I want a jet on the ground at LGA in twenty fucking minutes, without his knowledge, or you'll never fly again." I end the call, trying to calm the raging storm brewing inside me.

Fucking New York City. That's where this asshole held me captive. This whole ploy has Byron's name written all over it. Not only is he a native to New York City, but he also attended law school at Columbia and his largest firm is in the Big Apple.

I fucking hate the city. I hate crowds and I hate people. It's why eighty percent of my hotels are on private islands, with the exception of one that is actually here...in the city. It's on a smaller scale and doesn't have all the same luxuries as the other resorts, but it brings in good revenue, so I keep it open.

A call from my head of security, Anders, comes through, and I take it immediately. "Anything?"

"Actually, Boss. We've got reason to believe he's taken her back to Cori Cove. Jeffery confirmed the coming and going of a few different watercrafts over the last forty-eight hours."

"All right," I grumble. "I'm headed to the main island. I've got a crew waiting to be transported. We have to do this right. There's no room for fuck-ups."

"You've got it. We'll get her back, Boss."

"Damn straight we will." I look up at the gray skies, feeling the snow fall on my face. "Any word from Peter yet?"

"Nothing. I can only assume he's there with them."

"Keep me updated on any changes. Otherwise, I'll see you within the hour."

Byron's gone too fucking far this time. It seems the entire world believes I'm dead, and he's out there living my life with my girl.

"Stop here," I tell the driver. He slams on the brakes, likely out of fear of pissing me off further by going a foot too far. I've had a few choice words with everyone I've encountered today. It seems that coming back from the dead isn't an easy stint.

I get out, button my suit jacket, and knock my knuckles to the driver's window while taking in my surroundings at the airfield.

His window comes down and I lean forward, invading his personal space. "You didn't give me a ride. In fact, you didn't even see me. Got it?"

His response is a coy, "Yes, sir."

The last thing I need is Byron catching wind of my escape and doing something to harm Bella out of spite.

After standing around wasting time I don't have, the private jet finally arrives.

I get in, get comfortable, and begin making calls to the men I know will have my back. Loyalty and trust have nothing to do with it; it's because I pay them and I pay them well.

Deep down, I know I can't trust anyone. Never have, never will. Every single person in the world is out for themselves, no matter what bullshit lies they tell you. My past is proof of that. My future, on the other hand, will ensure that those who deemed themselves untrustworthy suffer the most extreme consequences. If they've placed themselves in my life, they should know better than to double-cross me because payback will be had. It seems there are more than a few that do not.

I'd like to think I can trust Peter, but you can never tell. The guy's been with me since the beginning, and he's never betrayed me, but he's no spring chicken and he needs the comfort of food and a roof over his head. If he had to take Byron's side, while assuming I was dead, he's the one person I'd consider forgiving. My only hope is that Byron has treated him well.

When the pilot announces we're clear to land, I stick my phone in my pocket, check my gun in the holster around my waist, and mentally prepare for any possible outcome.

I'm coming for you, Bella.

CHAPTER TEN

Nothing matters anymore. Another person who I thought I could trust has turned on me. This time, it's Trent. The man I spent two years of my life with and considered marrying at one point.

Now he's forcing me into a wedding gown, so I can marry someone else.

"Put your fucking foot in, Bella."

I don't. I just stand there in the laced bodice he managed to get on me. After quite the quarrel on the floor, I lost. My strength is no match for his.

One thing he should know by now is that I do not go down without a fight.

Trent kneels at my feet, trying to get me into a wedding gown, because that's what Byron told him to do.

"All this for money. You're despicable, you know that?" I begin unstrapping the ties of the bodice, undoing all the work he just did. It doesn't matter that I'll be standing completely naked in front of him.

As I said, nothing matters anymore.

"It's not about money. Consider it helping an old friend."

"Old friend?" I laugh. "Because you went to law school together? That hardly makes him your friend. He's using you, Trent, and the sooner you realize that, the better off you'll be." I scoff. "Wouldn't surprise me if he kills you when he's done with you."

"Byron contacted me once he put two and two together and realized you were my girlfriend, or ex-girlfriend. He made me an offer I couldn't refuse. An act of revenge, per se. Look," he drops his hands, peering up at me, "I've worked my ass off to get where I'm at and I've got nothing to show for it. A partnership with Davis & Davis law firm would be a dream come true. It's not like I've got anything to lose here. You made it clear where we stand."

I could kick him in the face right now. I really could. Just one lift of the leg and he'd be eating my toes. Then I could run. But running has proven to be a waste of time because I have nowhere to fucking go.

"Cal can help you. If you just stop all this and take my side, he will help you."

Trent stands up, nostrils flared and chest puffed out. "Fuck Callum Ellis." He leans closer. "And fuck you for fucking him."

Running might not be an option, but nothing stops me from raising my hand and slapping him across the face. "No, Trent. Fuck you!" The sting on my palm is actually gratifying. That was the best decision I've made all day.

Standing here arguing is getting me nowhere so I do what's asked of me in hopes that I'll find a way out of this mess.

I reach down and pull up the dress that's pooled around me. It's actually a beautiful dress. Off-white—because Byron said whores don't get to wear white—with an impressive floral, lace overlay. It's much too poufy on the bottom and nothing like I planned to wear on my wedding day. Not the wedding I dreamt of, anyway.

"Zip it up." I give Trent my back, and he does as I say without a word.

Not even looking back at him, I walk out the door, barefoot. The dress is the only beautiful thing about me right now. I didn't even brush my hair again because I have no interest in looking acceptable for my soon-to-be husband.

I also have no plans to actually marry him.

Instead of taking the elevator to the ballroom, where the ceremony is being held, I go straight to the kitchen.

I'm not sure why I didn't think of this before, but a butcher knife straight to his heart should do the trick.

"Good morning," I say to the cook. It's not the same one who was working here during my last stay on the island. In fact, Byron has taken on all new staff. Peter has been replaced with an uptight doorman who smells like green beans and farts and never smiles. The position might have been filled by someone else, but Peter himself is irreplaceable.

"You shouldn't be in here, ma'am."

I spot a knife block and walk straight to it. Reaching down, I pull out the biggest one. It illuminates under the dome light hanging from the ceiling, and it's so big I can see my reflection in it. "And you shouldn't be working for a criminal who kidnaps women and forces them into marriage."

His eyes widen, darting from me to the pointed blade. I wink back at him before leaving with the knife in one hand, and my dress balled in the other to stop me from tripping over it. That would be just my luck—fall and stab myself in the gut. That's one way to end this madness.

No. I prefer to die while trying to live. At least then I know I gave it my damnedest.

I go up to the seventh floor, where the ballroom is, and I'm prepared for what I have to do. Actually, I'm not, but it's best this way. If I think too much about it, I'll cower.

The elevator doors slide open and I'm greeted with a very angry Byron, dressed in a black tuxedo with a cream-colored bow tie to match my dress. He shoots daggers at me before dropping his gaze to the knife at my side.

"Clever, Bella. If only you had the guts to use it."

"You'd be surprised how gutsy I am, Byron." I hold the knife out and walk forward. Each step has him walking backward. "Tell me why I shouldn't slit your throat right now."

Trent comes walking toward us, spots the knife, and throws his hands up, halting his movements.

Two more men follow behind him—men I've never seen before.

"Restrain her," Byron orders the men.

I look at the guys, waiting for them to do as they're told, but no one moves.

"Now!" Byron barks the order.

The smaller of the guys, who's actually shorter than I am, starts my way. I hold out the knife, testing him. "Stay the fuck away from me." I choke on my words. "I'll do it."

"Bella," Byron says in a high-pitched voice, "think of Mark."

My attention snaps to him, the knife swinging with me. "I am thinking of Mark. And the rest of the world who I'd be doing a favor by taking you out. I will not marry you, Byron. Not today, not ever. I'll die first." I hold out my wrist, resting the knife against it.

Would I do it? Would I really die before marrying this guy? He'd end up killing Mark, probably Cal, too. I know he has him somewhere. I heard the conversation. He wants Cal to watch us get married, then he will probably kill them both.

"Go ahead," he nods toward the knife pressed to my wrist, "do it and save me the trouble of having to marry you. With you gone, I get everything I want."

"How?" I huff. "How am I standing in your way? What the hell do I have that you want?"

"Sir," the taller of the guys cuts in. "Sir, we have a problem."

Byron looks at me, the knife, then the guy. "What the hell is it now?"

The guy tips his head, calling Byron over.

With his back to me, I eyeball Trent, challenging him to stop me before I hit the button on the elevator.

Byron and the guy exchange some heated words and I tap my foot anxiously waiting for the doors to open. When they do, all eyes shoot in my direction. "Get her!" Byron shouts.

I step into the elevator and hit the button to close the door repeatedly. They begin to close, but a hand slaps between them, causing the doors to open back up. It's the smaller one of Byron's goons. I swing the knife at his hand, slashing it. His howls echo through my head and I turn away so I don't see the deep wounds pouring blood onto the doors and the floor of the elevator.

With my head turned, I begin vomiting. It all just comes out with no chance of holding it back.

The next thing I know, arms wrap around me and the knife is taken from my hands. "The boat is coming. We need to get the hell out of here now. Give me your fucking phone," Byron snaps at Trent.

Still holding me, Trent reaches into his pocket and pulls his phone out. Asshole told me he didn't have any service. How did I not see what a snake he is?

Vomit hangs from my mouth, and I'm unable to wipe it

away as my arms press tightly to my chest in Trent's hold. Byron and the other guys ride the elevator down with us.

My mouth tastes like ass and I'm on the verge of emptying the rest of whatever is in my stomach. "We're leaving the island?"

Byron taps into Trent's phone and doesn't even look at me when he speaks. "Seems we're getting some unexpected guests."

The elevator stops, and he slaps the phone in Trent's hand. "I'll take her from here. Go wait for the boat."

Trent shoves me into Byron's arms in the corridor of the main entrance. Everyone leaves, so it's just us. Byron holds me from behind and I can feel the tiny hairs on my arms standing up when his hot breath rolls down my neck.

"Seems I've got a decision to make, Bella. I can bring you with me and keep you, even though I don't need or want you. Or I can kill you and leave your body right here on this floor for my good friend and former client, Callum, to find."

"I thought...I thought you planned to marry me?"

Something happened. For some reason, everything has changed.

"You know, the first time I saw you, I knew you were trouble. I fought like hell to get you out of Callum's mind, but he fought me harder. I used to watch you for him. I saw you sleeping peacefully in your bed at night, not a care in the world. I jerked my cock while you were showering once. That was a good time. Then there was the time I saw you fingering yourself on your bedroom floor while your parents watched the evening news. Talk about rebelliousness."

My heart kicks into high gear because what I'm hearing is sickening. All those days that I went on with my life as a normal person, and I was completely oblivious to being watched.

"Each day Callum got closer and closer to getting you,

until finally, you came, just like he knew you would. You fought him hard for a while, but eventually, you caved and fell under the spell of the infamous Callum Ellis. Such a fucking fool you are. You see, Bella, you can call me a crook and a liar, but you fell in love with a monster. What I could do to you wouldn't touch the betrayal he bestowed upon you."

"I don't believe anything you say. So shut the hell up!"

"Is that so? What if I told you that you were never protected when you had sex with him? What if I told you that instead of taking birth control, you were taking fertility pills because Callum was trying to impregnate you? Still want me to shut up, Bella?"

"I'd say I don't believe a word that comes out of your disgusting mouth." My head tilts down, and I bite into the flesh of his arm. My teeth sink deep, piercing his skin, and the bitter taste of salt and blood seeps into my mouth.

"You fucking bitch." Byron tries to shove me away, but my mouth is latched so tightly that he'd risk losing a chunk of his skin.

When he grabs me by the hair and jerks my head back so hard I get whiplash, I finally release my bite. My head swings and thrashes as he pulls and the next thing I know, my head is crashing into the wall. My body slides down slowly as everything blurs around me.

"Hurry your ass up. We gotta go," someone says, though I can't make out the face or the voice. "There's a lot of them, Byron. We gotta go, right fucking now!"

I can feel him lift me up, but I'm unable to fight him off.

My eyes close, and I allow myself to drift away to a time I was happy.

"Come on," Cal says, taking my hand and leading me out the back door of the church.

I laugh as he pulls me, though my resistance tells him I'm not so sure about this. "Cal, we can't. If Mrs. Webster finds out, she's sure to kill us."

"Nah. She won't even know we're gone. No one will."

When the door closes behind us, I drop my head back, letting the warmth of the sun kiss my cheeks. It's a beautiful day without a cloud in sight.

"Still wanna go inside for youth group?" he asks, his hand still holding mine.

My head comes forward, and I look at him, our smiles matching. "No way."

Cal leads me over to the side of the church. Not a person, car, or house to be seen. We sit down in unison, backs pressed against the building, legs bent at the knees.

Once a week, we take a bus to youth group. Now that I'm eleven, I've been moved up to the same class Cal is in. It's a two-hour break for Mrs. Webster and a chance for us to get right with the Lord—aside from our regular Sunday morning service.

"Is this where you disappeared to the last couple classes?"

Cal smirks. "Maybe."

"And why wasn't I invited then?"

He grabs my hand, flips it over, and begins tracing the lines on my palm. Something happens inside me. My stomach does this weird flip-flop thing and my heart begins beating superfast.

"Didn't know you'd wanna hang out with me outside of the home."

"Cal," I blow out his name in one breath, "I always want to hang out with you. You've been my best friend since I got here. Why would you say that?"

He doesn't look at me, just keeps drawing on my hand and causing goosebumps to ride up my arm. "Saw you with Mark and Trent a couple weeks ago. They were poking fun at my pants being too short and you laughed with them."

The flip-flop of my stomach stops when my heart settles inside it. "I'm sorry, Cal. You never should've heard that."

"You never should've let 'em get away with saying it."

"You must've missed the part where I told them to both eat a bag of dicks."

Cal's eyes widen, finding mine. "You didn't?"

"Oh yes I did." I laugh. "And I'd do it again, even if it meant getting my mouth washed out with the nasty dollar-store soap."

Cal's expression gets serious, though I find it hard to take him seriously at all. "Always go for the blue bar if it's available. The green one tastes like perfume-infused ass."

We both burst out laughing.

"Really, though, Cal. I'm so tired of trying to fit in with these kids. Me and you. It's me and you. Ride or die."

Cal holds out his pinky. "Promise?"

I wrap my pinky around his and give it a shake. "Forever and ever, until kingdom come."

CHAPTER ELEVEN

"GET HIM!" I shout through gusts of wind as pelts of ice lash at my face. I'm running as fast as I can, unable to see a damn thing. But I won't stop. I will not stop until I have her.

I watch in slow motion as Anders takes Byron down to the ground, Bella's body falls weightlessly from his arms, and she topples face-first into the snow.

The two of them begin a wrestling match, rolling, punching, kicking, but I offer no help to my guard as I go straight for Bella.

My eyes skim over her body. Bruised, cold, and bloody.

"Jesus Christ, Bella. What did he do to you?"

Her eyes flutter open, lips smacking, and as much as I want to warm them with my mouth, I have to make sure she's okay first.

"Am I dreaming?" she asks through parted, cracked lips.

I breathe a sigh of relief at the sound of her beautiful voice. "No, baby. You're not dreaming."

Scooping her into my arms, I head for the castle. Looking over my shoulder, I shout to my men. "Rough him up. But keep him alive."

I don't even look back. I may have lost some men when the world assumed I was dead, but the ones still standing by my side are an army of soldiers. They have what it takes to restrain Byron and they'll be on guard until I'm one hundred percent certain Bella is safe. Not that I plan to take my eyes off her.

Her lashes bat snowflakes off them as I carry her in my arms like a small child. "Cal. Is it really you?"

"It's really me. You're safe now."

A sigh of relief escapes her, followed by a gasp. "Oh my God, Cal. Your face. What happened to you?"

She's taken notice of my swollen eye and bruised cheek. That son of a bitch holding me captive thinks he's got away with what he did because I paid him a measly seventy-five grand. He also expects the rest by this evening. Joke's on him. "It's nothing. Don't worry about me."

Bella locks her arms around my neck, peppering my face with kisses through cries of happiness, while sharing my breath to fill her lungs.

"You're alive and you're here."

I look down on her, smiling, though my insides are screaming for what she's endured. "I'm here and I'm never letting you go."

"Mark," she whispers through parted lips. "Byron has Mark."

"Don't worry. We'll find him."

This day has been like a repetitive kick in the gut. I'm not sure I'll ever stop blaming myself for what has happened to Bella. She's in a wedding gown. *Why the fuck is she in a wedding gown?* I can't even think about what would have happened to her had I not made a deal with the prison guard.

Once we're inside, I go straight up the elevator to the sitting room. Every few steps, I peer down at Bella and see her soft, green eyes staring back at me, trying to figure out if this is real or not.

We reach the sitting room and I take her straight over to the fireplace. It's like a moment of déjà vu, only this time, I'm not the monster she took me for that night. At least, not to her. Everyone else in this world? Well, they are about to see just how much of a villain I really am.

I lower her down to the ground and reach over, grabbing a throw blanket off the chair. My legs straddle her from behind. I quickly wrap the blanket around her cold body and squeeze her tightly in my arms.

My chin rests on her shoulder, and I inhale the scent of her damp hair. "Tell me everything."

"I...I don't even know where to start." She turns to the side, legs draped over mine. I press a chaste kiss to her cheek, still reeling from this unexpected reunion with her. "I've missed you so much, Cal." Tears slide down her cheeks and I use my thumb to sweep them away.

"I've missed you, too. But we're together now and nothing is going to tear us apart."

She begins sobbing, head resting on my chest, and I stroke her hair in an attempt to calm her. "Is Byron really gone?"

"He's gone, baby. I swear over everything, that guy will never touch you again. *No* guy will ever touch you again."

Fuck. The thought of him putting his grubby hands on her makes me fucking crazy. Like boiling water coming to the surface, ready to implode all over anything and anyone who comes near me.

"Bella," I tip her chin with my thumb, looking into her eyes and searching for the courage to ask what I'm about to, "did he...did he touch you?"

If she says yes, so help me God, I will go out there and dismember that son of a bitch before I'm able to get any answers. I will chop his body up into tiny pieces and use it as bait.

"No. Not like that."

A heavy breath of relief parts her hair and I pull her head against my chest. "You have no idea how happy I am to hear that."

We sit quietly for what feels like hours. Warming by the fire, just breathing and holding one another when the sound of heavy footsteps grabs our attention.

I look back first and see Anders, holding up another one of my men. He's severely injured and in dire need of medical assistance.

I tuck the blanket around Bella and scoot out from beneath her. She grabs my leg. "Don't leave me."

"I'm just going over there. I'm not leaving."

Once I'm on my feet, I walk steadfast to Anders. "What the hell happened?" I whisper, trying not to alarm Bella.

"He got away. Greg and Nico are dead. Ben, here, was shot in the abdomen."

I look at Ben, who begins coughing, spewing blood from his mouth. My eyes wander down to his stomach, where Anders has his hand pressed firmly. Blood oozes from his wound, dripping onto the hardwood floor. "Lay him down," I tell Anders.

He helps him down to the ground and I kneel over him, until the coughs and groans subside, then I sweep his eyes shut.

One glance over my shoulder and I see Bella coming toward us. I hold up my hand. "Stop. Don't come over here." Her movements halt, but it's too late, she sees him.

Her hands clap over her mouth, and she points her finger at Ben. "Who did that?"

I get to my feet, hurry over to her, and lead her toward the door. "Call for another boat for me and Bella. You guys go with Leo to the main island. I'll meet you at the docks." I keep walking, then shoot Anders one last look. "And get rid of all the bodies."

Anders nods and I take Bella out of the room.

"It's okay. I promise. We're going somewhere safe. We just have to get Peter first."

Bella bows her head, breaking eye contact. "Cal," she begins.

Something isn't right. I can feel it in my bones. I tip her head up, forcing her to look at me. "What is it? What happened?"

"Peter died over a month ago. Byron all but admitted to killing him."

"What did you just say?" It doesn't need repeating. I heard her loud and clear. I'm just having a hard time processing the words that just came out of her mouth.

"Peter is dead, Cal."

It feels like the world has stopped spinning. My hollow heart cracks beneath the surface, unable to feel it beating. All the blood drains from my face and it's also in this moment that I realize how human I really am. I've never felt loss. Never knew what it was like to feel that sort of pain.

No. It's not true. It can't be.

Peter was like a father to me. He was a mentor, a friend, a confidant. Aside from Bella, he is the only person in the entire world I ever gave a damn about.

"He's gone?" I ask, unable to believe it, even though the words were clear as day.

Bella nods before throwing herself into my arms and holding on to me like our lives depend on it.

Peter is dead, but I push the pain aside as something awakens inside me. I pull myself together and prepare for war.

CHAPTER TWELVE

Bella

NOTHING I SAY or do will ease his pain. He won't even admit that he feels any, but I can see it in his eyes. Those wide, dark orbs roaming around the abyss. Lost in his thoughts, while I'm curled against his chest.

I want to ask him if he's okay, but I know the answer. He'll lie and say he is. Put on a front because that's what Cal does. He wears this rock-hard exterior, even though he's crumbling beneath the surface.

Instead of saying anything at all, I just sit here quietly and savor this moment. We're finally together. After weeks of sheer torture, while everyone told me he was dead, he's here.

The boat slows, and I straighten my back on Cal's lap. My hand rests on his cheek, and I turn his face toward mine. "I'm here for you," I whisper, before pressing my mouth to his. It's a soft kiss, with no effort on his part. I can feel his sadness bleeding into my mouth, so I pull away. Looking into his eyes, he looks past me.

My hand drops and I put little thought into the distance he's putting between us. He's been through a lot and needs time to process everything. Peter was the closest thing he ever had to family, to a father. He was so much more than just a butler, and I know this because I felt it in my own friendship with Peter.

There is a lot we need to talk about. So many unanswered questions that are gnawing on my insides, tugging at my heart and begging to be asked. And I will, in time.

We come to a stop at the dock, and Cal pats my thigh, telling me to get up. I do, and as I go to reach for his hand, I stop myself. His attention isn't on me. It's on the men waiting at the end of the dock.

Right now, Cal has a one-track mind. I'm not upset about it. He saved me, and now he will work tirelessly to ensure my safety, while also avenging Peter's death. I know Cal will keep me safe, even if it won't be an easy task. Byron is smart —though a menace to society—and he will not make the hunt for him an easy one. I just hope in the process, we do not become the prey. For whatever reason, Byron is hell-bent on taking over Cal's empire. He could go out and steal from anyone, but he's after Cal. There has to be a reason for it.

Cal surprises me by taking my hand in his and leading me off the boat. The sun has dipped behind the clouds, making for a gloomy setting. A group of men await us. Some wearing suits, some looking like they just rolled out of bed. My bet on the most badass are the grunge-looking dudes. They look like they're ready to take care of business, scowls and all. One in particular catches my eye.

I squeeze Cal's hand, and he looks down at me. "Hey," I tip my head toward one of the familiar faces, "that guy with the bruised eyes and swollen nose. Who is he?"

"Ah, you remember?"

I snort. "Yeah. Actually, I think I'm the one who did that to his face."

Cal laughs, and it's a sound I've missed. "Yeah, babe. Yeah, you did. He was hired to watch you, and he failed. In fact, he shouldn't even be here." Cal picks up his pace, taking me with him. "Ludwig," he shouts, "I thought I fired your ass."

We approach the guy and Cal drops my hand before stepping up to him. "What the fuck are you doing here?"

"I called him," Anders chimes in. "Look, we need all the help we can get and regardless of a little mishap, he's a good one to have on our side."

Ludwig—I assume is his last name because it's a ridiculous first name—watches me as I join Cal's side. "Hey, sorry about your nose," I say to him, and he completely ignores me. *Jerk.*

Cal nods to the left, looking at Anders, and he takes me with them as they leave the group. "I'm taking Bella to the Manhattan resort. I want you to work with these guys and find that son of a bitch. Once you've got him, call me. But keep him alive. I wanna be the one he's looking at when he takes his last breath."

"You got it, Boss."

Cal wraps an arm around my waist and takes a step to leave, but stops. "Oh, and Anders, find out what happened to Peter's body. He deserves a proper burial."

Anders gives a sympathetic nod with his lips pressed together firmly.

We leave the docks, and the army of men Cal has rallied together. A shiny black car awaits us, and Cal opens the back passenger door. I slide in, and he joins my side.

For the first time in days, I feel safe as he wraps his arm around my shoulders. My head nuzzles into the pit of his arm as he says, "Tell me everything you know about Peter's death."

So, I do. I tell him how I found him on his bedroom floor. How Byron showed up on the island right after and told me about a body that was pulled from the bay.

"It was a former guard. Anders's brother. He was a fuck-up, and I won't deny I had him killed. I'm a monster, Bella. No matter how hard I try to be good, it's what I am."

I go on to tell him how Byron escorted me off the island and promised to keep me updated and that I didn't hear a word from him until two days ago at the performance hall.

Cursing and fuming, he listens to it all.

Cal decided it was best to drive to the hotel we're staying versus taking the private jet. He thinks Byron has access to the pilot logbook and will be able to find out where we're going if we use one of his. Fortunately, it's only a three-hour drive, and we drove past a fast-food restaurant and got greasy burgers, fries, and shakes for the ride.

I swallow down my last fry and place my hands on my bloated stomach. "I'm stuffed."

"I bet you are. You scarfed that food down like you haven't eaten in days." Cal takes a drink of his shake. I watch as his mouth wraps around the straw and then his tongue licks the excess liquid from his lips.

Food isn't the only thing I'm starving for. I've almost forgotten what it feels like to be with him intimately. He was my first, and naturally, he was my last. Once I got a taste of what sex was like, I've craved it ever since.

Cal catches me looking at him and smirks. "Why are you looking at me like that?"

My hand rests on his lap, climbing up until it's sitting on his crotch. "I've missed you."

He places a hand on mine, squeezing it until I'm squeezing him. His erection grows little by little, until he's rock-hard beneath my hand. He leans over and whispers, "Have you now?" Warm breath hits the nape of my neck, sending chills down my spine.

"Mmmhmm," I hum, rubbing his cock through his pants.

His eyes burn into mine, biting at his bottom lip. "Well, I'm here now. What are you gonna do about it?"

I look past him at the driver's rearview mirror and catch him watching us. He immediately returns his focus to the road. I move my hand to my lap and sulk. "Absolutely nothing because we have company."

Cal shoots a look at the front seat. "Who? Him?" He says in a breathy voice, "Fuck that guy. I'll fire him when we're finished to remove all awkwardness." Strong hands grab my waist, and he lifts me up until I'm straddling his lap. "There, now he can't even see you."

I chuckle. "He can see me. I just can't see him."

His mouth finds my neck, and I welcome it by tilting my head. "Same thing."

When his hand slides up the sweatshirt I changed into before we left the island, I give in to the desire. Reaching under my bra, he pinches the bud of my nipple and a whimper of pleasure climbs up my throat.

Cal moves his hand back down, trailing his fingers delicately across my stomach and beneath the waistband of my sweatpants.

"Maybe you're right. Maybe we shouldn't do this," Cal says, taking me by surprise.

"What? Of course we should. I need this. I need you."

"You've been through a lot today. You sure?" he asks, eyes wide and full of mischief. I think part of him likes that we have an audience, and part of me is also turned on by that fact.

I lick my lips and nod. "Positive."

His hand slides down, thumb grazing my sensitive nub. My heart picks up speed and I pull his face to mine, cupping his cheeks in my hands. Our mouths collide recklessly. My back arches as I roll my hips, forcing pressure on his hand down my pants.

Curled fingers dip inside me and I lift up just a bit, giving him better access. I can already feel my desire for him pooling around his touch. I shouldn't want this right now. But after all I've been through, I just want to feel something other than terror and torment.

Before long, I'm riding his hand, and we're full-blown making out like two teenagers in the back seat of the car. There's no hiding how much I want this, how much I've missed this. Cal and his magical fingers continue to work me, bringing me to the brink of orgasm.

His hand grips my hip, teeth dragging across my lower lip and sucking it in his mouth before releasing it like a rubber band. We resume tangling our tongues and stealing each other's breaths.

"Fuck, Cal," I cry out as he pushes harder and deeper. I bounce up and down on his hand, driving his fingers farther inside me.

"That's right, baby. Show me how much you've missed me. Come around my fingers."

His words turn me on even more. Pushing me over the edge as I come undone. I don't even try to muffle my cries of pleasure. My thighs tighten, walls clenched as my orgasm spills into his hand.

When I come down, I smile through the aftershock rippling through me. His fingers leave me and I miss them already.

Cal slides his fingers in my mouth, feeding me my arousal. My lips close around them, tongue swirling, licking my own juices while gazing into his molten eyes.

He pops them out of my mouth, then kisses me. "You taste so good, baby."

I purr into his mouth, our chests heaving together.

In one swift motion, Cal undoes his pants and his cock springs free. Hungry and ready to reclaim what's his. "Take these off," he commands, pulling on my sweatpants.

I look over my shoulder, catching the driver's eyes again,

but smirk inwardly. He's a driver for the rich and reckless, I'm sure this isn't the first time someone has fucked in the back seat of his car.

Cal grabs my face and presses his lips firmly against mine, teeth colliding and lips swelling. He mutters into my mouth, "Let him watch."

I'm not sure why that thought is satisfying, but it is. I'm learning a lot about what I find to be sexually satisfying. Like watching those people in The Grotto. I was highly aroused by it.

I lift up and tug my sweatpants and panties off, letting them fall to the floor. Cal pushes his pants all the way down, then pulls me onto his lap. His cock sinks inside me, wasting no time. Completely filling me up, I take all of him.

"God, I've missed you." His fingers sweep beneath my shirt, then pull my bra down, freeing one of my breasts. Leaning forward, he takes my nipple between his teeth. Biting, tugging, and sucking.

I kiss his swollen eye, down to his bruised cheek. "Not as much as I've missed you." My fingers dig into his hair, hugging his face to my chest. He moves to the next breast, sucking with so much tenacity that pain quickly becomes pleasure.

I ride him harder, faster. My tits bouncing with me. One hand pinches my waist as Cal holds me tightly, as if he fears I'll escape him. Our bodies meld together, a sheen of sweat coating both our foreheads.

"Holy shit, Bella," Cal grumbles, dropping his head back and watching me as I fuck him. His eyes burn into mine, while every inch of him consumes me.

I grip his shoulders, using them to balance myself as I move faster. I don't muffle my sounds, knowing full well that the driver hears me, sees us, and is likely jerking his cock as he takes us down the highway.

Cal's head comes back up; he plants both hands on my waist and squeezes as his breath holds and he grunts through his release.

We're both breathless, sweaty, and trying to calm our racing hearts.

My head rests on his shoulder, and he strokes his fingers through my hair.

As I'm sitting here, coming down from my high, I remember something Byron said.

What if I told you that you were never protected when you had sex with him? What if I told you that instead of taking birth control, you were taking fertility pills because Callum was trying to impregnate you?

I sit up, adjust my shirt, and broach the topic casually as I reach for my pants. "Hey, Cal. Remember those birth control pills you had Peter give me?"

He quirks a brow. "Yeah, what about them?"

I raise my shoulder nonchalantly and continue to fumble with my pants. "They were birth control pills, right?"

Cal goes quiet for a minute and I feel like he's sucked the air right out of my lungs. His silence is alarming. The tiny hairs on my arms stand up as I press for an answer. "Right?"

Cal lifts his waist and pulls his pants up, avoiding eye contact. "Why are you even asking about those pills?"

Once we're both wiped up and dressed, I curl one leg under the other and face him as he stares straight ahead.

Agitation takes hold of me and I'm not in the mood for this beating around the bush shit. "Just answer the damn question, Cal."

He finally looks at me, sorrow in his expression. He takes my hand in his. "No, babe. They weren't birth control pills. But let me—"

I jerk my hand away, cutting him off. "Don't!"

"Bella," he begins, though doesn't finish. Likely because he sees how upset I am.

I can't even look at him. All the words I want to say escape me.

It wasn't enough that I agreed to be his wife, because of some stupid will, but he intended to go one step further and trick me into getting pregnant.

CHAPTER THIRTEEN

THE REST of the ride is quiet. There's so much I want to tell her, but I use this time to let her collect her thoughts and calm down.

Yeah. I fucked up. What's new? I always fuck up. In a desperate attempt to keep her forever, at the possibility of her not agreeing to marry me, I made her think we were having protected sex, when really I was giving her medication to stimulate her ovaries. It's a safe medicine and has been known to aid in conception.

It was an asshole move, but at the time, I didn't care. Before Bella came to the island, I had the perfect plan laid out. I never intended to fall for her as hard as I did. If I'd known then that we could have a relationship built on trust instead of lies, I would have never done half the shit I did.

With the extra time, I was able to make a call to my new attorney, who's getting a new will drawn up for me as we speak. After reviewing my former will and testament, along with the contract Byron and I both signed, he's made it clear I'll be paying Byron a nice chunk of change for breaching the contract. I've agreed to the terms, but I also know that Byron won't be getting shit from me.

My accounts are in the process of transferring back to me, and I relinquished my rights to press charges against Byron. He'll get what's coming to him, and it won't involve any law enforcement.

We arrive at the hotel and it's past midnight. I fully expected Bella to fall asleep, but I don't think she's even blinked since I was truthful with her about the pills. Well, somewhat truthful. I'm not sure if she knows what they really were, but she does know that they weren't birth control pills.

I place a hand on her leg. She doesn't even flinch. "The driver will get our bags. Let me take you up to our room."

She scoffs, slides across the seat and exits the door opposite me.

My head drops, a pang burning in my chest and a sigh slipping through my lips. "Okay, then," I mumble. It seems she's going to make this harder than I expected.

"Eighth floor suite," I tell Gustav, the driver, who's lugging our bags onto a cart. "Oh, and I hope you enjoyed the show. You're fired." I don't even wait for a bitter expression or angry reply. I walk in through the automatic double doors, past the front desk, where a short brunette is biting into a crumbly muffin.

She has no idea who I am and I don't make my identity known. Right now, it's best to keep things under wraps. Bella and I both need to lay low until Byron is found.

I find Bella sitting on a beige sofa in the common room across from the elevators. Her arms are crossed over her chest, legs crossed at the knee, and the wry look on her face has creased her forehead.

I stick my hand out to her, though she's at least ten feet away. "Come on."

Blowing out a breath of annoyance, she gets up and walks toward me, bypassing my hand and standing directly in front of the elevator.

"Do you plan on being this much of a grump ass our entire stay?"

She huffs. "A grump ass? Why not use the word on the tip of your tongue—a bitch?"

I bite back a smile. "Okay. Do you plan on being this much of a bitch our entire stay?"

Her nostrils flare and she stomps a foot. "Did you just call me a bitch?"

Is she serious right now? "Yeah. Because you told me to."

"No. I was implying that you shouldn't lie."

I'm suddenly reminded why I've never had a relationship, or wanted one.

We take the elevator up and Bella walks slowly behind, following me to our suite. The entire eighth floor is ours. We have everything we need up here. Six of the eleven hotels I own have one floor specifically for me. All being the eighth floor. There's no rhyme or reason for it; I've just always liked the number eight.

Okay. I guess there is a reason.

I moved to The Webster House on the eighth day of the month. Bella was adopted on the eighth. I moved in with the Ellis family on the eighth. I killed my adopted father on the eighth. Some would say those are reasons to hate that number, but I use those incidents as a reminder of why I keep my walls up.

Slowing my steps, I wait for Bella to catch up. When she does, I place my hand on the small of her back. She grumbles under her breath but makes no attempt to remove it. "I'm sorry," I finally say, hating the way those words sound coming from me. I don't apologize often and when I do, it's because I truly mean it.

Her eyes roll but no nasty comment follows. We're making progress.

I use my master key to unlock the door. It's one key used to enter all the rooms. I have one for each resort—Cori Cove being the exception, since it's not finished, and we're still using skeleton keys.

I'm not sure what I'll do with that place now. Not even sure I want to open it up to the public. I bought it because it had special meaning to Peter. The entire process was planned with Bella in mind. I'd bring her there. Force her into marriage. Keep her there. I'm not sure when shit went awry, but plans changed fast when I fell in love with her. Then she reciprocated that love and days later, she was ripped out of my arms.

And here we are. Back together but miles apart.

We walk into the suite. It's the size of an apartment, with all the furnishings. A living room, full-size kitchen with all stainless-steel appliances, one bedroom, and two bathrooms. The best thing about this hotel is the view overlooking the city. I'm not a fan of the hustle and bustle of city life, but I can handle looking at the glowing lights atop the buildings from this viewpoint.

Bella must've caught a glimpse because she walks over to the patio doors and stretches the blinds open.

I come up behind her, arms wrapping around her waist, chin pressed to her shoulder. "What do you think?"

There's a beat of silence before she turns around. My chin lifts, but my hands never leave her waist.

Her tear-soaked eyes speak volumes about how she's feeling. My heart stings at the sight. "Why'd you do it?"

My thumb sweeps under her eyelid, catching a tear before it falls. "I was scared of losing you again." It's the truth, as painful as it is to admit.

"But you had me. I was there."

I give her more truth, and it hurts like hell. "We once made a pact and a promise of forever, and you left me. How was I supposed to know you wouldn't leave me again?"

"I was a kid!"

"You made a choice." My hands drop from her waist. I run my fingers through my hair. "Dammit, Bella. You were given two choices: stay or leave, and you left."

This is not going the direction I intended it to. I turn away from her and cross the room to the minibar between the kitchen and living room. I had the staff stock it with my favorite bourbon, and red wine for Bella.

I take the top off the decanter and pour myself a shot. Tipping it back, I take the contents down in one swallow.

"Is this what you're going to do every time you screw up? Turn everything around on me and throw it in my face how I left you behind when I was eleven years old?"

I pour another shot, taking that one down just as fast. My eyes close and I allow myself to feel the burn riding down my throat and settling in my stomach. Once it does, I set the top back on the bottle and turn around. My palms press to the bar behind me and my head tilts slightly. "You know, you're cute when you're mad."

"Fuck you."

"You're even cuter when you curse."

Bella spins on her heels, pouting as she looks out at the city beneath us. "In case you were even wondering, I'm not pregnant. I had my period two weeks ago."

I come up behind her, inhaling her hair and wrapping my arms around her tense body in the same manner I did minutes ago. "Good. That means you're ovulating. Maybe I should plant my seed in you right now."

Shoulders drawn back, she turns around to face me. "You already did it in the car, you idiot."

"Oh, so now we're name-calling?" It's a bad time for jokes,

but I'm having a hard time taking her seriously when she looks this cute. It's also been over a month since I've had a drink, and those two shots have me feeling pretty good right about now.

She pushes past me, making a beeline for the minibar. "How do you even know about ovulation and cycles? That's sort of creepy, Cal."

"I read books. I'm full of useful and useless information."

Bella opens up the wine cooler and pulls out a bottle of Cabernet Sauvignon. She begins fidgeting with the top, peeling off the foil, so I walk toward her to offer a helping hand.

"Corkscrew should be in one of the drawers." I rifle through a few until I find it. Hesitantly, she hands me the bottle. I grin in response because I know allowing me to help is torture for her right now.

A twist and a pull and the cork pops off. Bella startles at the sound, and I chuckle at her timidness, though she's not timid at all. She's fierce and a force to be reckoned with.

She goes to grab the bottle, but I hold it up, out of her reach. "Forgive me?"

She shakes her head no.

"Will you *ever* forgive me?"

Her shoulders shrug.

"I don't wanna fight with you, Bella." I lower the bottle, but she doesn't take it from me.

"I don't either. I'm just wondering how we're supposed to have a future together that's built on nothing but lies."

I set the bottle down on the counter, grab her by the waist, and pull her flush to my chest. "We start over and we build something better." My lips press to hers, but I can still feel resistance on her end. "Can we do that?"

Bella pulls away and my shoulders slouch when she leaves

my arms. "So much has happened, Cal. So many bad things, and I hate to say it, but it's all because of..."

Reality slaps me in the face, and it fucking hurts. "Because of what? Me?"

She doesn't have to say it. I know what she means. Bringing her to the island was the start of a series of unfortunate events. Bella has been emotionally beaten and had her heart shattered into tiny pieces. It is all because of me. I've hurt the only person left in this world that I give a damn about. And now, I don't think she can ever fully forgive me.

CHAPTER FOURTEEN

Bella

THE DAYS that follow are quiet. Me, lost in my thoughts; Cal, busy with his search for Byron. We haven't left this suite and it feels like the walls are beginning to close in around me.

Cal made some headway in finding Mark. It seems Cal was held in the basement of some building in the city, and he has a swarm of men heading there, because he's almost positive there were other prisoners.

I've been on pins and needles waiting to hear if Mark's been found. It's eleven o'clock at night and there hasn't been any word on him yet.

"Why don't you come to bed?" Cal pats the mattress beside him. We've slept in the same bed since the first night here, but Cal has never felt like more of a stranger than he has these past three days. Not even when I arrived at Cori Cove and saw him for the first time in twelve years. At least then I had hope. Right now, I feel like all hope is lost.

Regardless, I still slip my robe off and climb into bed, wearing the baby pink nightgown Cal bought me. He had bags upon bags of clothes delivered, and it was an assurance that we're going to be here awhile.

"Please just talk to me," Cal says with that same sadness in his voice he's had all day.

"I'm not really sure there's anything to say right now." Of all the things he has done that hurt me, giving me false hope of protection while trying to 'stimulate my ovaries' has been the one that hurts the most. Maybe I'm overreacting, but the way I see it, he tricked me. He stole the fight in me, and I feel breathless, without a voice. I trusted what he was having me take and he was using my body to try and create a baby that would be used as a pawn in this sick game he and Byron are playing.

I still love Cal. Don't get me wrong, I'm not throwing in the towel or giving up on him. I'm just stuck in this head-space of 'what-ifs' and 'what-now?' What does any of this mean for our future? Am I subjecting myself to a life in hiding because Cal has so many enemies? What other secrets don't I know?

Cal rolls onto his side, fingertips floating down my arms, leaving a wake of goosebumps in their path. "Can we please move on from this?"

He's been so sweet. So attentive and kind. I know he's hurting, but I am, too.

"It's late," I tell him. "Can we talk tomorrow?"

He blows out a heavy breath, drops his arm then rolls onto his other side, facing the wall. "You said the same fucking thing last night, Bella."

I don't react. Don't respond. Instead, I tug the blankets over my shoulder, turn away from him and lie there, replaying the events of the last couple months. Just like I do every night.

I'VE BEEN LYING in this bed still and quiet for two hours. Cal hasn't said a word and his heavy breathing leads me to believe he's asleep. Slowly, I sit up with my back pressed to the headboard. He's on his side, still facing the wall. I watch the rise and fall of his chest and my heart warms at the sight. There's something about watching him sleep. Being in a vulnerable state when he puts on such a badass front for the world.

I wrap my arm around him softly, nuzzling my face into his back. I'm so full of love for this man that sometimes I feel like I will burst at the seams. I know I'm being stubborn. I was born with the dastardly trait. I'm just not sure I'm cut out for the life he has planned for us. Half of my life was spent fighting against the world. I don't want that for my future. I don't want that for my kids.

Unable to sleep, I move my arm and crawl out of bed, taking care not to wake him up. Cal hasn't been sleeping the best either, and he could really use a good night's sleep.

I step into my slippers and wrap my black, silk robe around me, tying it at the waist. It's been made clear that I am not allowed to leave this room because someone could see me and alert Byron. However, I'm restless and I'm suffocating.

Leaving the bedroom, I close the door gently behind me. We're staying at one of Ellis Empire's infamous hotels; however, this one is much different than what we were planning for Cori Cove. Instead of being secluded, it's in the city. There isn't a Gothic, kingdom-like appeal as I've seen in pictures of the other resorts. But there is one thing that has curiosity gnawing at me. The Grotto. Cal said every hotel has one. They are strictly for VIP members, but with Cal's master key card that has The Grotto logo on it, I'm just that —VIP. I pick it up off the kitchen counter and drum my fingers on it. *What the hell, why not?*

I sneak back into the bedroom and pull on a pair of sweatpants underneath my nightgown, then leave again. This time, leaving the suite. I walk casually down the hallway to the elevator and take it to the lowest level of the hotel.

The scent of chlorine floods my senses as the elevator descends, telling me that this one has an indoor pool.

When the doors open, I step out into the hall of the basement. I was expecting it to be empty, but instead, there are a handful of people. One couple holding hands and a girl in a bright red costume made of feathers and black fishnet stockings. People pass by and walk away, not even giving me a second look, although it's apparent I just rolled out of bed, because I did.

The decor is similar to Cori Cove. Lit lanterns spaced out perfectly: a dimness that offers a sensual vibe.

Keeping my distance, I follow behind a younger couple, who are flirting and can't seem to keep their hands off one another.

My feet stop moving when I see a guard outside the door they stand in front of. The guy holds something up—a badge, maybe? A key card? The guard opens the door, granting them access.

I reach into the pocket of my robe and pull out the key card. It has the logo on it, so I'm hoping this is all I need to get in.

Approaching the guard, my nerves get the best of me. My hands tremble as I hold out the card from six feet away. He waves me closer, agitated at my pokiness. With it held out, I walk toward him.

"Nice outfit." He snorts before opening the door for me.

As soon as I step inside, my eyes shoot wide open.

Okay. I've seen The Grotto on Cori Cove. It was…interesting, to say the least. But this place, I never would have expected the scene in front of me.

People. So many people. Prancing around in barely anything. Disco lights, music, a dance floor, even a hot tub. There's a long red leather couch that extends the entire length of one wall. There are doors that lead to God only knows where. There are beds—some empty, some occupied. There are couples, trios, quads. My hand claps over my mouth when I see a guy wearing a thong with a leash attached to it and what appears to be a harness. The girl walking him seems very proud of her obedient pet.

I shouldn't be here. This is not my sort of thing. I'm more out of place in this room than I would be in a church completely naked.

"Mojito?" someone asks, snapping my attention away from the human dog.

A petite waitress, who looks younger than I am, stands beside me. Long, tight blonde curls, full lips with cheekbones that could chisel glass. She's wearing a black leather bralette, a pair of leather boy shorts, and five-inch heels. Extending a tray, holding three glasses with cute umbrellas and a cherry on top, she offers me a drink. "Umm, sure. Thanks."

I take a glass, bring the straw to my lips, and sip on my drink as I take in my surroundings.

"First time?" the waitress asks.

The straw leaves my lips, settling back into the glass. "That obvious?"

"Well," her eyes roam my attire, "you are hiding a night-gown and sweatpants under that robe. And don't get me started on those slippers."

"Hey. I happen to like these slippers." I stick one out, looking at the gray furry thing before laughing. "Okay. They're hideous."

"Cherry," she extends her hand, balancing the tray on the other.

"Cherry? That's a pretty name."

"It is. Unfortunately, it's not my real name. But it's what everyone knows me as."

With the straw parting my lips, I speak around it. "It's nice to meet you, Cherry. I'm B...Brooke." Fortunately, those few sips of alcohol haven't gone to my head yet; otherwise, I'd be spilling all my tea.

"You, too. Enjoy the festivities and holler if you need anything."

"Thank you."

Cherry walks off and I can't help but notice the confidence she ensues. Just the way she walks with her back straight, chest puffed out. It's an assurance I wish I had.

I walk farther into the room, sucking down my drink and trying to blend in as much as possible, for someone dressed to stand out. Even the girl in the business suit is getting attention, while no one even notices I'm here. I'm not sure if I should feel insulted or thankful. When the business girl turns around, I see exactly why the attention of three men is laser-focused on her. Beneath her open blazer is a pair of perky breasts with two hoops hanging from her nipples.

"Okay, then," I whisper under my breath.

I'm walking through the spacious room when a door opens just as I pass it. One glance inside turns into gawking on my end. It's a swimming pool. A very large pool full of naked guests. That explains the chlorine smell in the elevator.

"Going in?" a guy asks. He's tall. Bright blue eyes that are more blinding than the sun. Gorgeous shoulder-length blond hair and a rigid six-pack."

"Umm. No thanks."

Blue eyes pats a towel at his dampened locks. "You sure? It's pretty refreshing."

"Nah. I'm good. Need to work up a sweat first, if you

know what I mean?" I snort and immediately wish I could take it back.

The guy gives me a heated look, then closes the door, only to disappear into the crowd.

Yeah. I don't fit in here.

I keep sucking on my straw, until nothing comes back up. Another waitress walks by and I grab a drink off her tray. She doesn't even acknowledge me, just keeps walking by.

Somehow, I find myself sitting on the wall-length couch beside a couple making out. At least they're dressed, so I don't feel too uncomfortable. Suddenly, it feels like I'm back in high school at my freshman homecoming dance. The odd one out. The girl who always watched the fun instead of partaking.

Another door opens, this one straight across from me, and I see Cherry. She's serving up drinks to a few guys, one of which is getting a blow job. A hand lands on her ass, squeezing the tanned flesh of her cheek. She squeals in excitement and leans forward, whispering something in his ear. He gives her ass a slap, making it jiggle, and something ignites inside of me.

I'm not sure what it is or why. I'm not into girls, but just watching the action taking place inside that room, and all around me, is fascinating.

Cherry comes out of the room and her eyes immediately land on mine. "Now, what are you doing sitting there all by yourself?" She eats up the space between us, takes my hand, and pulls me up. "Since you're new here, I'll let you in on a little secret. But first, are you a voyeur or do you like to get in on the action?"

I clear my throat, unsure what she's even talking about. "A what?"

She giggles. "Do you like to watch or participate?"

"Umm..." I'm not really sure how to answer this. I could

tell her that I'm a nosey shit and just want to see what happens in places like this because I'm tired of being stuck in my room with my boyfriend/former boss/childhood friend/criminal who is hiding me, so I don't get us both killed. Instead, I opt for the easy response. "I like to watch, I guess."

Her brows dance across her forehead and she smacks her lips. "Perfect. Come with me."

"I, ugh... Look, I'm not really—"

"Have a little fun, Brooke. That's what this place is all about."

She's right. It's about damn time I have a little fun. Even if I have zero interest in joining in on any of this, there is no harm in watching and letting loose for a little bit.

A minute later, Cherry is taking me into a room. Not just any room, though. It's a dark room with dim red lighting. There is one ginormous bed in the center and a swing hanging from the ceiling. On top of the bed are at least six people having a full-on orgy. There's a girl in a swing, sucking on a lollipop and watching the action. Two guys in a corner are getting blow jobs from one girl. She literally has two cocks in her mouth. My tongue pushes against my cheeks just watching it. Then there's a girl fingering herself at the end of the bed. She's all by her lonesome. Just her and her own fingers, giving herself pleasure.

"Grab a seat. Grab a swing. Take your clothes off, or don't. Just enjoy the show. You'll thank me later." Cherry flashes me a wink before leaving the room. My heart jumps when the door latches closed and I expect everyone to look at me—but they don't. They don't even care that I'm here.

I decide to take a seat on a barstool that sits all by itself in a corner. With the glass clenched firmly in my hand, I take a small sip, uneager to finish the drink off because I need something to do with my hands.

On the bed, there are three guys and three girls. The guys and two of the girls are stark naked, while one girl wears a sexy lingerie getup. A blonde girl lies flat on the bed, sucking a big cock; her legs are spread as a brunette girl sweeps her tongue up and down her pussy. The girl eating pussy is getting fucked in the ass by a slender guy with glasses. Each pounce has him pushing the glasses back up on his nose while sweat dribbles onto the frames. He's also got an entire hand in his ass by a girl who's getting fucked three ways from Sunday. Okay, I've lost track of body parts. All I can focus on is the way that girl is sucking dick like it's her favorite meal. It glides into her mouth so effortlessly and she doesn't even gag, taking all eight, girthy inches down her throat.

My eyes skate up from the cock to the body of the man who owns it and I immediately jerk my attention away when I see him watching me. Staring at the wall beside me, I take a long sip of my drink, then slowly look back—and he winks.

My stomach somersaults and I begin watching the girl who's getting pounded from behind. The guy with glasses digs his fingertips into the meaty flesh of her hips. Rolling his hips and sliding his cock in and out of her. He grunts, taking her faster and filling her up completely. His pelvic bone crushing against her ass. His mouth falls agape and lust is written all over his face as he comes.

When their motions stop, I take a deep breath, feeling like I was on the verge of climaxing myself. I cross my legs, feeling the dampness pooling in my panties, tingles riding through my entire body. My nipples pucker against the thin fabric of my sheer nightgown and holy shit, I wanna get fucked. Like right now.

I finish off my drink, set the glass on a table, and leave the room without a word. I'm not sure what the etiquette is here, but I seriously feel like I should tip them for the show.

My feet don't stop moving as I tuck my hands in the pockets of my robe and walk toward the door I entered.

"Brooke," someone calls out behind me. It takes a second for the name to register when she hollers again, "Hey, Brooke. Wait up."

I spin around and see Cherry walking briskly toward me. "Well, how was it?"

There's no fighting the smile on my face. "Amazing. Thank you."

"You're welcome. Come back Friday. It's ladies' night and we've got a wet tee shirt contest in the pool room. It's always a good time."

"I wish I could, but I'm sort of…in a weird place right now."

Her expression shifts to one of concern. "Are you okay, babe? Is someone hurting you?"

"Oh no." I laugh. "Not like that. It's just my boyfriend. He wouldn't be too happy if he knew I was coming down here."

"Girrrrrl," she drags out, "never let a man tell you what to do." She checks me with a wink. "See you Friday?"

I smile back at her. "I'll try."

This wasn't what I expected; it was so much more. I've never felt so enlightened and free and so fucking horny.

I hurry back up to the room only to find Cal sleeping away. That doesn't stop me from crawling under the blankets and waking him up with my mouth around his cock.

CHAPTER FIFTEEN

I'M NOT sure if this is a dream or reality, but if I am dreaming, I have no intention of waking up. My cock twitches between the warm lips wrapped around it. Twitching and growing with each flick of her tongue. I know that tongue; I know that mouth. "Bella," I groan, my hand beneath the blanket, fingers wrapped in her hair as her head bobs up and down.

Warmth surrounds my balls, squeezing ever so gently. Nope. Not a dream.

I rip the blanket off of us, only to see her doe eyes peering up at me in the glistening beam of moonlight.

She smiles around my cock, sliding her beautiful lips up and down. Her nightgown dips in the front, giving me a peek of her tits. "Baby?" I moan out through my dry mouth and cracked lips. "Come here."

Her head shakes no as she continues to suck, and if she keeps it up, I'll be coming before I get a chance to get her off.

My cock pops out of her mouth and she slides her tongue up and down my length, hitting every nerve before taking me back in. I can feel my head reach her tonsils and I fist her hair tighter, rocking my hips with her motions.

One hand slides up my chest, running over my rigid abs, then sliding back down again and returning its attention to my balls.

"Fuck." I shiver when she rolls her tongue around my head and shoves my cock back down her throat. So warm, wet, and seductive. "I've missed the way that dirty mouth feels around my cock."

She looks up at me, and I point a finger, curling it and calling her to me. She shakes her head again and smirks like a devious child.

"Now!" I demand.

She finally does as she's told and climbs up my body on all fours. Once her bare pussy is straddling my chest, she peels her nightgown over her head. She must've taken off her panties before removing my boxers while I was sleeping. "Turn around," I tell her.

Doing as she's told, she twists until her ass is in my view. Both hands plant on her cheeks and I squeeze them in my palms before lowering her down until she's sitting on my face.

"Keep sucking."

Her mouth finds my cock again and my tongue sweeps up her slit. She tastes better than I remember. Sweet and salty. Her arousal drips into my mouth and I'm not sure what got her so turned on, but I want it to happen again and again. Every fucking night.

My tongue flicks against her swollen clit before I suck it between my teeth. Her body jolts, so I do it again, causing her to cry out in pleasure. Her head bobs up and down, mouth wrapped around my dick as she sucks it like it's her favorite flavor.

"God, your mouth feels so good, baby."

I part her ass cheeks with my fingers and swirl my tongue around her asshole. I'm not sure if she likes it, but she doesn't stop me, so I keep going.

"Cal," she whimpers.

"Want me to stop?"

"Hell no." She moans, lathering my cock with her saliva then sucking it off.

With my tongue still circling her hole, I slide two fingers in her pussy, feeling her walls clench around them. "So fucking tight and wet."

She moans, telling me she likes when I talk dirty like that.

"Do you like sucking cock, Bella?" My voice comes out cracked and gravelly.

"I like sucking *your* cock."

That's what I like to hear. Only me. Only mine. "This pussy is mine, Bella. Only I make you come. Do you understand?"

She nods through sucks and blows on my dick. Her hips flex and her ass shifts upward as I curl my fingers, pressing them as far as they'll go and tapping against her G-spot.

More moans around my dick and the vibration rides through me like a tidal wave. Hitting me head-on and sending me soaring. My tongue sweeps across my wet lips, watching her ass bounce in front of me as she fucks my fingers.

I slap a hand to her ass, squeezing as her skin separates my fingers and leaves a handprint behind, claiming her—owning her.

"Mine," I growl, before flexing the muscle of my tongue and licking her up and down.

"Oh God," she cries out. Squeezing my fingers and unleashing her orgasm.

At the same time, I warn her, "I'm gonna come." Thinking she'll pull out and let my jizz shoot all over her neck. Instead, she keeps going, taking me all the way in her mouth and opening her throat as she swallows my cum.

My cock twitches as it leaves her mouth, missing the warmth already.

Bella turns around, wiping her hand across her parted lips. She settles on my chest, blanketing my body with hers.

I stroke her hair, wondering where this sudden sexual desire came from, but I don't overthink it. She's here, and she's mine. That's enough for me.

CHAPTER SIXTEEN

Bella

I WAKE up to Cal standing over me, hair glistening from his recent shower and only a towel wrapped around his waist. He's got a steaming mug of coffee in his hand. "Good morning." He hands me the cup with a cheeky grin.

Smiling back at him, I scoot myself up and take the cup.

His lips press to my forehead and the scent of his cologne surrounds me. "Last night was amazing. I'm glad you've finally came to your senses."

I scoff. "Came to my senses? You sure do have a way with words, Callum Ellis." I take a sip of the coffee, black and hot. It burns my top lip a tad, but it's too good not to keep sipping.

He takes a seat on the edge of the bed. Beads of water rolling down his abdominal muscles. "I assume last night means you forgive me?"

"Cal," I say softly. "Last night was incredible but nothing has changed. I'm not mad at you. Not really. I'm just…stuck." I'm hurt by what Cal did to me. No amount of apologies can change the fact that he took advantage of my body as a woman and tried to get me pregnant without my knowledge.

However, I'd be a hypocrite to keep battling this out with him, considering we've been having unprotected sex. The difference is, it was my choice—or lack of restraint—and not his.

"Stuck?" He laughs, though it's void of any humor. "Bella, I have offered you anything you could possibly want. A kingdom, protection, all the money in the world. Most of all, I've offered you my heart, and now you're going to tell me you're stuck because I made one lousy mistake?"

It's too early for this. I take another sip, collecting my composure before I totally lose my shit on him. Then I set the glass on the nightstand and toss the blankets off me. "I'm going to take a shower."

Cal blows out an exaggerated breath but doesn't stop me.

This isn't how I wanted our reunion to go and now that it is going this way, it has me wondering how many days will be spent like this. Distant and bickering with a lack of trust.

As I'm lathering up my hair with the shampoo Cal had delivered for me, I think back to last night. How I snuck out of the room while Cal was sleeping and went to The Grotto. Here I am preaching about honesty and I'm pocketing secrets on night four of being back together.

Are we back together, though? I mean, he's here and so am I. After weeks apart, this is what I wanted. It doesn't feel like the relationship I expected. It's more like two people in hiding who are trying not to kill each other—while also sleeping together.

"Ugh." I breathe out a heavy sigh. How did everything get so messy?

Knuckles knock on the bathroom door, snapping me out of my thoughts. "Yeah?"

"Everything okay? It's been almost an hour."

Wow. An hour already. Feels like I just got in here. "Be out in a minute."

The next thing I know, the shower curtain is parting and Cal's standing there. He flicks the towel around his waist and it falls to the floor. "Want company?"

My eyes skate down his perfect body, stopping at his erection. "Umm sure. But didn't you just take a shower?"

He steps in, one foot at a time. "I did, but I'm not here for myself. Turn around," he demands, and I do.

I hear the sound of liquid squirting from a bottle. Standing under the stream of water, Cal begins rubbing his hands on my shoulders in a deep massage. My head tilts to the side, eyes closed, as I relax under his touch.

Smooth hands glide over my skin as goosebumps spill down my arms. "Cal," I say breathlessly.

He turns me around, eyes burning into mine. Hungry, yet vulnerable. As if he senses I'll push him away when all I want to do is pull him close.

"Baby," he whispers. "Don't do this to us."

A lump lodges in my throat and I swallow it down. Tears prick the corners of my eyes, but I fight them off. "I don't want to." My body connects with his, my head resting against his chest as the hot water pelts my skin.

Cal pulls my head away, cupping my cheeks in his hands. "Don't you love me anymore, Bella?"

My heart pangs with remorse. How could he even ask that? "Of course I do, Cal. I love you so much that it feels like my heart could explode at any given moment. That's what scares me."

His eyes dance across my lips, then back to my eyes, burning into them with so much desire that my soul catches fire. "Don't be scared, Bella. I'll never hurt you."

"But you do hurt me, Cal."

Saying the words hurts almost as much as the realization that I'm madly in love with this man.

Sadness sweeps across his eyes and the guilt of being so

honest gnaws on my insides. "I know I have and I'm going to spend the rest of my life making it up to you. If you'll let me."

It wasn't a question, but it felt like one. *If I'll let him.* Imagining a life without Cal in it is damn near impossible, but when I try to picture our future together now, all I see is darkness. I look down, watching the beads of water spill down my legs, to my feet, then slowly disappearing.

"Ever since I was a kid, I could look ahead and picture everything I wanted. Before my mom died, I imagined a dad. When she was gone, and I met you, I saw us as best friends in high school together. Going off to college and going to parties. I could even picture my wedding day. One night I was lying in bed after we had just finished an entire blueberry pie in the attic, and I saw us." My eyes skate up his body, finding him staring back at me. "We were holding hands and even though it was a daydream, I felt butterflies in my stomach. A few days later, I left and you stayed behind and I couldn't see you anymore. You weren't at school, or the parties, and we never held hands again."

"What are you saying, Bella? You don't want a future with me?"

"Let me finish. That's not what I'm saying at all. It wasn't until the dance in the ballroom, the night you took my virginity on that piano, that I was able to see you in my future again." A smile spreads across my face. "It was perfect. I imagined us living at Cori Cove and going to see my family for the holidays. I pictured kids and tubing behind a boat on the bay. I saw it all."

"And now?"

"Now I see a life on the run. Hiding out and looking over my shoulder because you have so much money and power that someone out there is always going to try and take it, the same way you took it from your adopted dad. I see our kids living in fear. Never seeing my parents because it's not safe to go home. I see loneliness. And that's exactly what I don't want in a marriage."

Cal shakes his head, disagreeing with me. I'm not surprised he doesn't see what I see. He's lived in the darkness since he was adopted as a teenager.

"You're wrong." He laughs. "You are so wrong. You wanna know what I see?"

I nod in response.

"I see breakfast in the courtyard. Dinners on the yacht. Flower gardens and sandboxes. Midnight swims when the kids are asleep. Smiles, laughter, and memories. Most importantly, love. I see all the things we wanted as kids that we never got. I don't see a second of my future without you in it. You think too much, Bella. For once, stop planning and just live."

I bite back a smile, my heart feeling all warm and fuzzy. "You really see all that?"

"I really see all that. Now kiss me and tell me you forgive me before all the hot water runs out."

I'm not sure forgiveness was ever a question. It was more about moving on from it all. Maybe Cal is right. It's time to stop trying to plan my entire life out. "Okay. I forgive you under one condition."

"A condition, huh?" He pulls me so close that I'm forced to tip my head back to look at him.

"And what's that?"

"Once this is all done. We go back to Cori Cove and finish the renovations."

"Actually. I was thinking about keeping that one for ourselves."

"No hotel?"

"Do we really want guests in our home twenty-four seven?"

I actually like the idea of running a hotel together. "How about we keep this conversation open for discussion."

His lips press softly to mine. "Deal."

Cal's attention is pulled away, lips leaving mine when his phone begins ringing from the sink vanity. Tugging me closer, his words whisper across my lips, "It can wait."

"It could be about Mark. You should get it."

Cal growls into my neck, resting his chin on my shoulder. "What about makeup sex?"

"Oh, that will happen. After you take the call." I push his shoulders back, forcing him off my body. The phone stops ringing but a voice message pings. "Please."

He kisses me once more, before opening the shower curtain. "Fine. But I'll be back. Wait for me."

Once he's out, I finish washing up. He must be listening to the voice message. "Who was it?"

Seconds later, the shower curtain parts, and he pops his head in. Wide eyes and water dripping down his forehead. He sweeps his tongue across his lips, catching a drop.

"You might wanna get out of the shower."

"No," I drag. "Please, Cal. Tell me he's not..." I can't say the words. I tear the curtain open and get out, immediately grabbing a towel from the hook and wrapping it around me. "What happened?"

"They found Mark. He's gonna be all right."

I blow out a heavy breath of relief. "Thank God. But what—"

"It's Trent." There's concern on his face that is surprising. He hates Trent as much as I do. Even if Cal doesn't know how much I've grown to hate him over the past week.

"He's dead, baby."

"Dead?" That's all I can say. I'm not sure how I feel. Trent was awful to me and I hoped I'd never see him again, but I'm not heartless. I didn't want him or anyone else to die. It's still a life and he has a family who loves him.

"Hey," Cal wraps his arms around my body, pulling me in for a hug, "you okay?"

"How?"

"From what my liaison said, it was Byron. Apparently, he went nuts and shot up an entire room of people."

I pull back and look at him. "But Mark got away?"

"Barely. But, yeah. Anders and a few others were able to make it in time and get him. We had an insider distracting Byron, and when he found out, he lost it."

I begin drying myself off quickly. "I need to see him. I have to go to my parents and tell them what happened."

"I can't let you do that, baby."

"Can't or won't?" I toss the towel on the floor at my feet, my hand lingering on the door handle.

"Both. I swore I'd never let anything bad happen to you again and I meant it. It's too risky to leave this place right now. It'll all be over soon, though, I promise."

"Will it, though? Will it ever really be over?" I tear open the door and go straight to the bedroom. My bag sits open on the floor and I shuffle through it and grab some clothes.

"What are you doing?" Cal asks, standing in the doorway with just the towel around his waist.

I clasp my bra behind my back and pull a black sweatshirt over my head. "I have to go, Cal."

Cal slams the door closed and closes the space between us. The towel dropped somewhere in between. "Dammit. Don't do this."

"Please don't try to stop me. I have to go to them. Mark is hurt and it's all my fault. All of this is my fault. Trent's dead and his parents are likely mourning their loss as we speak. Everything that happened is all my fault." Somewhere between shouts and cries, I fall apart in Cal's arms. Sobbing hysterically into the nape of his neck.

It is all my fault. If I'd never taken that stupid job offer then none of this would have happened. None of it. Not even us.

"It's not your fault, Bella. It's mine."

I don't say anything. I don't agree, and I don't disagree because, deep down, part of me knows that to be true. Cal started all this. He dragged me into his world, and in the process, it turned upside down. Now I have to decide if it's all worth it.

CHAPTER SEVENTEEN

SHE DIDN'T LEAVE. Thank fuck I was able to calm her down and convince her it was a bad idea. Byron's out there watching and waiting for his opportunity to take something else from me—namely her. I'll die before he lays a single finger on her delicate skin again.

I'll die fighting for her, so she can live. Bella deserves it all. A life full of happiness without worry. The kids, the yard, the white picket fence. She deserves everything I don't. But I have the power to give it all to her. Even if I don't deserve her.

I'm despicable compared to this goddess. She's vibrant and full of life and here I am sucking it right out of her because I can't live without her in my life. How selfish is that?

I'm lying on my side, watching her sleep. Each breath flares her nostrils and every once in a while, her lips part, cracking a smile, and I find myself smiling in response. She's perfection personified. The most beautiful art piece imaginable—a Mona Lisa.

Most people don't believe in soulmates and maybe I've

read too many novels, but I'm a firm believer that I was left in that alley as a newborn for Bella. So that one day, we would meet and our lives would be forever changed. She's the only person in the world who's ever given a damn about me and I'm not about to let some money hungry bastard take away everything I've fought my entire life for.

I haven't told Bella yet, but I'm thinking about changing my last name as well as the name of the company. I never wanted to be an Ellis. In fact, I hate the fucking name and everything it stands for. I'm not even sure what last name I was born with. Hell, I don't even know what time I was born. No clue if it was a hard labor or a C-section. Don't know my birth weight or how long I was. I could probably pick any name in the world and go with it. Blake, perhaps? It's Peter's last name and he was the closest thing I ever had to a family.

My head rests on the pillow right next to Bella's, and I watch her until my eyes don't allow me to any longer. Slowly, I drift into a deep sleep. And when I do, I instantly regret it.

"Mr. Ellis," I say, my voice soft and almost a whisper.

He doesn't even look at me, just keeps his eyes on the spread newspaper in his hands. "What the hell do you want?"

"I was thinking maybe we could talk about school. Ya know? Me, attending."

Mr. Ellis folds the newspaper in half as laughter climbs up his throat. "First of all, Caden," he enunciates the name he's plagued me with. "In this house, you call me Dad. Second of all," he stands, pressing his hands firmly to the desk in front of him, "you will never attend public school. Now get your ass back in your room and do your schoolwork before dinner. Mom's cooking tonight and I expect your compliance."

I go to walk out, tail between my legs and head hung low, but instead of pulling the door open, I shove it, so that it latches closed.

Slowly, I turn around and meet his gaze.

With drawn shoulders, he steps around the desk and pins me with a hard stare. "You got a problem, boy?"

"Actually. I do." My feet stay planted, fists balled at my side. His eyes wander to them, then back to my face, before erupting in full-blown laughter.

Heavy steps bring him closer. "Unclench your fists and walk your ass out of here before you make a big mistake."

My heart is going a million miles a minute, sweat dripping down my forehead. I'm gonna do it. I'm gonna punch this fucker right in the face. I've been doing lifts with my bed every day. It might not give me the brawn needed to lay him out, but I've got the mindset.

One more step and he's in arm's reach.

I'm gonna do it.

His hand extends, fingers spread as he goes straight for my throat. Before he can make contact, I cock my fist and aim right for his nose. Somehow, it lands, and I'm as surprised as he is as he cups his face.

Only, I didn't think ahead, and I'm not sure what to do now. So I go in for another, ready to pound my knuckles into his wrinkly flesh.

This time, he stops me. Catching my fist and squeezing before twisting my arm in a full three-sixty. Cries of misery fill the room, echoing in my own ears. But, I don't even feel the pain, all I can focus on is the sound of my bone snapping.

The look on his face is malevolent. This is no man; this is the devil incarnate. Inflicting pain on others is his favorite pastime. My punch to his nose didn't even draw blood. I'm almost positive he's not human. He doesn't have a heart, that's for sure.

Tears prick the corners of my eyes, but I use them as fuel as I jerk my hand away, now able to feel the pain shooting up my entire arm. My hand hangs freely, but I don't dare look at it out of fear of passing out. If he sees my weakness, he'll use it to his advantage.

"Maybe you'll think twice before you try that shit again. Now

wrap that hand up and do your schoolwork." He turns around and walks back to his desk. "Dinner is in an hour and if your mom asks, you fell."

I hug my hand to my chest, the pain almost unbearable. It's like my hand doesn't even belong to me anymore. It just hangs by a thread of bone on my wrist and I can already feel the swelling around it.

Without a word, I turn and leave quickly. Once I'm out of his sight, I scream at the top of my lungs and fall to the floor in the hall outside his office.

"Cal. Wake up." Bella shakes me, pulling me out of my dreadful nightmare. "Hey," she peers over me, beautiful green eyes looking into mine, "I'm here. It was just a dream."

I sit up, wiping the sheen of sweat from my forehead and rubbing my wrist. I look down and see the scar from the surgery. It's another reminder of how hard I had to fight for what I've earned. I grab my bottled water from the night-stand. "If only it were a dream," I tell her between sips.

I've been cursed with nightmares and rarely dream at all.

Bella places a calming hand on my arm. "You wanna talk about it?"

"Nah. It's nothing. Go back to sleep, baby." I kiss her fore-head, hoping she doesn't drag this out.

The only thing worse than a nightmare is having to relive it once you're awake.

CRAZY HOW A NIGHT full of monsters in your head can turn into the best night's sleep you've had in months. It's all because of the girl by my side. I smile, eyes still closed, and wrap my arm around her. Only, my arm sinks into the down comforter.

I open my eyes to see that Bella is not there. My mind

immediately goes to the worst possible scenario, and I shoot up to a sitting position. That's when I see her. Sitting at a desk in the corner of the room, blinds still closed and barely a wink of light.

"Whatcha doing over there?"

She spins around in the chair, my phone in her hand. "Trying to get into this thing. What's the passcode?"

I tear the blanket off me and walk toward her, my morning wood greeting her through the fabric of my boxers.

"That depends on what you need it for." I press my palms to the desk, caging her between my arms, and I kiss the top of her head.

Worried eyes look up at me. "Cal, please just let me call my parents."

"We've been over this, Bella. It's not safe."

I can feel the tension building between us, and I'm trying really hard to avoid another argument. But she can't make contact with anyone. Not yet.

"Dammit, Cal!" She pushes me back and gets up. "I want to know that Mark is safe." She's full-on yelling, hands shaking and tears welling in her eyes. "I want to see how Lucy is doing after the news of Trent's death. I want to talk to my fucking family!"

I take a deep breath, contemplating the best approach here.

"Give me my phone," I finally say, holding my hand out.

She slaps it in my palm, curses, and storms out of the room.

A quick call to Anders, and hopefully, we can come to an agreement that works for both of us.

"Hey," I say when he picks up on the first ring, "I need you to do something for me."

"Anything, Boss. What is it?"

"Go to the brother's hospital room and call me when you get there."

Anders laughs, though there is nothing comical about this situation. "He's at NYC General. I'm back at Cori Cove."

My teeth grind. "Did I ask where the fuck you were? Do it. Now."

I end the call and slam my phone down on the desk. There is nothing I hate more than an employee who questions a job I give. I pay Anders damn good money, and I do it because he's the best.

The sound of a door slamming has me hauling ass out of the bedroom. "Bella," I holler, searching the suite frantically. "This isn't funny, Bella. Where the hell are you?" I open and close closets, the bathroom door. "Fuck!"

She's gone.

And she took my damn key card with her.

CHAPTER EIGHTEEN

Bella

"CAN'T EVEN MAKE a damn phone call. What is this? Prison?" I'm halfway down the hall in the basement when I realize I'm talking to myself and getting strange looks from passersby.

Cal could be hot on my tail, for all I care, and that's the thing—I don't care. I'm twenty-three years old and if I want to leave that suite and go watch people prance around naked while getting groped, fucked, or both, then I have every right to do that. If I want to make a phone call to my mom to make sure she's okay, I can do that, too.

I quickly hold up the card to the guard, and he gives me access to The Grotto.

I'm so sick and tired of everyone trying to tell me how to live my life. Foster parents, foster siblings, case workers—I've dealt with authoritative people my entire life. I'm an adult and I'm free to make my own choices. I'll be damned if someone is going to tell me otherwise. Let alone impregnate me because it fits *his* plan.

No. Not anymore.

"Brooke." Cherry beams with too much excitement. Her

bright red lips match the nickname she's presumed. "You came back. And you're not in pajamas this time."

I snatch a drink from her tray and tip it back, gulping down the entire contents before setting it back on the tray, empty. "Sure did."

"Well, someone was asking about you after you left the other night. Maybe you could…give him a show." She angles her head toward the guy who winked at me mid blow job the last time I was here.

"Oh, no. It's not like that, Cherry. Actually, I'm in a relationship. I just…like the thrill, I guess."

"No worries. I totally get it. Trust me, babe. You're not the only one." She nods toward a lady wearing a leopard suit, only it's missing the crotch and the breast coverage. "Lady Leopard over there. Married to a state senator. Doesn't even know she frequents this place."

My eyes widen. "Really? That's crazy." I take a more serious note. "Cherry, can I ask you a question?"

She adjusts the tray on her hand, moving glasses around to balance it out. "Of course. Ask away."

"Is this…" I'm not sure how to word what I want to ask. "Is this considered cheating? Ya know, coming here without the knowledge of your significant other."

Cherry draws in a deep breath. "Well, that depends on how your significant other would feel if he found out. If he'd get mad, then yeah. Probably. But if he wanted to join in on the entertainment, then I'd say no."

"He has definitely done his fair share of joining in."

Her hand sets on my shoulder and she grins widely. "Then don't sweat it, babe. He'd be a hypocrite to judge you."

I nod. She's right. Cal has been part of this club for years. Hell, he owns the damn place.

"Listen," she continues, "if you're worried about upsetting

your boyfriend or getting caught, just disguise yourself. There is nothing wrong with watching. It's porn, only live."

"Thanks, Cherry. You've been extremely helpful." I point to a full glass of mojito, lime this time. "Mind if I have another?"

"Have all you want. You pay your dues and we supply the drinks." She picks one off the tray and hands it to me. "Holler if you need anything else."

"I will. Thanks, again."

With my drink in hand, I mingle through the crowd. I end up at the far side of the basement at a round table with two stools. There's a small stage with three poles, running from the ceiling to the hardwood platform. Two girls dance around in sexy lingerie while men gawk, and a few even jerk their cocks. One is in the midst of fucking a girl from behind. Though, his eyes are not on his counterpart, they're on the dark-haired stripper holding eye contact with him.

I wonder if he's fucking his wife and the dancer is his mistress. Maybe he's not married at all and doesn't even know the girl whose pussy his cock is stuffed in.

Then there's the beefy biker dude who's stroking his three-inch penis. I'd never guess a man of that stature was that small.

One of the things I like about this place is trying to guess the story behind each person. It's sort of fun and exciting. I wonder if anyone is watching me and trying to guess my story.

Girl is hiding out because some deranged man wants to kill her and her boyfriend, so he can take all his money. She gets pissy and wanders here out of vengeance while searching for a thrill.

If only I could predict my outcome in this messed-up situation. Will Byron win and kill me eventually? Will someone kill him first? Will Cal and I end up married? Most importantly, now that I've found this place, will I ever want to give it up?

"Ready for another?" Cherry asks, coming out of nowhere. Before I even respond, she sets a full drink on the table and takes my empty one. I didn't even realize I'd finished it off.

"Don't mind if I do." I smack my lips before wrapping them around the straw.

Cherry leans in, her lips practically brushing my ear. "See that dark-haired girl on the stage? That's his wife." She tips her head toward the guy who's pounding his cock in another girl.

"Really?" I drag. "I knew there was some sort of connection there."

Interesting. This *is* fun.

"Bella!" someone yells. Only, it's not just someone, it's Cal. I turn around and see him walking steadfast toward me. I look at Cherry, who's glancing back and forth from me to Cal.

"I thought you said your name was Brooke?"

"And yours is Cherry, right?" There's a sliver of sarcasm, but I think she gets the point.

"How do you know Callum Ellis?"

Before I can even answer her, Cal stops me from talking by throwing me over his shoulder.

"Put me down," I curse, slapping my hands to his back, and déjà vu hits me full force. I've done this a couple times.

"If you wanna act like a child, then you'll get treated like one."

He carries me across the room, grabbing the attention of everyone in our path. I look up and see Cherry watching us in shock. My shoulders shrug, and I mouth the words, "I'm sorry."

"Give me the card, Bella." Cal holds his hand up, expecting me to give it to him.

"I don't know what you're talking about."

"Oh. So it's gonna be like that." He slaps a hand to my ass. I shrill at the pain but crack a smile at his tenacity.

"Didn't you learn your lesson about sneaking around during your stay at Cori Cove?"

"And didn't you learn that I don't take orders from anyone?"

"Like I said, Bella. You act like a child, you'll get treated like one."

"This is absurd. I'm fully capable of walking." I'm no longer fighting to get down. The humiliation has passed and I know Cal, he won't free me until I'm holed up in the suite again.

Cal slams his thumb into the elevator button and the doors open, letting a trio of men out. They stop, looking at me with questioning eyes, likely wondering if I'm okay. It has to be due to the pinched eyebrows and furious expression on Cal's face.

"Mind your fucking business," Cal barks at them, then steps into the elevator. "Let me ask you something, Bella. Do you have a death wish?"

"I mean, we're all going to die sometime. Why not have it be in a place with live porn?" It's what Cherry called it, after all.

"You think this is funny?"

"Yeah, Cal. I think it is. For the past couple months, everything has been so serious. Maybe I just wanted to have a little fun for a change?"

We reach the eighth floor and he still doesn't set me down. For being hauled away over someone's shoulder, I should be angrier, but I'm actually feeling pretty good right now. I'd say it's attributed to the drinks I sucked down in a matter of minutes. I'm not a heavy drinker, and it doesn't take long for the effects to go to my head.

"You want fun? I can give you fun. In the safety of our suite where you're supposed to stay until we catch that son of a bitch."

"Oh yeah? What kind of fun, Cal? You wanna play checkers, maybe some Go Fish?"

We're halfway down the hall when my feet finally hit the ground. "Are you drunk?" Cal asks, eyebrows perched on his forehead and back stiff as a board.

"Maybe? Why? Will I get in trouble for that, too?"

He takes my hand, leading me to our suite, and I stumble over my feet with the first couple steps. "You shouldn't be drinking. We've had unprotected sex and you could be carrying my baby."

"Oh," I blow out a heavy breath, "is that so? Is that part of your devious plan, Callum? Are you still trying to get me pregnant?"

He shrugs his shoulders. "Not trying, but anything is possible when you're not protected."

"Yeah." I jerk my hand away from his. "Anything is possible because I probably still have those damn fertility pills circulating through my bloodstream and," I quote, "stimulating my ovaries."

Cal stops walking and I do the same. He looks me dead in the eye. "He told you about that, too?"

"Yeah. He did. At least someone is honest with me." My feet start moving again, getting a few steps ahead of him. I still have the key card, so I pull it out of my pocket and swipe it through the pad.

I don't bother holding the door for him, but he catches it before it latches. "Is this your new thing, Bella? Sneaking off to go to The Grotto?" My response is a smug grin as I drop down on the couch. "How often have you gone?"

He eats up the space between us, crouching down in front of me. "How often, Bella?"

Why does he keep saying my name like I don't know it? Normally, I like the way it rolls off his tongue. Right now, it's downright annoying.

"Twice, Callum." I emphasize his name. "I've gone twice."

"And...do you like it?"

I shrug my shoulders, almost embarrassed to admit that I do. "A little bit."

To my surprise, a smile spreads across his face, though it feels condescending. "Why didn't you just tell me?"

My hands fly up. "Because of this. Look at how you're reacting."

"It's okay to enjoy that sort of thing. For a while, I did, too. Eventually it gets old, though."

He's piqued my curiosity, so I lean into the space between us, hands resting on my knees. "How often did you go?"

"For a while, every night. It sizzled down to a couple nights a week or check-ins with the staff. Once you came back into my life, never."

"Are you mad that I...like it?"

His hands rest over mine, reassuringly. "I'd never judge you for your sexual fantasies. All I ask is that you let me be a part of them. Now," he drawls, "if I find out one of those men touched you, then we have a problem."

"No," I spit out, "No one's touched me and I'd never... I'd never do that to you. Or to us."

"Good." He pushes himself up, pressing his lips to mine and speaking into my mouth. "Now that that's settled. It's time for your punishment."

My heart skips a beat, excitement pooling in my stomach. I must be out of my mind for wanting this. "Take it easy on me. 'Kay?"

His hands slap to my waist and he lifts me up, tossing me over his shoulder again. "Don't count on it."

My smile never leaves my face as he hauls me off to the bedroom, slamming the door closed behind us.

He tosses me onto the bed and we begin tearing each other's clothes off like animals in heat. "Fuck me, Cal." I moan into his mouth.

"I'm gonna fuck you when I'm good and ready. You just lie back and take whatever I give you."

I'm not sure when I crossed the line from being vanilla to wanting all the dirty talk, while fulfilling sexual desires, I didn't even know I had, but now that I have, I'm never going back. Cal is so aggressive in bed, in such a way that has my body sweltering. Any time we've had sex, he's taken control. He's punished me, degraded me, and called all the shots. Feeling pretty brave, thanks to the alcohol I've had, I think it's time I turn that around.

My hands meet his chest, pushing him off me, lip curled and eyes burning into his. "Or, you take whatever I give to you."

Once he's on his back, I jump on top of him, straddling his chest and locking his hands over his head.

Too stunned to speak, he just lies there.

"You can move when I tell you to move, Mr. Ellis. Until then, lie down and keep your dirty mouth shut."

When his eyebrows hit his forehead and a smirk draws on his face, I know he's loving this. Even if he won't admit it. Even if he'll probably put up a fight for control.

"You're asking for it, baby."

In a knee-jerk reaction, I raise my hand and slap him across the face. My hand immediately claps over my mouth. "Oh, shit. I'm so sorry! I was trying to be...kinky."

His laughter eases my embarrassment, and when his fingertips pinch my waist, I'm completely over it.

"You don't have to pretend with me. We both know who's in control in the bedroom."

I feel like he's testing me. Trying to see how far I'll take this.

"Is that so?" I bite my bottom lip, observing the cocksure expression on his face. "Sounds like a challenge." He goes to sit up, trying to move me, being the control freak that he is. I push him back down. "Whoever comes first loses. If I win, you forgive me for running out and going to The Grotto."

He quirks a brow. "And if I win?"

I tap my finger to my chin, thinking. *I've got it.* "If you win, I'll let go of all the asshole things you've done to me."

"Including the birth control?"

"That's a big one. But, sure. Why not? I plan on winning anyways."

Cal laughs. "Oh, it's on, baby." He holds out his hand, ready to shake on the deal.

Even though it was my challenge, I'm hesitant. Mostly because I've always been one to hold on to grudges. I have a problem with throwing mistakes in people's faces, even when I've made my own fair share of them. Maybe it's time to change that.

I place my hand in his and give it a jerk, sealing the deal. Before I can even pull away, Cal is flipping me over until he's the one on top. I let out a squeal as his naked body cloaks mine.

Our mouths crash together. Hard and forceful, teeth clanking, lips bruising. When my tongue invades his mouth, he sucks the tip of it then moves to my bottom lip, sucking so hard that the taste of copper seeps into my mouth.

My hands coast down his back, nails digging into the skin as I roll my hips, trying to gain friction. Then I remember this is a challenge, not a quest. Sliding my hand between our bodies, I get a firm grip on his erection. He presses down, stopping me from stroking, while breathing heavily into my mouth.

In a swift motion, he pulls my hand out from between us and pins it over my head.

"Oh, this is war," I seethe into his mouth.

He grabs my other wrist, restraining it in the same manner. "Bring it on."

He devours every inch of my neck—nipping, biting, sucking—then moves to my ear. Tingles shoot through my entire body, and I'm half tempted to throw in the towel.

My need for him overpowers my desire to win. I can move on from everything he's done. I pretty much already have. What started as one thing, grew to something so much more with us. He couldn't have predicted that.

"Crumble, baby. You know you want to." His words sweep across my mouth in a gruff whisper.

Nope. I will not crumble.

Using all my strength, I push my hands to his chest. To him, it's laughable, but I manage to get a firm grip on his erection between our smoldering bodies. Cal works up a sweat, trying to gain the upper hand, but when I squirm out from beneath him and he flips on his back, I know that I've got this in the bag.

He tries to stop me when my lips wrap around his girth, tongue flicking against his under shaft.

"I was born with restraint, Bella. Suck my dick all you want...holy fuck!"

I smirk around him while I slide him in and out of my mouth.

His fingers wrap around the ponytail on my head and he tugs forcefully. So much that it feels like my follicles are on fire, though it only arouses me further.

I pop him out of my mouth, then lick my way down to his balls, sucking one in my mouth and humming.

"God, baby. Don't stop."

I question him with raised eyebrows as I suck his other ball into my mouth. It seems he's forgotten this is a challenge. My mouth presses to his pelvic bone, and I kiss my way up to his stomach. "Giving up already?"

I'm desperate for him to be inside me. So desperate I'd give up the win.

Once I'm straddling his thighs and his dick is lined up with my entrance, he lets out a gravelly breath and grabs me by the waist, lowering me onto his cock.

It slides in with ease, filling me completely as I begin bouncing on him. Two hands pinch my hips, gliding me up and down.

My nails rake against his chest, clawing their way down.

Cal presses his thumb to my clit as I ride him, rubbing in vicious circles that instantaneously bring me to the brink of orgasming. If I don't stop him now, he'll win.

His tenacity doesn't falter. He pushes hard, rubbing faster. Lust-filled eyes meet mine, the rise and fall of his chest mimicking my own unfulfilled breaths.

My head falls back, eyes closed as I give in. Climbing higher and higher. Electricity riding through my veins and hitting every nerve in my body.

I hold my breath, squeezing his cock as my walls close tightly around him. I'm not even sure how I stand a chance at winning now and I don't even care.

"I'm gonna lose," I cry out, bringing my head forward. My mouth falls open, and I'd swear my eyes roll into the back of my head.

"Give me your hand," Cal says, not waiting for me to offer it to him. He picks it up off his chest, takes two of my fingers and closes the others. Pressing my own fingers against my clit, he grumbles, "Rub it."

I do as I'm told. Rubbing slow circles with little pressure.

I've never done anything like this with an audience. It's exciting and new and the way his eyes watch my movements as I take control of my own pleasure turns me on. Each passing second gives me a new sense of comfort and before I know it, I'm vibrating against the pads of my fingers and screaming as I ride his dick.

Grinding against him, rolling his cock inside of me, I keep rubbing myself—watching him, waiting for him to explode inside me.

My orgasm hits me full force as I spill around his cock that's still engulfed in me.

Without warning, Cal grabs my waist and lifts me up, a stream of his cum shoots upward, hitting my fingers as I continue to rub myself, using his arousal as lube for my pleasure.

It's probably the sexiest thing I've ever seen—even more than watching the couples at The Grotto because I get to experience it.

When I become sensitive to my own touch, I stop rubbing and collapse on top of Cal. Our sticky bodies come together and he wraps his arms around my head, holding me close.

"Well, who won?" I ask breathlessly.

"Let's call it a tie. We both won."

I lift my head to look at him. "Or we both lost and we stick to our end of the deal."

"I like that idea." His hands grab my cheeks and he pulls me in for a kiss.

Looks like it's time for us both to forget the past and start planning for our future—together.

CHAPTER NINETEEN

"It's about time," I say to Anders through the phone, my eyes wandering to Bella, who's spreading cream cheese on a bagel, while sitting on the bed and watching *Friends*. "Give him the phone."

I walk over to Bella, grabbing her attention as she bites into her bagel.

"Everything okay?" she asks around a mouthful.

"What the hell do you want?" Mark growls.

I put the call on speaker phone, so I'm able to hear the conversation.

"Mark?" Bella tosses her bagel on the plate on the bed and jumps up, causing it to flip over onto the, was-clean, comforter.

She grabs the phone from my hand and I let her. Holding it up to her face, she talks into the speaker. "Mark, is it you?"

"Bella. You gotta run. You gotta do whatever it takes. Get away from that Ellis guy or you'll end up dead. I mean it—"

Bella looks at me as she tries to calm her brother down. "Mark, I'm okay. I promise Cal would never hurt me."

"That's what he wants you to believe. Listen, that Byron

guy and Trent, I heard them talking and Ellis is bad news. Lures young girls to work at some club and promises them the world only to—"

I cut him off by snatching the phone away and shutting the speaker off. "Listen here, you nitwit. Did it ever occur to you that those guys let you hear what they wanted you to hear?"

His response is just heavy breaths.

"That's what I thought. I'd never hurt Bella. In fact, I can ensure your safety, too, if you'd quit being a jackass and listen to what I have to say."

"Give me the phone back, Cal. I wanna hear what he has to say."

Ignoring her pleas, I finish up the call with Mark. "A guard will be outside your hospital room. Seems you're gonna be there for a while."

I tap End and stick my phone in my pocket, preparing for the wrath of Bella.

She looks past me, lost in thought. When she speaks, it's like she's talking to thin air. "I'm glad to hear he's going to be okay. Thank you for setting that call up for me."

"Of course. Everything is going to be okay, baby. I promise you."

Bella laughs condescendingly. "Okay? Everything is not okay, Cal. Everything is a mess."

I position myself on the end of the bed where she's kneeling. Bagel crumbs coat the white comforter and cream cheese has smeared on the pillowcase. "Eventually, it *will* be okay."

She drops onto her back, staring up at the ceiling. "What did Mark mean when he was talking about young girls working for you?"

"Bella, I swear he's lying. It wasn't me, it was—"

Her head shoots up. "I believe you."

I give her a sideways glance, finding it hard to believe that I don't have to go to great depths to explain myself. "You do?"

Bella sits up, crawls across the bed until her arms are around me. "Of course, I do. I wish I could believe that everything is going to be okay, but when you tell me you didn't do something, I believe you now."

I pull her onto my lap, burying my face in her hair. "Byron has pretty much always run things at the clubs. I'm still in charge, but I let him do his thing, thinking he was doing a good job. A few years ago, during the recession, we had a hard time finding girls to work at the club. He said he had it under control and I assumed he did. It wasn't until shortly before you arrived that I did some research on the employees and realized they were young girls. All of consensual age, but eighteen, nineteen-year-old girls straight outta high school. Do you remember me telling you that he was doing some shady business?"

"Yeah. I think so. It was the night you told me about the contract and how I'd basically agreed to marrying you without my knowledge."

One of my many fuck-ups with Bella. "Yeah. Yeah, I did do that," I admit.

"Hey," she turns my face toward hers, "in the past, remember?"

"Yeah. In the past." For now. "Anyways, he basically had men go out and find these girls who were living in poverty or needed some extra cash. Lured them in and promised them the world. Once they were in, he gave them no choice but to stay."

"I mean, if they agreed to it and they were old enough to make the decision, I don't see how it's that bad."

"It's the way he treats them that's wrong. A couple nights after you arrived at Cori Cove, I found him slapping a girl around and belittling her. A minute later, he was consoling her and apologizing, behaving like the sociopath that he is. He uses his narcissistic behavior to manipulate these women. Makes them think they need him and the job."

"So, what are you gonna do about it?"

"Well," I drawl, rubbing my thumb across my chin. "Once Byron is no longer a problem, I'm hoping to find someone to help these girls. Rehabilitate them and find them jobs that will help them in the long run, maybe even help them with schooling."

Bella's eyes light up as if she's had an epiphany. "Let me help. Please, Cal. If these girls are in trouble, then I want to help them."

"I think we could work something out. I think I'm shutting the clubs down, so a lot of employees are going to be out on their asses. I might offer a small severance, but I'm not sure what more I can do."

She looks surprised. "You're shutting the clubs down?"

"It was never my thing. It was always Vincent's and Byron's. Sure, I enjoyed them from time to time, but it's no loss to the company if I close up shop."

Bella doesn't say anything, just gives me that voided look as if her wheels are spinning. "What if I help run the clubs? If the girls choose to stay, then I can be their boss."

That warrants a laugh on my part. "Not a chance. Those men have grubby hands that like to touch every ass that walks by. I'd have to sit in a corner with brass knuckles and a shotgun in my hand." I crane my neck to get a better look at her. "Why is it so important to you?"

"It's not...important to me. I just kind of like the environment and I can tell others do, too."

"Of course they do. It's sex. Everyone loves sex."

Bella shakes her head. "No, it's more than that. For the employees, it's a job. For the members, it's an escape. A chance to be more than a spouse or a parent or a businessman. It's a place where you can be and do whatever you want without judgment."

"All right. I'll put this on the list of things to revisit once we're out of this damn suite."

Bella grins, then softly kisses my lips. "Deal."

CHAPTER TWENTY

Bella

I CAN'T STOP THINKING about Cherry. She doesn't look a day over twenty. I get the feeling that Byron is using manipulation tactics and abuse to keep her there, the same way Cal said he was doing to the other girls.

I have to talk to her. I know we're not friends, but she's such a sweet girl, and if there is anything I can do to help her, I have to at least try.

"Do you trust me, Cal?"

Concern sweeps across his face. "Of course I do. Why do you ask?"

"Just making sure." I kiss his lips, knowing that I'll be asking for forgiveness later.

Cal falls asleep only minutes later with me in his arms. I close my eyes, trying like hell to do the same, but my mind keeps wandering back to Cherry and all the girls who were victimized by Byron.

Peering up, I look at Cal's face. His nostrils flare with each breath, and I smile at his vulnerable state. These past couple months have been tainted with bad luck and bad experiences, but Cal is right, eventually, this will all be over and we'll be able to start our lives together. For the first time in a long time, that glimmer of hope has returned.

Part of putting all the bad behind us includes making sure Cal's company is running smoothly. He's been so caught up on protecting me and the search for Byron that I'm worried his employees are suffering—particularly the young females who were brainwashed. Possibly Cherry.

I lift Cal's arm slowly and rest it on his chest. He squirms a bit but falls back into a deep sleep. In just his tee shirt, I climb out from under the comforter and get out of bed.

One last look at him and I'm grabbing some clothes from my bag on the floor. Cal has told me many times that I should unpack, but unpacking means accepting that we'll be here awhile, and I refuse to do that.

I tiptoe out of the room, leaving the door slightly ajar to keep from waking him when I return. Instead of using the bathroom in our room, I go to the extra bathroom and change out of my clothes.

Fuck. I forgot my bra, and it just so happens that I grabbed a white tee shirt from the pile and Cherry had mentioned it was ladies' night, complete with a wet tee shirt contest—not that I'll be participating.

My fingers run through my hair and I wipe my thumb under my eyes to try and force the bags away. It doesn't work, though. Those bags are a sign that I need to start getting more sleep. Maybe tomorrow I'll try. Tonight, I have something to take care of.

Quietly, I grab the key card, from the drawer I stuck it in yesterday, and my black zip-up hoodie that's lying on the barstool, so I can cover up my breasts showing through my top.

I go out the door to the hall, and a few minutes later, I'm flashing the card at the guard. He gives it a double take, looking from me to the card, then holds up a hand. "Wait a damn minute. You're the girl Mr. Ellis escorted out of here the other night. Are you sure you're supposed to be here?" His hand rests on a walkie-talkie attached to his jacket, like he's about to rat me out.

Think fast, Bella. "Mr. Ellis happens to be my fiancé and if you know what's good for you, you might not wanna piss me off."

My heart is racing so fast, but I think I handled it well.

He sighs heavily, before opening the door and letting me inside.

I smirk, rolling my eyes like a bitch, though I feel really bad for threatening the poor guy.

Ignoring all the action going on around me, I skim the open room for Cherry.

This place is completely packed. Way more than it was the last couple times I was here, and it's mostly all men. I'm pushing through crowds of people who are standing around talking—likely waiting for the contest to begin.

I walk straight toward the pool room, remembering where it is from the time I was invited in. As I reach for the door, the crowd behind me begins shouting profanities. I turn around, catching the stare of a grouchy man. "Hey, lady. You can wait in line like the rest of us."

Stretching my neck, I look down the line of men and woman, and it extends all the way to the door I just entered.

I look down at my zipped hoodie, bite my bottom lip, and go for it. In a swift motion, I jerk the zipper down, exposing not only a white tee shirt, but also my puckered nipples that peek through the see-through fabric. "Actually, I'm part of the show tonight." I smile, hoping they all bought it.

No one says a word, so I open the door and step inside. Standing around the pool are about two dozen girls, all in white shirts. Some tank tops, some swim tops, and some tee shirts like my own. I seem to be the only one wearing jeans and a pair of flip-flops, though. But at least I've got half the outfit right.

The oval-shaped underground pool isn't huge, but I'd say it could hold at least one hundred people, assuming they want to touch body-to-body. The entire wrap-around area is furnished with lounge chairs, some round tables with stools, and even a tiki bar in the far corner.

"Brooke," Cherry hollers, and I catch her making her way toward me from the other side of the pool. "Or should I say, Bella?" Her arms cross over her chest, pushing her cleavage up through her V-neck bralette.

"Look, Cherry. I'm really sorry about that. It was a nickname, much like yours."

With a scornful look, she plants a hand on her hip. "It's not the name I'm upset about. It's the fact that you're one of them."

I have no idea what she's talking about. "One of who?"

She shakes a finger, pointing around the entire space. "Them. The owners. The assholes. The ones who treat us like dirt."

"No. I'm really not. Cal…err, Mr. Ellis and I are together, but I promise he's not like Byron and the other guys who run the clubs."

"Uh-huh. Sure. It's your word, baby girl. But I don't trust ya." She checks me with an eye roll and spins around, strutting back to her girl gang.

I jog after her, grabbing her by the arm. "Cherry, wait."

Sneering, she snaps back around and pulls her arm away. "Do you have a death wish, Bella?" She emphasizes my name for added effect.

"I know what Byron, or Mr. Davis, or whatever the hell you call him, does to you all and I want to help you."

"Help me?" She laughs, the sound mocking, but fully loaded with sarcasm. "Help me, what? Make more than minimum wage? Work less than seventy hours a week? Or are you referring to my cracked and bloody feet because I'm forced to wear high heels with no breaks?"

"I...I had no idea it was that bad."

"Of course you didn't. Because you're living up in your ivory tower with the riches, while we're all down here in rags," she snaps the waistband of her black miniskirt, "literally."

I look around at the girls who are all watching us, some looking like they're ready to attack if I so much as make the wrong move. "Can we talk somewhere more private?"

Cherry looks over her shoulder then back at me. "Fine," she breathes heavily, "but make it quick. In about two minutes, those doors open, and men will be swarming."

I follow behind Cherry, and she opens up a door to leave the pool room. Inside is a long hallway, with more rooms that section off.

We walk into a large room that's decked out with vanities covered in makeup, racks upon racks of costumes, and open boxes scattered all over.

I reach down into one and pick up a platinum blonde wig, wanting to try it on for good measure. I've always wondered what I'd look like as a blonde.

Cherry clears her throat, grabbing my attention. "You wanted to talk?"

"Yes," I clutch the wig, running my fingers through the golden locks, "listen, I know this all seems very odd to you and I'm not even sure why I'm about to fill you in on what's going on, but I like you, Cherry, and I'm also worried about you."

An annoyed smirk replaces her indignant look. "Worried about me? You hardly know me."

"I know enough. You were kind to me and made me feel welcome."

She waves her hand through the air, trying to move this conversation along.

"Anyways, my name is Bella, and I've known Mr. Ellis since I was a child. He's a bit rough around the edges, I know. At the end of last year, I fell in love with him, but it didn't come without a cost. You see, Byron is after me…well, Mr. Ellis. He wants his money and he's hell-bent on killing one or both of us to get it. I've been hiding out here until Byron is found so that—"

"So that Mr. Ellis can kill him first?" She's not as taken aback as I thought she'd be. In fact, she's abnormally calm after everything I just told her.

"Yeah. Pretty much. I know it all sounds crazy."

"Girl, you don't know crazy until you've lived my life."

I blow out a breath. "You'd be surprised."

"So, what does this all have to do with me?"

"Last night, Callum told me he was recently made aware of how Byron's been treating the female staff. He had no idea and I swear if he did, he would have stopped it sooner."

"Yeah," Cherry sighs, "it's quite a nightmare working for that asshole, but it's a job and most of us can't afford to quit it, not that he'd let us." She drops down into a swivel chair in front of a vanity and begins dabbing some blush on her cheeks. "Mr. Byron Davis has made it very clear that if we want out, we will pay the ultimate price."

My eyebrows rise, hoping she doesn't mean what I think she does. "What price is that?"

"Our bodies, our livelihood. He's threatened to go as far as shipping us off to Mexico and selling us to the cartel. I think he's probably talking out of his ass and he's just desperate to keep the place staffed, but there was one girl who quit six months ago, and she's been missing ever since."

"Oh my God," I gasp. "Look, Cherry, Callum and I are

going to help you all. Soon, Byron will be out of the picture and some big changes are coming to these clubs."

Cherry drops a lipstick back on the vanity and smacks her lips while looking at me through the mirror. "From your mouth to God's ears." She spins back around and stands up. "I gotta get back out there, but thanks, Bella. And I hope you're right about the changes. We sure as hell could use them." Cherry takes the wig from my hand and flips it until it's placed on top of my head. Her fingers comb through the stray strands, and she smiles at me. "It suits you." Then she heads out the door while I'm still standing here.

My eyes dart over to the vanity. My cheeks could use a little color. Going with a shimmery rose color, I run the brush up and down, highlighting my cheekbones.

I stare into the mirror, appreciating the girl looking back at me. She's full of mischief and capable of raising hell, given the right opportunity. My palms press to the makeup-stained vanity and I look closer. "Hello, Brooke."

Feeling carefree, I go out the way I came in, still wearing the wig. I'm already here, might as well see what this event is all about. Nothing wrong with sitting back on the sidelines and watching the action.

Cherry wasn't kidding when she said the place would be swarming. Men flock over every foot of space in the pool room. There are girls jumping around in the pool, tits bouncing through the wet fabric of their white shirts. Some have even removed their tops altogether.

In a matter of minutes, the place went from radio silent to sex-party central.

There are a couple waitresses walking around with drinks, Cherry included, though she's on the far side of the room. I opt out of drinking tonight, knowing that I can't stay here long.

Before Cal fell asleep, I asked him if he trusted me. I knew exactly what I intended to do tonight, but I also knew he'd stop me. I had to talk to Cherry. Now that I have, I'm surer than ever that I was brought here for a reason. I have this aching desire to help these girls and show them that they are more than just a body to be slapped around and mishandled. If they want to work here, then more power to them, but they don't deserve the disrespect they've had to endure.

I'm walking around, trying to find a corner to tuck myself in, so I don't stand out in the crowd, when my eyes meet Cherry's wide ones. Red flags immediately rise when I see the expression of dread on her face.

Her head shakes no, but I have no idea what she's referring to.

"Well, well, well. I can't say I've seen that ass around here before." That voice. I'd know it anywhere. His hands get a firm grip on my ass as he pulls me down until I'm sitting right on his lap.

My heart gallops in my chest, hands trembling and lip quivering as I try to come up with a plan of escape.

Eyes deadlocked on Cherry's, I mouth, 'help me.'

"I must say, you fit pretty well on my lap, little girl. Why don't you turn around, so you can shove those tits in my face?"

My entire body shivers, chills skating down my spine. I hold my breath, afraid to breathe, afraid to move.

His hands come around, squeezing my thighs. Fingers begin riding up, pressing into my crotch through my jeans. "I bet you've got a nice, tight pussy on ya, too."

I have to get up. I have to get out of here before Byron realizes it's me.

Cherry struts over with her tray balanced on one hand and a fake smile plastered on her face. "Hey there, Mr. Davis. I wasn't expecting you tonight. Can't say I'm disappointed."

She forces out a bout of fake laughter, and I'm officially indebted to her, assuming she can get me out of this.

Byron leans forward, me still in his lap. "And I wasn't expecting you to stand around doing nothing. Get to work."

Asshole.

While I want to scream it from the rooftop, so everyone knows what scum this man is, Cherry takes it with stride. "See my hand? It's a tray holding drinks." She grabs one off and hands it to him. "Would you like one, Mr. Davis?" She smirks.

He scoffs a bit, then takes the drink from her hand. "One for my new friend here, too."

Cherry looks at me, bewilderment in her eyes. I nod, accepting the offer, and she hands me a glass, too.

"Actually, Mr. Davis," Cherry begins, "there's someone I wanted you to meet. A potential new hire who I think would do a damn good job."

"If I wanted to know what you think, Blueberry, I'd ask."

Cherry grimaces, and I can tell she's offended. "It's Cherry." She grabs a toothpick stuck in one of the full drinks and pops the cherry on the end into her mouth. "And you'd be a fool to let this girl go. She's got a way with the gentlemen."

Byron squeezes my thigh tightly. "What about you, little girl? Are you in need of a job? I'm sure the men would love to get a look at that tight ass while you serve them drinks...and maybe more."

My stomach twists in knots, bile rising up my throat. I don't say a word out of fear he'll know who I am.

His hand moves to my cheek and he tries to get me to look at him. "Turn around. Let me see that pretty face."

I have to get out of here. I feel faint and my rapidly beating heart feels like it's going to explode from overexertion.

In a swift movement, I push myself off his lap and walk steadfast to the doors out of the pool room.

"Hey!" Byron hollers. "Where ya going?"

I reach the doors, and in a knee-jerk reaction, I look back, instantly regretting it when our eyes meet. Byron's blue orbs stay affixed on me, and his mouth drops open.

Shit.

I pull open the doors and run across the club toward the exit. There are so many people shuffling in and out that I'm forced to push my way through the crowd, knocking down a petite, young woman who spews profanities at me while I keep moving.

There are more people in the hall, lined up and waiting to get in. I pay them no attention as I hustle to the elevator. There's a line and it's taking forever. My foot taps impatiently when I finally give up, knowing that Byron is likely on his way to find me.

I keep going down the hall to the door that has a sign above it that says 'Stairs.' I push it open and go up them as fast as I can, tripping over my own feet a few times. As I'm hurrying up, I tear the wig off my head and toss it behind me.

I'm out of breath and my anxiety is so high that I fear I'll pass out and topple down the staircase along with the blonde wig.

When the sound of a door below me opens and closes, I stop momentarily and look down the winding staircase. As soon as I hear footsteps thudding up the stairs, I move faster.

He's going to catch me. He's going to grab me and take me away again. This time, he'll make sure I'm not found. This time, he might even kill me.

"Bella," Byron singsongs, sending shivers through my entire body.

There is no way I can keep going to the eighth floor. He'll

catch up before I make it and then he'll know exactly what floor we're staying on. Though, I'm sure he already does. He's well aware of Cal's private space at the hotels.

I reach another level and the door has the number five on it. Hoping like hell that it opens, I give the handle a turn and internally scream with excitement when it does.

As I run down the hall, I'm well aware that this feat is far from over.

I'm mid-panic, practically hyperventilating and ready to curl over and give up, as the elevator takes its precious time to come up.

It's likely from the event downstairs. All the people going in and out are holding it up, and I'm expecting the doors to open to a full crowd.

I look over my shoulder as the bell dings and the doors slide open. Still no sign of him.

There are two people—a man and a woman—looking back at me, waiting for me to get on, and they have picked up on my unease.

"You okay, hun?" the lady asks, stepping aside and making room for me.

Just as I step on, the door to the staircase flies open, and Byron comes running down the hall.

"Yeah," I tell her in a panic. "Just go. Make the elevator go. Eighth floor." I'm almost crying at this point. On pins and needles, hoping the doors close in time.

"Hold the—" I hear Byron shout, just before the doors seal and his voice becomes a whisper that quickly fades.

I curl over, grabbing my stomach as I catch my breath.

I made it.

"Was someone chasing you?" the sweet lady asks.

"No." I shake my head. "No, I'm fine."

The truth is, I'm far from fine. I'm watching and hoping we're not stopping at any other floors on my way up because there's a good chance Byron will be waiting outside the door for me. He's no idiot, and he knows this place like the back of his hand.

Dread washes over me when we stop on the seventh floor.

He's going to be there. I know it. I can feel it.

The doors open, and I'm half tempted to grab the burly man and ask him to save me.

But, Byron isn't there.

"Take care, hun," the lady says with concern written all over her face.

I force a smile and thank her before she disappears, and I'm pounding on the button to close the doors.

One more level. I'm almost there.

Seconds later, I'm getting off on the eighth floor, and I still don't see Byron. I run as fast as I can down the hall to the suite with my key card ready in my hand.

As soon as I swipe it and the door opens, I go inside, slam it shut, and slide down the door onto my ass.

"Cal," I scream at the top of my lungs between breaths. "Cal!"

My head rests between my shaking knees. My entire body trembles and my lungs still fail to fully inflate.

Cal comes hurrying out of the bedroom, rubbing his eyes in a pair of black briefs. He drops down at my side. "Baby, what's wrong? What happened?"

"Byron," I choke out. "He's here and he saw me."

CHAPTER TWENTY-ONE

"What do you mean he saw you?" I'm half asleep, and I've got no idea what the fuck is going on. All I know is Bella is sobbing and shaking uncontrollably on the floor in front of me.

"He saw me," she says again, her lip quivering and eyes pooling with tears.

"Saw you where?" I shout, not at her, but out of frustration. "Where the hell were you?"

She lifts her head slowly and looks at me. "I went back. I'm sorry, Cal. You said you trusted me, and I had to go see her. You shouldn't have. You shouldn't have trusted me because I screwed everything up."

"You're not making any sense, Bella. Went where? Seen who?"

"Cherry. A girl I met at The Grotto."

My face drops into my hands, massaging my temples as she continues, "She works there and I wanted to make sure she was okay, after everything you told me about Byron and the way he treats the female employees. Byron was there. He didn't see me at first—"

"Byron was at The Grotto?"

"Mhmm. He was being the total douchebag he was. Before he even saw my face, he pulled me on his lap and was—"

Rage builds inside me, unleashing in a shout, "He pulled you on his fucking lap?" She nods. "Aside from pulling you on his lap, did he touch you, Bella?" God, please tell me he didn't touch her. I can already feel the heat rushing to my head, my fists clenching, veins bulging.

"He was very touchy-feely. Grabbed my ass, rubbed my thighs, and cupped my crotch. I tried to get up, but I was so scared he'd know who I was." I feel gross just talking about it. Like tiny spiders are crawling all over my skin.

I don't even hear anything except the sound of my knuckles crashing into the wall beside the door. I bust through the drywall. Blood streaming down my hand and dripping onto the hardwood floor.

"Cal! What the hell?" Bella grabs my hand, looking at the cuts.

I pull my hand away and get up, ready to run out that door, to find him and kill him. "Give me the key card." I hold out my bloody hand, waiting for her to give it to me.

"Why? Where are you going?"

My fingers roll against my palm, hand still extended as I wait impatiently. "Give me the damn key card, Bella. He must've been out searching all the resorts, knowing we're at one, and now, he's found us."

"Please don't go out there. I'm scared, Cal. Don't leave me. Don't do anything stupid."

"Stupid?" I laugh. "There will be nothing stupid about me slitting that bastard's throat."

Bella throws herself into my arms. "Don't leave me."

The fire inside me slowly begins to subside from a boiling point to a slow simmer. That's all it takes to calm me down.

Her touch, her scent, her soft voice. I kiss her head, stroking her hair as she presses her face to my chest. "I won't leave you."

I hold her for what feels like minutes, knowing that he's out there somewhere—either trying to find us or trying to escape. Once I've got her calmed down and I'm ready to think clearly, I step away to make a call in the bedroom.

I'm standing in front of the window, looking out at the city, as I tap Anders's name. He picks up on the first ring and I cut right to the chase. "He's here at the Manhattan resort. Bella blew our cover tonight by sneaking down to The Grotto." Sensing her presence, I turn around and see Bella standing there. Her hip pressed to the doorframe and a look of remorse on her face.

"Baby, I didn't mean—"

She holds up a hand, stopping me. "It's okay. It's the truth." She turns and walks away and as much as I'd like to chase after her and apologize while explaining myself, I have to get things rolling.

My attention returns to the call. "I need all of our top men here. Put this place on lockdown. Contact Edward, Jason, Pedro, and all the head guards at the other locations and alert them of what's going on. If Byron shows his face anywhere, they are to detain him and contact me immediately."

"I'm on it, Boss. You want me there, too?"

"Yes, I want you here. You're my head of security and I need you to fucking catch this guy." I end the call before I blow up and say shit I'll regret. It seems I've already put my foot in my mouth enough tonight.

With my phone still in my hand, as I anticipate a call back from Anders once he's made contact with everyone, I leave the room. "Bella," I holler out. She shouldn't have heard that. Hell, I shouldn't have said it. I was trying to get as much information out as I could, as fast as I could. "Baby, I didn't mean it like that. Don't be mad."

Noticing the light on in the bathroom, I go toward it. "Bella?" I push open the door, but she's not there. All I see is the pajamas she had on when she went to bed. She must've changed here before going to The Grotto.

I scoop up her pajamas and let them fall back to the floor, wondering where the hell she's at. Something doesn't feel right.

"Bella," I holler again, now frantically searching the entire suite. When she doesn't turn up, I scream. "Fuck!"

Why the hell does this girl keep sneaking off? Since the minute she came back into my life, she's constantly disappearing and getting herself into trouble.

I hurry into the bedroom, pull on a pair of dress pants that were lying on the floor and fasten my belt. Skimming the room for a shirt as I try to hurry, I don't see one. I rifle through the drawer I unpacked in. I go for the first white undershirt I find and slip it on, along with a pair of socks.

Once I'm in my shoes and ready to search this entire fucking property, I go to the door—without my key card, because she still has it.

What a fucking mess.

Just as I open the door, I hear her sniffling. My head snaps around and I see that the balcony door is open a tad.

Relief washes over me. I kick my shoes off and cross the room.

Sliding the door open, I see her leaning over the railing, looking down. She flinches; I know she's aware that I'm here. I come up behind her, pressing my arms to the railing on either side of her.

"I'm sorry," she says as I go to speak, "I didn't mean to blow our cover."

"That's not what I meant. I had so many thoughts running

through my head, and I was trying to tell Anders what went down and it came out wrong."

Bella turns around. Her eyes are swollen and it's obvious she's been crying. "No. You were right. I've been careless. Hell, I'm always careless. I should have never left this suite to begin with."

I sweep my thumb under her eye, then the other, before resting my hand on her cheek. "I love the careless side of you. The carefree, vibrant, 'never giving a shit' side. When you get something in your head, there's no stopping you."

She looks down at the space between us. "Yeah, I'm a royal pain in your ass."

I tip her chin up, feeling the warmth swimming through my chest like it does each time I look at her. "That you are. But you make life interesting. Did you know that before you came back in my life, I did the same thing every single day? Wake up, drink coffee and have breakfast—alone—make a shit-ton of business calls, feed Amara, have lunch—alone—handle more business, have dinner—alone—and I'd attempt to sleep only to be haunted by my nightmares. You've shaken things up in the best way possible. I'd hide away with you forever if it meant being with you forever."

Finally, a smile. It's just a little one, but it's something.

She raises a brow, chewing on her bottom lip and driving me wild like she always does. "You mean that?"

"I absolutely mean that." I kiss her lips, tasting a hint of saltiness from her tears. "Without you, I'm nothing."

Her hint of a smile grows to one that pushes her cheekbones up, showing her pearly white teeth. "I feel the same way."

"Good." I tuck a stray strand of hair behind her ear. "Now that we have that settled, I need you to promise you'll quit sneaking off all the time. I'm not even thirty years old and you're giving me gray hair."

She laughs. It's a beautiful sound that I want to hear every day for the rest of my life. Bella has given me life. She's made me feel things that I swore I'd never allow myself to feel. My heart is no longer empty, it's so full of love for this girl.

"I promise I'll try to run things by you first."

"Okay. That's a start." I kiss her again, and when I go to pull away, thinking she needs some sleep while I handle this business with Byron, she pulls me back in. Hands wrapped around my head, fingers intertwined in my hair. She kisses me hard and every emotion spills into my mouth. I feel it all. I feel her, the woman of my dreams, in my arms, and a permanent fixture in my life.

CHAPTER TWENTY-TWO

Bella

"CAL," I grumble, rolling over to my side. I watch him in a pair of gray joggers as he paces the bedroom with his face in his phone. "It's two in the morning. Come to bed."

He holds up a finger, eyebrows dipped in a deep V as he finishes reading whatever is on his phone.

It was after midnight before I finally fell asleep, even then it was broken chunks. All I could think about was Byron's dirty hands all over me in the pool room. The look on his face when he realized it was me is etched in my mind and will likely haunt me in my dreams.

Cal finally lifts his head and cracks a smile. "Anders has a lead. He'll be updating me as soon as he has more information."

"That's great." I pat the mattress beside me. "Now come and sleep while you can." I've gotten used to having Cal by my side every night, and I sleep so much better when I'm in his arms.

Giving in, he drops his joggers to his ankles and kicks them off.

I lift the blanket, inviting him in, and he slides beneath

the covers. His warm body engulfs me, arm wrapped around my waist as he pulls me close.

My head nuzzles up to his scruffy chest and everything is perfect.

I'M WOKEN up to the slamming of drawers. When I spring up on the bed, I find Cal pulling on clothes like he's in a hurry.

Hugging the blanket to my chest, I watch him, blinking a few times to adjust to the light shining in the room from the open door. "What are you doing?"

"I have to go, baby," he says, his words as rushed as his movements.

I throw the blanket off me and get out of bed. "What do you mean you have to go?" I walk over to him, putting my hands on his shoulders to stop him from moving like a crackhead in need of a fix.

"Anders called. They found him." For a brief moment, he looks into my eyes before he begins hustling again.

"Found him? Is he dead or something?"

He pauses, stares at the window, then resumes slipping his socks on. "If only." He reaches for his dress coat that sits on the dresser beside me, and I grab it before he does.

"Would you just stop and tell me what the hell is going on?"

"I have to make a little trip. I shouldn't be gone long. There will be a guard outside the door twenty-four seven."

"Twenty-four seven?" I spit out. "I thought you said you wouldn't be gone long?"

He takes the jacket from my hand and slides one arm in, before pressing his lips to mine in a hurried kiss. "A day, maybe two." He puts the other arm in, zips his long black coat, and walks past me.

I follow behind him, not letting him get away with only the few details he's sprinkled on me. "Where is this trip taking you?"

He stops. Turns slowly with a shoe in his hand. There's a beat of silence that has my heart pounding in my chest. He finally says, "Rhode Island," before putting on his shoes.

"Rhode Island? But, what the hell would Byron…" My hand claps over my mouth, and I shake my head.

"He's got your parents, Bella."

"Oh my God," I cry out. "What do you mean he's got my parents? Please stop with all these one-liners and tell me what the fuck is going on?"

Cal closes the space between us, places one hand on my waist, and looks deep into my eyes with a serious and concerned expression. "I didn't wanna tell you. I know how you are. You can't go and try to play the hero, Bella. Do you understand? Let me handle this."

Tears stream down my cheeks as I think of every possible scenario. Did he kill them? Is he going to kill them?

"What did he do?" I choke out, my words muffled with my cries. "Did he hurt them?"

"No. At least, not yet. He's two steps ahead of us and baiting us to him. I got a cryptic text and a picture—"

"Show me."

He stands idly, not wanting to show me the image he was sent.

"Show me the damn picture and text, Cal!"

Dropping his hand from my waist, he reaches into his pants pocket and pulls out his phone. A second later, he's holding it up, and on the screen is a picture of my mom, my dad, and Mark—all gagged and tied up in our dining room. I gasp, feeling like the air has been sucked right out of my lungs.

"And the text?"

He swipes up, showing me the words on his screen.

Unknown: These should have been your parents. You seem to have forgotten that bitch left you. She's the only one to blame.

"Did you respond?" I grab the phone from his hand, scrolling down and reading the exchange of messages.

You son of a bitch! Touch them and I'll be sure to cut off your nutsack and use it as bait on my next fishing trip.

Unknown: I'd like to see you try. You've got until noon, or they all die. Come alone or they die anyways.

I toss the phone back at him and he catches it in midair. I spin around, burying my face in my hands as I break down.

Cal comes up behind me, turns me around, and lets me fall apart in his arms. "You see why I have to go."

I nod through sniffles and tears. "Okay." I look up at him, seeing the worry in his eyes. He's putting his life on the line to save my parents—parents he thought would be his, too. "Be careful." I don't want to let him go. I want him to stay here where he's safe, but I know that no matter what I do or say, he'll go anyway. We're alike in that way.

His lips press to my forehead, then he takes a few steps back and pulls his phone out of his pocket, though it's different. It's not his phone at all. He hands it to me. "What's this?" I ask.

"A temporary phone, so I can reach you. Under no circumstances do you leave this room. I mean it, Bella."

I nod in agreement, clutching the phone in my hand. "Call me as soon as you're all safe."

"I will. I promise."

"Don't get yourself killed, Cal. I can't live in this world without you."

The corners of his lips tug up. "I love you, baby."

I throw myself into his arms one last time before I let him go. "I love you, too."

Cal opens the door and I see the guard. As soon as I lay eyes on him, I know I'll be safe here. He's about seven feet tall and at least three hundred and fifty pounds of solid muscle. His tattooed arms are folded in front of him and he tips his head to Cal.

"That's my whole world in that room," Cal says. "Don't let anything happen to her."

"You got it, Boss. She's in good hands."

Cal gives me one last look before he pulls the door shut. The latching sound mimics a prison cell being closed. Only, I'm not in prison; I'm in hell. With Cal out there and me in here.

He's going to be fine. He'll save them, and everyone will be okay.

It's the only ending I'll accept.

CHAPTER TWENTY-THREE

It's a quick flight to Rhode Island. We touch down at a private airfield, about twenty minutes from Bella's house. As we're bussing through the space, I send Bella a quick message to check in, just to make sure she hasn't knocked out Stanley, the guard, and hopped on a commercial flight to try and save the day. I can't help but smile, knowing it's totally something she would do.

She responds right away with a picture of her sitting on the couch in our suite. She's wearing one of my black tee shirts, her legs crossed like a pretzel and her eyes swollen from crying so much. Fuck, I miss her. It's only been two hours, but I'm ready to be back by her side. I long to dry her tears and sweep her hair out of her face while kissing her until our lips bruise.

Me: Good girl. I'll be in touch. Love you.

I put my phone back in the front pocket of my coat and unbuckle my seat belt as soon as I'm given the green light to get off the jet.

Lloyd, the pilot, bids me farewell with a handshake.

I go down the short staircase and my car is waiting about

three yards from the jet. The driver exits, pulling the back door open for me. Inside, I see Anders waiting.

He's got a scowl and he's shaking his head, and I know this isn't good.

I pick up my pace and slide in the back seat. "What's with the pissed-off look?"

"I got a call from one of my new guys. It seems Byron has the entire Jenkins house surrounded. He wants you alone, and I worry he'll go to extremes if we carry out the plan and have an army of men showing up."

"What do you suggest?" It's not often that I take advice—I prefer to give it—but in this case, it's necessary. Anders is highly trained, and he's handled situations much worse than this.

"We'll have the driver drop me off somewhere near the Jenkins' house. I'll have everyone gather there." He hands me a small object that looks like a black thumbtack. He reaches over and drops it in my front pocket. "We'll be listening the entire time. The minute we think you need backup, we'll be there."

I should be scared. Should fear for my life. Going up against Byron is one thing, but a flock of men who are likely trained assassins, members of the militia, and mafia partners is risky business. But, I'm not. Growing up, I had so much fear inside me. Fear of ending up alone, fear of failure, fear of living. I'm not sure I'm even able to encompass those feelings anymore. Now, I thrive when danger lies ahead. I seek out a challenge, and I fight like hell for what's mine.

"Fine. Let's just get this shit done. I've got better things to do with my time."

Anders makes a call and relays the plan on an untraceable phone. A few minutes later, we parallel park on the side of the street in front of a quaint little bed and breakfast that looks like something straight out of a country magazine. It looks like a house that was built in the early 1900s. All white siding, a white picket fence, and what I imagine is a well-cared-for lawn, though it's covered in snow. In the summer, there's probably flower gardens surrounding the place. A sign hanging in front of the house reads, 'Betsy's Bed and Breakfast'.

"Looks cozy." Anders laughs. It's a far cry from what we're used to, but I actually kinda like it. It does look cozy, mostly because it's quiet. There aren't dozens of people lurking around. No clubs, no bars, no noise.

"Yeah. Now get your ass out and round up the troops."

Anders's hand lingers on the handle. "Code word: Nuggets."

"Nuggets? What the fuck kind of code word is nuggets?"

He shrugs a shoulder, a smirk on his face. "One that works." The door opens, and he gets out. He taps the hood as he walks by and the driver pulls back out onto the street.

As we travel down the road, I slide on my black, leather gloves and double check the microphone in my pocket. Still there, let's just hope the damn thing works.

I contemplate texting Bella one last time before going in, but when the driver slows the car, I realize there is no time. We pull up in front of the house, parking on the side of the road instead of using the driveway.

At first glance, I don't see anything that appears to be out of the ordinary. No men, no fresh tracks. In fact, it looks as if the last car in the driveway was before the heavy snowfall began.

The driver looks at me in the rearview mirror and says, "I'll be waiting, Mr. Ellis."

I nod, then open the door and put one foot on the ground. The packed snow on the road makes for a slippery step, so I'm cautious as I get to my feet.

Closing the door behind me, I look at the house. It's just

as I remember it all those times I checked in on Bella, without her knowledge.

I've never been inside, and I'm curious to see what the house she spent her teenage years in looks like. I imagine it smells like freshly baked cookies with family pictures covering the walls. Nothing like the home I had at the Ellis mansion.

There's a sheet of ice on the road so I take care as I walk toward the driveway. Once I make it down without falling on my ass, I pull one hand out of my coat pocket and knock on the screen door. It rattles against the frame a bit, and when no one answers, I knock again.

"Doesn't look like anyone's here," I say in a whisper, yet loud enough for Anders to hear me through the mic.

This time, I open the screen door and knock harder on the main door. Stretching my neck, I look over the railing on the small cement slab and try to get a peek in the window to the living room.

It's eerily quiet, and my gut tells me to just go inside. I knock a couple more times before I turn the handle, but it's locked.

"Door is locked. No answer."

I go back down the stairs and step beside a big bush in front of the picture window, trying to get a look inside.

There's a haze on it, or maybe it's fog from the cold temperatures. I move even closer, shielding my eyes and getting a better look.

Then I see them.

"Fucking Christ!"

Three chairs, holding three people. Tied with their hands behind their backs, ankles restrained, and duct tape across their mouths.

Duct tape, Byron? Really?

Just proves he's as classless as I thought he was.

Trudging through the snow, as it seeps into my socks, I hurry back up the stairs and tear open the screen door. With it wide open, I stretch my leg out and kick, hoping to knock the main door open. I try a few more times, before giving up and running around the side of the house to try and get in through a back door.

There's a sliding glass door on the deck. With the snow now soaking my feet. I run up the deck, knowing this door is likely locked, too.

And it is. *Dammit.*

"I need backup. I can't get in this damn house and Bella's parents are tied up. I've got no tools on me to pick the lock."

I pull my phone out of my pocket, wondering if Byron's attempted to call. I'm not sure what his endgame is here, but he's definitely got a plan.

Bella.

What if this was a decoy? A distraction so I'd leave her. He would have known I'd come to try and rescue Bella's parents if they were in harm's way.

I pull the mic out of my pocket, speaking directly into it. "Hurry the fuck up."

When Anders and the guys are still a no-show, I give him a call.

He picks up immediately. "We're thirty seconds away. Listen, Boss, it could be a trap. Don't enter until we get there."

"Just hurry your ass up." I end the call and stick my phone back in my coat pocket. As soon as it drops down, it begins vibrating against my side.

Retrieving it, I look at the screen and see it's Bella calling from her dummy phone. I tap End, knowing that if I take this call before I have answers, she'll panic.

I leave the deck and go back around to the front of the

house; Anders is already here, along with a train of six or seven, matching black cars lined up in front of the house.

"'Bout fucking time."

"Came as soon as we could, Boss." He's got a pick in his hand and he wastes no time picking the lock.

Simultaneously, the car doors all open and out steps a dozen men who are armed and ready. Anders gives them a quizzical look before picking at the lock again.

This is why he's head of security and the reason I pay him so well. Anders is the best of the best, and the only person I know who could throw together a team like this at the last minute.

A minute later, he looks over his shoulder at me as I stand in the snowy yard at the bottom of the porch steps. He tips his head at the door, asking if I'm ready to go in, and I nod in response.

We move silently as Anders retrieves his gun from the holster then opens the door. The army of men scurry across the yard, ready to take action.

Following behind Anders, we enter the house and the men follow behind me.

Anders waves his arm around the room. "Search it top to bottom," he tells them. "Even if you come up empty-handed, search it again."

I go straight into the living room. My eyes land on Bella's mom first, then to her dad. Lastly, Mark. Anders begins helping Bella's parents, so I pull the duct tape off Mark's mouth. They shrill and immediately begin flooding our ears with what happened. I can't make out a word they're saying because they're talking so damn fast.

I hold up a hand, hoping to shut them up. When they continue to speak at the same time, I shout, "Shut the hell up."

Bella's mom and dad appear stunned at my outburst, but

Mark just grits his teeth, staring me dead in the eye. "If anything happens to my sister, I'll kill you, you son of a bitch!"

Ignoring him, since he's obviously got a stick up his ass, I start with Bella's dad. Crouching down, I level with him. I've learned to never untie someone you need answers from. It's the one useful bit of information I learned from Vincent.

I reach into my pocket and pull out my phone, bringing up a picture of Byron. "Was this guy here?"

His eyes squint as he tries to get a better look, so I bring it closer to his face. "Ugh, no. Doesn't look familiar. The guys that were here were heavyset with leather jackets and combat boots."

I look over my shoulder at Anders and we speak without words. He taps into his phone and makes a call as I continue my questioning.

Just as I go to speak, I catch a glimpse of Mrs. Jenkins, Bella's mom. Something jabs inside my chest, and it's a strange feeling, knowing that she was supposed to be my mom. Short brown hair, glasses, dressed like a librarian. She looks sweet. Like someone who would listen when you've had a bad day and hug you when you're hurting. It's a surreal moment that I quickly snap myself out of because I can't handle any more what-ifs.

I push myself up and turn my back to Bella's family. "Were you able to track him?"

Anders shakes his head no, still holding the phone to his ear. He walks away, into another room, and I return my attention to Bella's dad.

"Bella is safe. I can promise you that."

"Liar!" Mark shouts. "None of this would have happened if it weren't for you. Why couldn't you just stay dead like we all thought you were?" He squirms and curses, trying to free himself.

"I'll admit, much of this is my fault. But," I pause for a moment, looking Mark dead in the eye, "one could say it's your fault, too. After all, I should have had your place with this family."

He doesn't say a word, just continues to wriggle against the ropes on his wrist.

"Cat got your tongue, Marky? Don't your *parents* know what you did all those years ago? Lying and setting me up so I'd miss out on the adoption?"

"Mr. Ellis," Bella's mom begins. Her voice is just like I imagined it: soft, sweet, compassionate. "We all make mistakes, myself included. But we can't change the past. Everything worked out the way it was meant to."

I turn around, unable to look at them any longer. They'll always take Mark's side. He's their son, after all. My fingers run through my hair, dampened by the snow. "Yeah. The way it was meant to."

I'm not here to make friends with this family. Sure, they'll be my in-laws one day, but I don't fit in here. I'm too broken while they're all so well put together.

Putting the past where it belongs, I focus on the future. "How'd he get you, Mark?" I spin around, looking at him as he sits there with a fat lip and a scorned look on his face. "Was it through Trent?"

"Fuck Trent and fuck you!"

Seems we're not getting anywhere by playing nice. I eat up the foot of space between us and press my hands to the arm of his chair. "Answer the fucking question if you ever want to be untied."

"Yes. Okay? Trent invited me over to his place to play poker, and as soon as I walked in the door, I was knocked over the head. It was the last time I saw him before he was found dead on the Elizabeth Islands. I'd just heard of his death when I returned after being tied up for a fucking month! Don't even try to pretend that you had nothing to do with that or Trent's murder."

I blow out a heavy breath of laughter. "I don't pretend. But I didn't kidnap you. In fact, I was held in a room in the same building. Had no idea you were there. And I didn't kill Trent. He's lucky Byron got to him first because I would have tortured the fuck out of that piece of shit for what he did to Bella."

Mark's eyes widen. Now I've got his attention. "What the hell did he do to Bella?"

"Lied to her. Tricked her into believing he was a good person."

"Oh, you mean pretty much what you did to her?"

He's got a point, so I don't argue it, even if my motives were different.

Anders returns and grabs my attention. There's panic in his eyes. "We gotta go."

My heart jumps into my throat. Fear consuming every inch of my body. "Where is he?"

The men all begin hustling out the door, except for two, who enter the living room and begin untying the Jenkins family. "These two will be guarding the house until we know it's safe," Anders assures the family as he moves quickly to the door. "In the car, now!"

I don't even say anything to Bella's family before hauling ass out the door. As we're hurrying to the car, I press for more information. "Tell me what the hell is going on!"

"He's at the Manhattan resort. He's going for her, Boss."

CHAPTER TWENTY-FOUR

Bella

"DON'T PANIC, BABY," Cal says through the speaker before I can even get a word out. Him telling me not to panic has me jumping off the couch.

"What's going on? How are my parents?" The blanket that was wrapped around me drops to the floor, and I walk over to the balcony doors, looking out into the night, fearing someone is going to bust through the glass at any given moment.

"They're fine. I'll fill you in later, but they're safe."

There's a knock at the door that has me spinning around. "Someone's knocking, Cal. Should I answer it?"

"No!" he blurts out without a second thought. "Do not go near the door, Bella."

I grip the phone tighter, chills running down my spine. "You're scaring me."

"Go in the bedroom and lock the door."

"What if it's the guard?" Regardless, I do as I'm told and head for the bedroom.

"It very well could be, but we can't take any chances."

There's a worry in his voice that tells me there's no way it's the guard.

"Please tell me what's going on. Why did you tell me not to panic?"

He takes an audible breath and exhales slowly. "We lost Byron."

My heart jumps into my throat, my pulse throbbing in my neck, and it only gets worse when the knocking on the door becomes erratic. "They're not going away, Cal." My voice cracks, hands trembling. "What do I do?"

"We've got more men on the way. Just stay put and do not leave that room."

My entire back vibrates off the bedroom door from a loud bang outside the room. "Cal," I whisper, frantically, "I think someone's inside."

"Baby, stay on the phone. Anders has men on their way up. Do not leave the room!" His voice is as panicked as mine, and it does nothing to calm me. Not that he could at this point.

"Come out, come out, wherever you are."

Every alarm in my body is set off by the sound of Byron's voice. My heart is beating so fast that I fear it will jump right out of my chest. "It's Byron," I manage to choke out.

I step away from the door, not taking my eyes off it as the handle begins shaking. "Open the door, Bella."

"Leave me the hell alone!"

Cal is still on the phone, mumbling words I can't comprehend when the bedroom door flies open. I walk backward until I hit the bed and the phone slips out of my hand, crashing onto the bedroom floor.

Byron wears a devious grin on his face as he walks toward me. The closer he gets, the more I try to get away, but I'm cornered.

I fall back onto the bed, immediately trying to roll to get off, so I can run, but his hand grabs my ankle.

"Ya know, I'm getting really tired of having to chase you down, Bella." He yanks my ankle, pulling me back down the bed. My nails claw into the blankets, trying to climb my way back up, but he takes back each inch I gain.

Once Byron has me right where he wants me, he presses a firm hand on my stomach, holding me in place. I can hear Cal shouting through the speaker of the phone on the floor and it grabs Byron's attention. He bends down, picks it up, and brings it to his ear.

"Hello, old friend." He smirks, eyes still pinned on me.

I snarl, raising my knee and kicking him in the gut. It hardly fazes him as he squeezes my stomach with all his strength, fingertips digging into my skin. "You're gonna pay for that, you little bitch."

Cal's voice raises through the phone and Byron releases a menacing laugh. "She's mine now, fucker. I've been wanting to taste this pussy for a long time."

Dread swarms in my belly. I have to get out of here. My eyes scan the room, taking in objects I could potentially use as a weapon. Damn you, Cal, for not leaving me a gun.

Byron ends the call and whips the phone over my head. It crashes into the wall behind me.

"Now, let's have a little fun, shall we?"

In one swift motion, he tugs my satin pajama pants down until they're lingering beneath my ass. My legs flail, trying to kick as I scream at the top of my lungs. "Someone help me!"

The sound of the button popping on his pants is deafening. It's nothing compared to the sound of his zipper sliding down. He pushes his pants, letting them drop to his ankles as his belt clanks together.

"You should have been mine, Bella. And now you will be."

"Byron, please. Please just stop this."

"I can't stop now."

His cock springs free from his boxers, and he begins stroking it over the top of me. "I'm gonna fuck you, Bella. Then I'm gonna kill you and fuck you again."

I'm past the point of tears as anger ripples through me. He can try, but he won't take me without a fight.

"Fuck you!" I shout in his ear as he begins slobbering kisses all over my neck.

He fidgets with his cock, and when he raises his hips, lining his dick up with my entrance, I squeeze my legs together and lift my knees to my chest. My feet press into his abdomen and I use all my strength to kick him back. With the upper hand, I shove him hard until he flies off the end of the bed.

In one fluid motion, I roll off the mattress and drop to the floor.

Byron gets up quickly and stands over me with a clenched jaw, "You little whore!"

I scream again, fearing no one can hear my cries. As Byron stoops down, I notice a figure behind him and relief sweeps through me.

Cherry.

Byron catches my gaze and spins around, but before he can react, Cherry smashes him over the head with a lamp. His body goes slack and tumbles on top of me, and I immediately shove him off.

The base of the lamp drops to the floor before Cherry kneels beside me. "Are you okay?"

Blood rolls down the side of Byron's face and I've seen enough horror movies to know that he will wake up in about thirty seconds. I grab the base of the lamp, push myself up and smack him in the face with it. His head moves a bit, eyes still closed. "I am now." I grab my sweatpants off the floor and pull them on before throwing myself into her arms like she's an old friend. "Thank you. How the hell did you get in here?"

Cherry pulls out of the embrace and sets her hands on my shoulders. "I came to make sure you were okay. I saw him chasing after you. It took me a minute to find you, but when I saw the dead man outside your open door, I knew exactly where you were." Her tone shifts quickly as she grabs my hand. "Come on, we need to get out of here."

I look from her to Byron, still in shock about what just happened. "No," I blurt out.

Cherry gives me a puzzled look and stands up. "No?"

"If we leave him here, he'll escape, then he'll come after me and Cal again."

Cherry raises an eyebrow. "Do you suggest we kill him?" The casual tone of her voice is astounding. She asks the question in the same manner one might ask someone if they want crackers with their soup.

"I'm...I'm not sure. Do I want him dead? Yes. Do I want to be the one to do it? No." I'm not a killer, but if I had to be to save mine and Cal's lives, I think I could do it.

"Then don't. It will stay on your conscience forever, and you don't want that burden." She bends down and grabs one of Byron's limp feet. "Help me get him in the kitchen. We'll tie him up until someone who will feel no remorse can do the job."

Byron's pants are still hovering around his ankles. "Ugh," I cringe. "Can we cover up his penis? I'm gonna be sick."

Cherry laughs and grabs a sheet from the bed and tosses it on him. "Better?"

"Much." I grab his other foot, and we pull him across the room. He's heavier than I expected.

A trail of blood streaks across the hardwood floor as we drag him. His jacket ruffles up around his head and the sheet begins to slide off, but it's still covering enough of him to appease my stomach.

We're pulling him out the door, trying to maneuver him to fit through the doorway, and his hand bangs against the frame. "Oops," I say, sort of hoping it happens again.

We finally make it to the kitchen and drop his feet to the floor. "What are we gonna use to tie him up?" I look around the room, as if something will just pop out that we can use.

"Look in the drawers and cupboards."

I highly doubt we have anything, but I begin searching. As I'm opening and shutting cupboards and drawers, Byron lets out some muffled sounds, and I move quicker. "I'm not finding anything."

"Wait," Cherry says, holding up a finger. "The guard outside. He has to have something. A gun at the very least."

"Yes!" I cross the room to the open door. I look out and see the guard lying there, dead. Cherry's standing behind me and I'm thinking she'll have to take on this task.

"What are you waiting for?" she asks. "Search him."

I'm looking at a guy with a bullet in his head. "I…I don't think I can do it."

She huffs, brushing past me. "Move. I'll look."

I step aside and watch as she digs into his many pockets and retrieves a gun, a baton, some pepper spray, and a ball of twine.

"That should work, right?"

"It'll keep him restrained temporarily, but we need backup to hurry their ass up, because it won't hold him long."

Cherry carries everything she took from the guy back in the suite and drops them on the counter, except the twine, which she begins unraveling. "All right, let's get to work. Grab his hands."

I'm reaching down, ready to grab Byron by the wrist,

when his head begins moving around. I look at Cherry who waves her hand, rushing me along with the twine spread in her hands.

I take one wrist, then the other, and just as I'm bringing them together on his chest, Byron's eyes shoot open and he grabs my arm. "Ahhh," I scream, trying to pull away, but he overpowers me.

Out of nowhere, Cherry kicks him square in the temple, knocking him out again. I look up at her, stunned. "Damn, girl."

Her shoulders shrug. "What can I say, I've had to fight off my fair share of men."

With both hands together on his chest, Cherry wraps the twine around them so tightly that it digs into his skin.

Once we're sure it's secure, we move to his ankles. "Ya know," Cherry begins, "we could just wrap this around his throat and end him now." There's a glint of humor in her eyes, and I can't tell if she's serious, or joking.

"I think Cal will appreciate us leaving him alive, so he can get the answers he needs."

"You really like that guy? Mr. Ellis?" She seems surprised, as if he's unlikable. I suppose to many people, he is.

"Yeah. Yeah, I like him a lot. The Mr. Ellis you all see isn't the one I get. He's had a rough life, but he's a good man."

"If you say so." Cherry ties off the twine on Byron's ankles, then drops her butt to the floor.

I know that most people won't understand my relationship with Cal—my family included—but that's the beauty of it being *our relationship*, it doesn't matter what they think. It's ours and ours alone.

"What now?" Cherry asks, getting to her feet. "Should we call someone?"

"Oh shit!" I get up quickly and hurry into the bedroom to

find my phone. Cal is probably a mess with worry right now.

I find it lying on the floor, screen shattered, as suspected. Fortunately, it seems to still work. I tap the button on the side to open the home screen then hit the phone icon. A piece of glass sticks into my finger, and I shriek, pulling the glass out then sucking my finger into my mouth.

There are like fifty missed calls and messages from Cal, and when I go to call him again, it rings before I have a chance.

"Cal," I say into the speaker.

"Thank God, Bella. I've been worried sick. Listen, I'm here. I'll be in the room in a minute. Are you okay? I swear if that son of a—"

"Babe, I'm fine. He didn't hurt me."

Cal breathes out an audible sigh of relief. "All right. I'm coming down the hall."

I run out of the bedroom, stopping in front of where Byron lies on the floor. Cherry gives me a weird look, and I return the gesture when I see that she's eating a handful of pretzels while standing over a passed-out body. Girl's got a strong stomach, I'll give her that.

"Help is here," I tell her, before stepping over Byron and going out the open door.

Cal's walking steadfast down the hall with his phone still pressed to his ear. A smile draws on my face and I toss my phone onto the floor as I run to him. Tears of happiness stream down my cheeks. I wasn't sure I'd ever see him again, but here he is.

I throw myself into his arms, jumping up and wrapping my legs around his waist. "I'm so happy to see you."

"You have no idea how fucking worried I was, baby. I had men on their way, but they were delayed, and I thought for sure...it doesn't matter. I'm here. Fuck! The thought of him touching you, hurting you." His head shakes, eyes closing momentarily. "I can't even comprehend what I'd do if I lost you."

"I'm here. I'm okay." I kiss his lips over and over again as he carries me into the suite.

As we approach the room, I figure I should probably give him a warning about what he's walking in on. "I had help," I tell him. "It's the girl I was telling you about. She saved my life, Cal."

Cal sets me down on my feet. "The waitress from The Grotto?"

I nod, my words scratching at my throat. "Byron was planning to rape me and she came just in time and knocked him out." Cal pushes past me to go into the suite as I keep talking. "So, we tied him up." I wave my hands over Byron, who is now wide-eyed and alert.

Cherry points at Byron with a pretzel rod in her hand, then takes a bite. "Shithead woke up."

I can't help but laugh at this very non-humorous situation.

"Well," Cherry continues, "I'm gonna let you two deal with that, so I can get back to work." She brushes off her hands and swallows down the last bite. "It's Gentlemen's Night tonight, and I've got some waiting for me." She goes to leave the room, but I stop her.

"Thank you, Cherry. You saved me, and I'm forever in your debt."

Cherry looks from me to Cal. "Giving me a new boss is a good start. Mr. Davis was a fucking prick."

Cal extends his hand to Cherry, and she looks down at it like it's tainted. "Callum Ellis. It's a pleasure to meet you, Cherry. You'll be compensated fully for your help tonight. And I can promise, you'll never see this son of a bitch again."

She nods, half-smiling, and shakes his hand. "You've got a tough girl, here. Don't fuck it up."

Cal looks into my eyes. "Wouldn't dream of it."

Once Cherry's gone, Cal practically begs me to wait in the bedroom. Says I don't wanna see or hear what's about to go down. There are a dozen men outside our room, Byron's tied up, Cal's here—I'm safe now. So I do as he asked.

CHAPTER TWENTY-FIVE

PACING UP and down where Byron lies on the floor, speechless and staring back at me, I grind my molars and restrain from stomping his face in. My fists clench so tightly, I can feel the blood draining from my hands.

I'm tempted to lift the sheet to see why his lower half is covered, but I know it'll only infuriate me more. There's a good chance he's pantless, which means he had intentions that I can't fathom at this moment.

"You've done a lot of things to piss me off," I begin, slouching down and putting my knee to his chest. He blows out a heavy breath as I deflate his lungs. "You tried to steal my empire, stabbed me in the back, and took the life of my good friend, Peter." I press harder as I try to pull out the words while leaving my emotions behind. "But nothing you've done has pissed me off more than you hurting my girl." I cock my fist and release it right on his nose.

"She's mine," I scream. "She will never be yours. Yet, you tried to force her to marry you and..."

Fuck! I can't even say the words, but it's necessary to get this out before I kill him. "You fucking touched her. What gives you the right?" It's a closed question and I want no response. No bullshit excuses or creative lies.

Now that I got that out, it's time to ask the questions I *do* want answers to. "Why the fuck did you do it? I know damn well it's not because you caught feelings for her?"

A smirk tugs at the corner of his lip, and my blood hits a boiling point. "You think this is fucking funny?" I punch him again, this time, hard enough to crack his nose. He shrills as blood spills down the side of his face. His legs begin kicking, trying to free himself from whatever the hell he's tied up with.

"You son of a bitch!" Byron shouts. "If you don't kill me, I will kill you. So you might as well end this shit right now."

"No! Not until you answer the damn question."

"And why the hell should I answer questions that will give you peace of mind? If you must live, I want you to live a miserable life, wondering why I tried to destroy your life."

I scream so loudly that my words echo off the walls surrounding us. "Whyyyy?"

It's obvious that there is nothing but hatred between this asshole and me. It wasn't always like this, though. It's like one day, something snapped inside of him and he thought it would be fun to try and wreck my life.

"You were my fucking friend, Byron. My attorney. My business partner. What the fuck happened to make you do a complete one-eighty. To go as far as kidnapping me, killing Peter, and trying to take over my men, my money, and my company. Not to mention, the woman I love. It's like you wanted to be me."

Byron pushes his hands against my leg, trying to get me off him, but it only makes me push down more. Putting my full weight on him, I guarantee he's not going anywhere. "Answer me, dammit!"

He inhales a deep breath, as deep as he can with the little

air that can get through, and he stares back at me. "Because it should have been me." His voice is tranquil with little to no fight in him.

"It should have all been mine."

"You really are a delusional motherfucker." I'm not sure why my father's attorney—one who helped change his will, stating that I was the sole beneficiary—thinks he should have gotten everything I have.

Byron groans, squirms, and finally gives up again. "You call it delusional and I call it the truth."

Getting bored with this conversation, I'm ready to get it over with. "All right. I'll bite. Why should it all have been yours?"

"Lift your fucking leg off my chest, so I can breathe, and maybe I'll tell you."

"Ah. There it is. You just want me to move, so you can try and overpower me. Not happening. Now, if you've got nothing left to say..." I pull my knife out of the holder clipped to my pocket and flip the blade open. "Let's get this over with."

Byron's eyes shoot wide open. It seems I've got his attention now. He had to know how this would end. Bella and I will never be free until he's done. He'll never stop.

I press the tip of the blade to his throat, and he sucks in a breath, trying to escape what's inevitably coming. "Wai... wait. Okay. I'll tell ya."

"You've got ten seconds. Nine...eight...seven..."

"Because I'm Vincent's son!"

This time, I laugh. He's really pulling out all the stops. I press the knife deeper, piercing his skin and drawing blood that trickles down his neck.

"It's true. That love child I told you about, it was me. He wasn't planning to leave everything to a son he'd had out of wedlock. His beneficiary on the will was some distant cousin of Delilah's, before we changed it. He barely even knew the kid. He just wanted to be a dick and leave us nothing."

I don't believe a word he says. Why the hell should I? Byron has proven to be a loose cannon. "So that's your lie. That's the story you're going to tell me to try and escape death." I breathe out a laugh, though it's empty of humor. "You're gonna have to try harder."

"I swear to you, Callum. It's the truth. Believe me or not, but I am Vincent's son." My leg lifts a tad, giving him a little more breathing room. He takes advantage of the extra breath in his lungs and keeps on with his story. "Vincent had an affair with my mom. It wasn't until I was going through some of my mom's things, when she passed away, that I found out who my dad was. A DNA test confirmed it. I was only eighteen years old, never had much of anything, not to mention a backbone. I cowered to the man. He asked me to keep his secret and promised to be part of my life, while helping me financially. He put me through law school and eventually hired me. It was all for show, though. He didn't give a damn about me. He just didn't want his wife to know, so I went along with it and milked him for everything he'd give me."

I'm trying really hard not to buy into this story, but his details are astounding. Even if it were true, there are still some things that don't add up. "Why not just change his entire will over to you. Why use me as a middleman and allow me to have all the control?"

"Undue influence. As the attorney in charge of his estate, it was impossible."

"Impossible and illegal are two different things, and I don't think you care much about the latter. Besides, you were the executor of my will and you were fully prepared to have me killed so you could take it all."

"I knew you'd be a pain in the ass. Eventually, you would

have looked into it all and I'd be investigated. It was a risk I wasn't willing to take. You were the last person alive who had any interest in his money. So, the easiest thing for me to do was get rid of the one thing standing in my way. It was a solid plan—until she fucked it up."

There's a good possibility he's telling me the truth, but it doesn't change anything. "Well, old friend, I guess we'll never know how things could have panned out, had you told me the truth from the start. Instead, the empire is mine, the kingdom is still standing," I lean forward and whisper into his ear, hoping to hit a nerve, "and I got the girl."

When he begins trying to fight me off again, the blade returns to his throat, and he settles back down.

"I didn't want that washed-up bitch anyways. She's a headache and a pain in the ass."

That she is. All the more reason I love her.

"I just wanted to see your face when I told you I took everything from you. I wanted to look you in the eye and see that pain before I killed you."

"Well, it looks like the roles have reversed." I press the blade deep into his neck and drag it across, slitting it wide open.

There was nothing left for me to say and nothing he could do to prevent what was coming. He double-crossed me, and for that, I could never let him live.

I drop the knife to the floor and climb to my feet. Once I've scrubbed the mess from my hands in the kitchen sink, I go into the hall and call in the men to get him out of here.

It's finally over.

CHAPTER TWENTY-SIX

Bella

IT'S BEEN ALMOST a week since Byron died. I've talked to my parents, who are hell-bent on me coming home and leaving this life behind me. I tried to make them understand, but I don't think they ever will. My life is with Cal now.

After staying in a separate hotel, one not connected with the Ellis name, Cal is taking me on a little trip. He won't tell me where we're going or for how long, so I'm just sitting back and enjoying the ride, or flight, rather. He's assured me we'll be there within the hour, which leads me to believe we're going back to the place where it all began. It's the one little hint he dropped that sort of spoiled the surprise.

I'd love to return to Cori Cove. It's become one of my favorite places. It might have a lot of bad memories, but it's got some pretty great ones, too. Regardless, I'm happy to go anywhere with Cal, as long as we're together.

He squeezes my leg, winking at me and sending a swarm of butterflies through my stomach. He's on the phone, talking business, and his serious voice is sexy as hell. What's even more sexy is when he drops the tough guy facade and shares a glimpse of his humanity with me. It makes me feel pretty special—knowing that everyone else gets his ruthlessness and I get the sweet stuff.

"All right, Anders, I'll be unavailable for the next thirty-six hours, so if you need anything, it'll have to wait." Cal looks at me again, biting his bottom lip as his hand slides up my thigh.

I put mine over it, pushing it up farther and curling his fingers with my own until they're pressing against my sex.

"Yeah. Yeah. Yeah. Gotta go." Cal ends the call and sets it on the rooted round table in front of us. He hums, leaning into my space and tickling my neck with his breath, causing the tiny hairs on my arms to stand up.

Cal's mouth finds mine and he pulls me in by placing a hand on the back of my head while his other rubs my crotch through my leggings.

There is nothing gentle about the way his lips devour mine. It's unruly and fervent. Raw and profound. My hand wraps around his head, weaving through his hair that's in desperate need of a cut. I get a firm grip, shoving his face closer to mine, feeling as if I can't get enough of him. I rest my other hand on his cheek, fingers grazing his short stubble.

We tear into each other like wild animals, not giving a care that the members in the cockpit could see us. Cal lifts up my shirt, our mouths parting momentarily, and I miss his taste already. They reunite as his hand sweeps around my back and unclasps my bra.

"I want you, Cal." I hum into his mouth, sharing his breaths.

My bra drops to my waist, exposing my breasts. My back arches, legs spread wider to give him better access. "Now," I beg in desperation.

Pulling out of the kiss, he looks lustfully at my breasts. "You've always been such an impatient little thing."

It's true. Patience is not my strong suit. And right now, it's downright torturous.

I reach over and grab his cock through his pants, giving him a taste of his own medicine as I rub my hand up and down his length. "That's because you like toying with me."

"Hmm. Seems you're picking up on that. I might need to up my game."

I squeeze him harder, smirking against his lips. "Bring it on."

My need for him to do something, anything, is agonizing. My insides are practically quivering. I'm not above begging at this point. "Please, baby."

It seems my pleas are working. Cal grabs my waist in a viselike grip and pulls me on his lap effortlessly, as if I'm as light as a feather in his hands.

My legs straddle his lap and his hand drags down my leggings, finding my want for him pooling in my panties. "You probably should've taken these off." He hints at my leggings, knowing I'm about to soak them.

I look over his head at the front of the plane. It's a small jet and there's only three seats and a curtain separating us from the cockpit.

The old me would never. The new me says *screw it.*

I lift up and let Cal strip me out of my clothes. Once I'm fully undressed, I tap my chin with my index finger. "Your turn."

He wastes no time ridding himself of his pants and boxers, letting them drape around his ankles. His cock springs free and my eyes land on his smooth pink head. Legs spread, balls resting against the seat while the tiny black hairs on his legs stand tall. He strokes himself a few times, giving me a show. "You want this?"

My tongue sweeps across my lips as I slouch down

between his legs and take the shallow end of him in my mouth.

He rubs my head like I'm a pet. "That's my good girl."

I take more of him, feeling his head hit the back of my throat while I swirl my tongue around the bulging veins of his length.

An airy moan escapes him and it's an assurance that what I'm doing feels good. It's a satisfying feeling, knowing I'm the one bringing him this pleasure. That I'm able to make my man feel good.

Cal taps my shoulder. "Come here, baby," he says in a raspy voice.

I peer up at him with questioning eyes, wondering why he wants me to stop. "I wanna come with you." His voice is a low growl, one that sends waves of shivers down my spine. "On my lap. Now."

Pushing myself up, I climb on his lap, knees locked on either side of his torso. Fortunately, the seats on this private jet are good-sized or this wouldn't work so well.

Cal leans forward, cupping my left breast, massaging as he sucks my nipple into his mouth, and my stomach pools with hot desire. His lips glide upward, hitting my neck, and I tilt my head instinctively, savoring the tingling sensation that rides down my body from his touch.

His warm fingers sweep across my lower abdomen, and when he begins pressing them against my sensitive nub, I raise my hips to give him better access. Bridging my back, I roll into his touch. Electricity ripples through. I need more, my body aches for him.

Cal pushes his fingers inside me, and I begin riding his hand. I cry out in pleasure, not caring who might hear us. These men are on Cal's payroll; I'm sure what they're hearing is expected from a man of Cal's stature.

Curling his fingers, he presses deeper, hitting the spot that has me screaming. Our mouths collide, masking my whimpers, and I kiss him hard. So hard my lips swell and bruise and bust, metallic liquid seeping onto my tongue as I share the taste with Cal. "Ugh. Fuck me, Cal." I want him so damn bad. I also don't want him to stop what he's doing. I shut off all thoughts, falling into his touch and the way his fingers work their magic on my pussy. My man makes me feel so fucking good.

Moving faster, he digs his fingers in so deep that I'm on the brink of explosion. I clench my walls, squeezing him, as I reach the height of my orgasm.

"Did that feel good, baby?"

I lock my lips, grinning. "Mmhmm." Just as I kiss his mouth, Cal shoves his cock inside me. Filling me and gliding me up and down with his hands gripping my waist.

"That's right. Fuck me like you love me."

I moan in a high-pitched voice. "I do love you."

"Tell me you love fucking me."

I feed him the words he wants to hear, giving him the truth. "I love fucking you."

A raspy groan climbs up his throat as he meets me thrust for thrust. His hands move from my hips to my breasts, squeezing and using them as friction as he pounds me from the bottom.

My head rolls back, eyes closed, while I grip his shoulders and bounce on his cock.

"Fuck, Bella. You're so damn sexy." Soft lips find my collarbone, peppering kisses all the way up to my ear. He sucks my earlobe in his mouth, teeth grazing the sensitive skin, and I whimper in delight. Chills shimmy down my body as I chase my second orgasm of the night.

"I'm gonna come," I cry out. My mouth falls open, and I don't even recognize the sounds that escape me.

"Come for me, baby. Soak my cock."

And I do. I completely come undone, and he fills me up at the same time.

Our motions slow until we're completely still. My head rests on Cal's shoulder while we both steady our breathing.

We stay there quietly, holding one another for a few minutes before I finally climb off him. Proof of our orgasms spill down my legs. "I need to clean up before I get dressed."

"No one can see you. Just carry your clothes to the bathroom."

I'm hesitant to walk through this jet nude, but it's not like I didn't just ride my boyfriend completely naked, while I'm sure everyone in the cockpit was listening.

I really don't want to soil my clothes with our bodily fluids, so I ball them up in my arms and walk hurriedly to the lavatory. As I reach the door, the pilot announces that we're preparing to land. I clean up quickly, wiping myself down and washing my hands before getting dressed and heading back to the seat next to Cal to buckle my seat belt.

"I'm anxious to see where we're going," I tell Cal as I snap the buckle. He's already cleaned up and dressed with no evidence of our rendezvous.

His hand rests on my leg, and he smiles. "Don't get too excited. You might not like this place as much as I do."

"As long as I'm with you, I'll go anywhere you take me." I rest my head on his shoulder, closing my eyes as the wheels touch down on the runway. I could peek out the window and try to make a guess, but I'll let him keep his surprise a little longer.

We're told we can exit the jet, and Cal takes my hand as I walk behind him down the aisle. He thanks the pilot, and we walk down the steep staircase out into the fresh, night air. There's a running car not far away with its lights on. All the cars that we get in and out of are the same—sleek and black.

I can tell just by the moisture in the air that we're near

water. It's crisp, clean, and cold. There's snow on the ground, but only a light dusting.

I know exactly where we are.

Squeezing Cal's hand with both of mine, I nuzzle against him as we walk to the car. "We came back."

He looks down at me, a glint of a smile along with a sliver of disappointment. "You know?"

I shrug my shoulders. "I can feel it. We're going back to Cori Cove, aren't we?" I squeal a little bit, excited to return to the place where we fell in love.

Cal stops walking, reading my expression. "Are you okay with that? I know there are some bad memories there."

On my tiptoes, I kiss his cheek. "I'm more than okay with that. The good memories override the bad ones. I fell in love with that castle the moment I fell in love with you."

THERE'S STILL daylight left when our boat arrives at Cori Cove. We took the small charter over, so we could haul all our luggage. We're only staying for a weekend, but it looks like I packed for the rest of winter.

Cal steps off first, offers me his hand, and ushers me down the dock. I look up at the stone structure and smile. So many memories hit me at once, but I only let the good ones infiltrate my thoughts. Like my conversation with Peter on the turret when he told me about the love of his life, Carolina. How this castle was special to them both. It's ironic that his life was taken at such a monumental place. My heart should ache for the loss of him, but it actually squeezes when I think about him and his Carolina being reunited.

As we walk toward the main entrance, I think of seeing Cal for the first time in his study. I knew there was something familiar about him, but I didn't put my finger on it until he spoke of my eyes. "Your eyes. They once spoke to me. I could read your thoughts with just a look," he said. The weeks that followed were brutal. I felt like a prisoner by a stranger and I mourned the loss of my friend. Slowly, I started to see fragments of the boy I once knew. Before long, he held the key to my heart. Now, I can't imagine life without him.

I look over at him and he catches my stare. Squeezing my hand, the corner of his lip lifts. "What?"

I smile back at him. "Nothing. Just thinking."

"About?"

"Us. Our past. Our future."

"Oh yeah? What do you see in the future?"

My lips press together, biting back a smile before I finally say, "you."

We walk hand in hand through the main doors and I'm stunned when we step inside. "Wow, Cal. Who did this?"

The patched-up hole in the ceiling that once leaked is now unrecognizable. The cement floor is now a sleek gray that's so glossy it looks like marble. A large chandelier hangs overhead from the finished ceiling, and the doors that were put up on the back wall are now gone. I'm grateful for that. I didn't like those doors. There's something comforting about the opening to the back yard. But, Cal didn't know I felt that way.

Ignoring Jeffery, who is carting our luggage to the elevator, I glance up, down, and around the entire space. "How did you have time to do all this?"

"Time isn't an issue when you have money. I made some orders and told them to finish by the time we arrived."

It's perfect. Everything I would have done if I had designed it myself. "This is why you wanted to stay in a hotel for a week. You were having the entrance renovated."

"Maybe," he raises a shoulder, smirking in delight, "or maybe I had it all renovated."

"You didn't?" My eyes widen, excitement taking over. "The guest rooms? The design ideas I had?"

"No," he deadpans, crushing my spirits.

My shoulders go slack. "Oh."

"Not at this place, anyways. Your designs are great and they'll be used, but this one's just for us." He pulls me toward the elevator. "Come on. I'll show you."

Just for us. I'm okay with that. "Wait," I say, stopping him before he presses the elevator button. "Does that mean—"

"This is our home. Yes. That's exactly what it means."

"Ahh," I squeal, clapping my hands together before throwing myself into his arms. "We're going to live here?" I pull back, looking up at him. "You're serious? You better be serious."

"Would I lie to you?" He stops me before I can speak. "Don't answer that. Would I lie to you...again?"

Cal has lied to me. The job I was supposed to have when I came here the first time and countless other white lies. It didn't ruin my trust in him, though. Not once I broke through those barriers he put up. "No, you wouldn't."

He stands there, staring at me. "Hey, what's wrong?" I give his hand a squeeze. It's not the fact that he's staring at me that has me perplexed. It's the look in his eyes. They're almost...sad. As if he just had a self-realization—a moment of truth. My heart twinges at the realness in him that I've been seeing more often. Like he's ripping off old Band-Aids and letting emotion spill from his scars.

"Nothing. I just...thank you." His forehead crinkles and I place a hand on his cheek.

"For what?"

He doesn't shy away. Doesn't look down at his feet or brush this away because vulnerability is a weakness to him.

Instead, his brown eyes bore into mine. "Not giving up on me. For staying and not leaving. For just...being you."

I can't explain what my heart does next. It's a feeling so new and raw and stronger than any sensation I've ever felt. To the point that tears prick at the corners of my eyes. "You never have to thank me for loving you. It comes naturally and it's infinite. You are worthy of love and I'm not going anywhere."

"*We* are worthy of love."

Those words speak a thousand volumes. Born into madness, passed around like we were bags of old toys, surviving the loneliness. Yet, somehow, we found our way back to one another.

We are worthy of love.

I press my lips to his in a soft, subtle kiss. One that I can feel in my bones. "I love you so much."

"I love you more," Cal breathes into my mouth. "Now, let's get on that elevator, so I can show you the rest of your home." He smacks a hand to my ass and I yelp before jumping back and tapping the elevator button.

As the doors open, Jeffery steps off the elevator, and Cal and I both thank him before he leaves.

I'm so anxious to see what he's done with the place. I wonder if my room is the same. Or if I have a room. We didn't talk about the living arrangements, but I'd assume we'd probably share a room now. Or maybe Cal wants his own space, which is understandable...for now. I mean, eventually, when we get married, we'll share a bed, but we're not even officially engaged yet.

My hand hovers on the panel, waiting to hit the button. "Which floor first?"

"Lucky number eight."

"Eight it is." I tap the button and curl up to his side, wrapping my arms around him. "So, what do we do now? We have this entire island to ourselves."

"Now," he kisses my head. "We relax like we're on a honeymoon. I don't know about you, but I've had a stressful couple months and I could use a little R and R."

"You," I chuckle. "Relax? I don't see it happening."

"Oh, it's happening. No business, only pleasure for the next couple days." He snatches me up, hands gripping my ass. "You've got me all to yourself. So, tell me what you like. Chick flicks? Walks along the waterfront?"

"Foot massages," I blurt out. "Yep, I love foot massages while watching chick flicks."

He scoffs teasingly, reaching into his pocket and pulling out his phone. "Oh damn, looks like I do have work to do."

I grab his phone from his hand and stuff it in the pocket of my zip-up hoodie. "Nope. A promise is a promise."

"Never promised," he teases again.

"Ohhh, but you never lie to me."

"I did say that, didn't I? All right. I guess I'll rub those things."

I stretch up on my tiptoes and lay a gentle kiss on his lips. "I know you will."

The elevator stops on the eighth floor, and we get out. Our luggage is all placed on the floor, right in front of Cal's room. Hand in hand, we walk down the hall and I ask the question burning on my mind. "So, I assume I'll be in my old room."

Cal stops unlocking his door, jerks his head around, and gives me the stink eye. "What? No. You're in my room, baby. Or should I say, *our* room."

I smile inwardly, biting my bottom lip. "Okay."

Guess I got my answer.

CHAPTER TWENTY-SEVEN

We're finally settling back into life. Bella seems to be happy we're back on the island. I'm thrilled to be with her, no matter where we are. For the first time…ever, I think I'm finally getting the happiness I so desperately wanted all my life.

I watched her sleep for a good thirty minutes before peeling myself away to go down to the dining hall. Everything has to be perfect and the only way to ensure it is, is by doing everything myself. Well, almost everything. Some of the staff returned last night. I've hired more live-in guards for the time being. Byron had a lot of enemies, but I'm sure somewhere out there he had a friend or family member who would want to avenge his death. Or not. I just can't be too sure. My personal chef has returned, as well as the housekeeper. Peter's position has yet to be replaced, and I'm not sure I'm ready for that.

For breakfast, we're having Bella's favorite—blueberry pancakes, greasy bacon that she loves so much, and lemonade.

I've got some instrumental music playing through the

speakers that are perched in every corner of the room. Four vases holding white roses are placed up and down the length of the dining room table. Then, there's the box. It's safely placed under the lid of a platter.

I rub my sweaty hands together, making sure everything is in place. I suppose there isn't much that could be out of place, considering it's just a breakfast setup.

Albert, the chef, is in control of the music, and he's been instructed to begin a special song at exactly eight o'clock. I glance down at my wristwatch. It's seven-fifteen now, which means I need to get Bella up and get her fed before it begins.

Leaving the dining room, I run my hands down my pants. Didn't think I'd be this nervous. She's already agreed to marry me. She was under pressure then, though, since I had coerced her with a contract. Agreeing and wanting are two different things.

There's no doubt in my mind that Bella loves me. I'm not just some egotistical man with a big head—I can feel it. The connection we share is extraordinary.

Once I'm in the bedroom, I close the door and walk over to the bed where she's still sleeping. Only, she's not there. Panic ensues. It's a feeling of dread I've experienced with this girl one too many times. Seems like every time I turn around, she goes missing. "Bella," I shout, looking around the room. "Bella. This isn't funny."

"Good morning," she finally says, stepping out of the bathroom with a toothbrush in her mouth.

I immediately grab my chest in relief. "Don't ever do that to me again." I cross the room and squeeze her waist.

She giggles and continues to brush her teeth, speaking with foam on her lips. "I'm sorry. You were gone, and I was ready to get up." Going back into the bathroom, she leans over the sink and spits, then rinses her mouth out before turning back to me. "You have to stop worrying so much." She pats a towel to her mouth and sets it back on the sink.

"Eventually I might. Right now, I'm still on high alert. It's only been a week. Be patient with me."

On her tiptoes, she presses her lips to mine, and I can taste the sweet mint from the toothpaste. "And you need to trust me. I think I've proven I can take care of myself, if worse comes to worst. Cherry and I did manage to restrain Byron."

"Oh, I know you're tough. But I also know you seek out trouble."

"Mr. Ellis," she smirks, "are you calling me a troublemaker?"

I grab her ass cheeks, peering down at her. "That's exactly what I'm calling you."

Her hands rest on my chest, and she kisses me again. "Then you'd be correct. And I'm about to show you just how much trouble I can cause." She begins walking me backward toward the bed. My body rushes with heat, wanting her so fucking bad right now, but I have to be the asshole who turns her down.

"Later, baby. Breakfast is waiting." I instantly regret the words. Fuck breakfast. All I wanna do is fuck her.

Her head twists, and she grins. "Wait. Are you seriously rejecting me to go eat breakfast?"

I exhale profoundly. "Yes." Dammit. I hate that I'm such a stickler when it comes to plans. I've got everything set and ready.

Bella takes a step back, still questioning me with squinted eyes. "Who are you and where is my dangerous boyfriend?"

"It'll be worth it. I promise." I take her hand and begin leading her out of the room, hoping she doesn't drag this out. As we're walking, I adjust my erection in my pants nonchalantly, but she takes notice.

"I'm glad to see it wasn't an issue of impotence."

I let out a roaring laugh. "You never have to worry about that. All I have to do is look at you and my dick twitches."

We make it to the dining room with twenty minutes to go. I pull out a chair for Bella, and she takes a seat, inhaling a deep breath as she lifts the lid on the pancakes. "Blueberry? My favorite!"

"Everything blueberry is your favorite."

"And lemonade? What's the special occasion?"

I take a seat right beside her, adjusting my napkin in my lap. "Didn't know we needed a special occasion to have lemonade."

"Well, usually it's orange juice. I'm just surprised." She takes a bite of bacon and points to the lidded platter holding the box, speaking as she chews. "What's that?"

She knows. Dammit, she fucking knows. I can't put anything past this girl. "Dessert. Just eat your breakfast, Sherlock."

I can't even look at her because I know she's observing me as I poke my fork around at my food, not even taking a bite. My appetite is nonexistent. My hands are shaking; my heart is racing. I need to just get this over with.

"Are you done?" I ask her, my eyes still on my plate.

"Cal," she chuckles, "what the hell is going on with you? I've never in my life seen you nervous, and you're acting like you're about to propose or something."

Yep. She knows.

"No." I finally take a bite, a big-ass bite that fills my entire mouth.

Bella drops it and continues eating. "What's the plan for the day?"

"I thought maybe we'd tour the castle. I could show you some of the finished rooms. Maybe have lunch in the courtyard."

"Sounds nice."

Why does it suddenly feel like we're a fifty-year-old married couple who has nothing to talk about? Is this what marriage will be like? What if she gets bored with me—with us? What if, suddenly, I'm not enough, and she wants more? She'll leave me eventually. I know she will.

Maybe this is a bad idea.

I'm not sure where all this self-doubt is coming from. *What am I thinking?* Bella has always been mine, and she always will be.

Bella sets her fork beside her plate, turns her entire body toward me, and places a hand on my lap. "Then maybe we could take a nice hot shower together." She waggles her eyebrows, and it's cute as hell, because she has a smear of syrup on her chin.

I set my fork down and run my thumb over it, then lick off the sweet maple. "I could use another shower."

"Maybe we could talk about some ideas I had for the clubs."

"You've really taken a liking to the clubs, haven't you?"

Her cheeks tinge pink. Also cute as hell.

"Don't be embarrassed." I chuckle. "I'm excited to hear your ideas because I seriously think we should just shut them down. I hope you're not expecting one here, though, because the only show you'll get at this castle is from me."

She leans in, the scent of pancakes and syrup spilling from her breath. "I only need you." Her lips press to mine.

Okay. I can do this. We're good. No matter what obstacles we face, we'll face them together. She's not going anywhere.

I lift the napkin from my lap and pat my mouth before dropping it on my plate. A glance at my watch tells me it's time.

My chair pushes out and I stand between *it* and the table.

Reaching over, I pull the platter toward us, without lifting the lid.

Bella sinks back in the chair, her hands resting on her stomach. "I'm so stuffed. I'm not sure I've got room for dessert."

My lip twitches with humor. Maybe she doesn't have any idea.

My entire body is trembling. Pretty sure my face is pale, too.

I turn toward Bella, still standing, and take both of her hands in mine. "Do you remember the day we made the pact, Bella?"

She nods, looking at me like I've lost my mind. "Of course I do. We were in the attic and you were upset about breaking the Beckhams' window with that baseball. Mark and Layla had just ratted you out and you thought for sure Mrs. Webster was going to send you away."

"That's exactly right. You told me, in no exact terms, soulmates come in different shapes and sizes. That best friends can be soulmates, even if they don't love each other."

Her lips tug up in a smile and my heart skips a beat. "That was before I knew what love even was."

"But you weren't wrong. You said we were soulmates and that nothing could tear us apart. I think we've proven that to be true. Bella," I drop to my knee, "you are my soulmate. You are my best friend."

"Cal?"

The music begins, soft, but audible. It's *Our Song*. The one Bella composed.

"Oh my gosh." She gets choked up. "This is our song."

"Let me finish," I press as she claps one hand over her mouth. "Against all odds we found our way back to each other. Through oceans and mountains. Downpours and blizzards. Our hearts cried for one another and we followed the sound. I can't promise it will be easy. But I can promise to smile with you when you want to cry, hold you when you want to run, and love you when you don't feel strong enough to love yourself. I can give you that same promise I made all those years ago—a promise to never part. Until kingdom come."

Tears fall from the corners of her eyes. Tears of happiness that clench my heart. Her hand drops, and I see the smile on her face.

"Will you marry me, Isabella Jenkins?"

She squeals, throwing herself into my arms, and shouts, "Yes! Hell yes, I will marry you."

I lift the lid on the platter and reveal an ivory box with gold-encrusted embroidery. Picking it up, I take her hand in mine, then flip the top. Inside is a custom-made, ten-carat ring. Engraved on the inside, it reads, *until kingdom come.*

Her eyes light up, and she gasps at the beauty of it. "Oh my God, Cal. It's exquisite."

I take her left hand and slide the ring on her finger. It fits perfectly. Just like us.

Bella looks from the ring to me with puffy eyes and a red nose. "I love you so much."

"I love you more."

AFTER BREAKFAST AND THE PROPOSAL, Bella and I decided that it was a good day to just lie in bed. It's exactly what we've done for the past week, but it doesn't matter. I could do this with her every day, and it would never get old.

I was an idiot for questioning things. What we have is solid and real. Bella is never going anywhere, and neither am I.

My phone buzzes on the nightstand, but I ignore it.

Bella lifts her head from my chest. "Should you get that?"

"Nah. If it's important, they'll leave a message."

It buzzes again, and again. And when it stops, it starts right back up.

I huff, leaning forward and reaching for it. "Unknown caller." I glance at Bella before finally accepting the call.

"This is Mr. Ellis." Bella lays her head back on my chest, fingers floating over my stomach.

"Yes, Mr. Ellis. This is Jim from Water Express Delivery. We've got a package for you from Gunders Cremation Services. We're docked at Cori Cove, but the guards won't let us up to deliver the package, and we need your signature."

"I'll be down shortly."

I end the call abruptly and go to get up. Bella lifts her head, tugging the sheet over her chest. "What is it?"

"Peter's remains are here."

My feet hit the ground, and I snatch my clothes off the floor.

"Do you want me to come with you?" Bella asks, still lying in bed, looking so inviting.

"No. You stay here where it's warm. I won't be long."

Ten minutes later, I'm at the dock, wearing nothing but a tee shirt, joggers, and a pair of boots as the snow falls from the sky.

I greet the delivery guy, and he hands me a rectangular box. "Sign here," he says, holding out an electronic keypad with a pen attached.

I scribble my name, thank him, and head back to the castle with Peter.

So many emotions take over as I make the trek. There is so much I want to say but talking to a box seems ridiculous, so I think the thoughts instead.

I never got to say goodbye. I never got to thank you for picking me up from The Webster House that day. You were there for me when no one else was. Cleaned my wounds when Vincent got out of control, adjusted the thermostat when he'd crank it up and try to roast me in my bedroom. You taught me how to ride a bike when I was fifteen years old, when Vincent took Delilah to a clinic out of state. I was embarrassed as hell that I was a teenager and didn't know how to ride one, but you never once judged me. And you never gave up when it took all day. You were a good friend. The father I wish I'd had. I won't let you down, Peter. Bella and I will live out the dreams you and Carolina had—right on this island. It'll be a home full of laughter.

Before I know it, I'm standing in the sitting room on the staff floor where Peter would often have his nighttime tea.

His chair is still there, weathered and used. It was his favorite chair. He didn't care what it looked like. Always said it was the comfort that mattered.

He was right. What we see is not always what we get.

I sit down on the chair and begin peeling away at the packaging tape on the box. Inside is a heavy-duty, wooden box. I pull it out, letting the shipping box fall to the floor. Holding it up, I read the engraving on the front.

Peter Blake
February 8, 1948 - December 8, 2021

"Happy Birthday, Peter."

CHAPTER TWENTY-EIGHT

STANDING in the doorway of the sitting room, I just watch him. It didn't take me long to find where he'd gone. When I rang the guard and he said Cal had picked up the delivery twenty minutes ago, I knew he just needed some time.

Ten minutes later, I checked the cameras.

Slow, soft steps lead me over to him. I wrap my arms around him from behind as he sits in Peter's chair. "Hey. You okay?"

He runs his fingers over the top of the box. "Yeah. Just wish I could've been there for him. I let him down."

His words are like a knife to my heart. "Babe, no." I round the chair, keeping one hand on his neck as I slouch beside him. "Don't think like that. There was nothing you could do."

"I should have acted faster when I knew what Byron was up to. I should've never left the island that day."

"You had business to tend to. Peter would never want you to blame yourself."

"There was no business."

I tilt my head. "What do you mean?"

"I said I had business to take care of on the note I left you, but I lied." He turns to look at me, and I can see the sorrow in his eyes. "I went to the main island to get you this. While I was at the jeweler's, I got a tip-off that Byron was rallying men for some big scheme he'd been planning that involved you. That's when I called Peter to get you out of here. I left the purchased ring with the jeweler, with plans to return and pick it up. As I was heading back to you, someone stuck a bag over my head and knocked me out. Anyways," he lifts my finger that has my engagement ring on it, "I knew this one was perfect for you."

I had no idea Cal was going to buy me a ring. Sure, I told him I'd marry him the night before that day, but at the time, it was all because he needed me to. "I can't believe you went and bought me this."

"It was never about the contract or my will. It was always because I loved you so much that I couldn't imagine spending another day without you."

My fingers graze his as the glow of the fire in the fireplace hits my ring, illuminating the ceiling with glimmering oracles. "Well, I have a confession, too. When I agreed to marry you, it was never because I thought you needed me to be your wife. It was because I *wanted* to be your wife."

Cal flashes a half of a smile as he still looks down at the box. I can tell he's pretty down on himself still.

"Peter would be so proud of how far you've come. Don't beat yourself up over what could have been."

He nods, though I don't really think he's accepting what I said. It'll take time, but lucky for both of us, we have all the time in the world.

"I decided on my new last name."

"Oh yeah? What's it gonna be? Stanford, Vanderbilt?"

"Blake. Callum Blake."

"I think it's absolutely perfect. Peter would be honored, and I'm honored to take the last name when we're married."

He looks at me then, light finally showing hope in his eyes and replacing the sadness I saw moments ago. "Bella Blake."

"I like the sound of that."

Cal doesn't have a middle name. He was never given one, and I'm not even sure how he got a last name to begin with. Obviously, Ellis was given to him when he was adopted, but he was never an Ellis—he's said so himself.

I'm glad he decided to take Peter's last name. It's one that he can be proud of.

"What about the company?" I ask, curious if he'll keep the Ellis name for the resorts. A cramp in my leg has me standing up, and Cal does the same, still holding the box.

"I was thinking, Blake Hotels and Resorts."

"Oh, wow. You've already figured it all out."

"It's got a nice ring to it, don't ya think?"

I wrap my arms around his neck, our noses brushing against one another. "I think it's a great name."

Cal presses a chaste kiss to my forehead. "All right, let's get back to bed. We're supposed to spend all day there."

I smile against his mouth, kissing him over and over again. "I like the way you think."

Cal sets the box down in the chair. "We'll leave him here for the night and find a good spot for him tomorrow."

"I think that's a good idea. He always liked this room."

I take Cal's hand and we head back to our room. It's obvious he's hurting and I wish there was something I could do or say to make him feel better; I just don't think there is. He needs time.

We get back to the bedroom and crawl into bed. My head rests on Cal's chest as he stares wide-eyed at the ceiling.

Before long, I'm drifting off to sleep.

CHAPTER TWENTY-NINE

Bella

I WOKE up before Cal for a change. He didn't sleep well last night. I felt him toss and turn for hours as we battled for the blanket. Each time he'd roll, he'd pull it off me. Each time I pulled it back, he rolled again. Finally, I took the whole damn thing and covered him with the flat sheet.

Sharing a bed will take some getting used to, but I'm sure that's the case for all newly-engaged couples.

I've already showered and have coffee in the room for us when it occurs to me that I should cook breakfast this morning. I love to cook, but I've never had the chance to cook for Cal.

I sneak out of the bedroom, closing the door gently behind me. I'm half tempted to go check out the other levels to see what changes are being made. We never did a tour last night, so I'm still not sure what his plan with all the extra space is. Cal wasn't feeling up to it and I honestly wasn't either.

Deciding against it, I go to the kitchen and find that the chef is not there, so I help myself. It's a large, commercial kitchen with anything you could ever need to make any food you want. I find a large refrigerator stocked full and decide on scrambled eggs and hash browns.

I get all the ingredients out on the counter and begin my search for utensils. A big kitchen is nice and all, but when I'm a mother and wife, I'd like to be able to cook for my family in a room that doesn't feel like I'm serving up a restaurant full of people.

My agitation gets the best of me when twenty minutes have passed, and I can't find anything I'm looking for.

That's it. We need a smaller kitchen. Cal will argue and say I don't need to cook and that we have people to do it for us. Same with the housekeeper. He'll insist that she can do all the cleaning and I never need to lift a finger. I wasn't raised that way, though, and Cal wasn't either. We know hard work and we also know that it pays off. I don't want someone else taking care of my family and I'll certainly never hire a full-time nanny to watch them while I do absolutely nothing. An occasional sitter, fine. We all need a break, but my dreams of being a mom and wife include doing all the things that moms and wives do.

I'm pulling out pans, dropping them to the floor with a thud and making an obscene amount of noise, when I hear laughter from behind me.

My head jerks around and I see Cal standing in the open doorway. "Good morning, beautiful," he says, arms crossed over his chest and humor on his lips.

I drop down on my ass, feeling defeated. "I wanted to cook you breakfast." I bury my face in my hands, on the brink of tears.

"Baby, we have a cook for that." He crouches down beside me and rubs a hand up and down my back. "I put in an order for omelets. Come to the dining room, it will be ready shortly."

"No, Cal," I raise my voice, not meaning to, but really

wanting to get my point across. "I wanted to cook for my fiancé. How can I, though, when this kitchen is the size of a house? I can't find anything."

"You really wanted to cook me breakfast?"

I look up at him, a serious expression on my face. "Yes. I want to do all of those things. But this place is...too...big."

"I thought you loved it here?"

"I do. As a vacation or even a place of work. But not as a home."

I'm being so selfish. My face drops back in my hands and I begin sobbing like a baby. "I'm sorry. I know you went through all the trouble to have these renovations done that you want to surprise me with, and here I am acting like a brat."

Cal laughs and the sound calms me slightly, knowing that he's not angry. "Stand up." He gets to his feet. I look at him, and he's holding out a hand. "I want to show you something."

I place my hand in his and he pulls me up. "What is it?" I ask, never being one to have an ounce of patience.

He leads me out of the kitchen and we begin down the hall. "I told you I had some changes done, but I never told you what they were."

"Well," I drawl, "what are they?"

"You'll see."

We end up in the elevator and back on the eighth floor, where our room is. Cal takes me down the hall, and we stop in front of the room I stayed in when I was here. "Ready?" he asks, wide-eyed and excited.

I nod, anxious to see what's behind the door. He pushes it open, and I look inside. "Cal," I gasp. "Are you serious right now?"

I'm no longer looking into my old room. I'm now looking at a baby nursery. Gray carpet, with white walls, a white crib with matching dressers, and even a rocking chair in front of the balcony doors. "This is..." I fall into his arms, ready to cry again, "I love it so much."

"I know we're a long ways away from having a baby, but I figured we could at least be prepared. The plan was for you to decorate however you want, but now, I'm thinking we need to talk about what exactly it is you want. I'm not so sure anymore."

Our hands clasp together, bodies level, and I look up at him. "I just want something...smaller."

"So you want to leave Cori Cove?"

"No!" I blurt out, "I don't want to leave here. I absolutely love this island. It's surrounded by beauty and I love the way I feel when I'm here."

"Okay, then it's settled. We'll build our own house, just the way we want, on the backside of the property."

My eyebrows hit my forehead. "Really?"

"Sure." He shrugs causally. "Why not?"

"And what will we do with this place?"

"What do you want to do with this place?"

I grin, biting my bottom lip. He knows what I want. "How about we stick to the original plan. Open it up to guests. We have our own home separate from the resort, and I can help out here when needed."

"As in, you can work at the club? No. Not a good idea. There'd be too many bodies to get rid of, and I just don't have the time for that."

I can't help but laugh. I know he thinks I'll get hit on left and right, and he'd have to take guys out, but I also think he's letting his mind wander to the worst-case scenarios.

"I don't want to work at the club. I want to manage the waitstaff and help the girls. I've actually been thinking about it and I have a plan."

Cal walks into the nursery and takes a seat in the rocking

chair. For a brief moment, I see it. Him holding a baby and being a daddy. It's a beautiful picture painted in my mind that will someday be a reality.

Cal blows out an exaggerated exhale. "All right, tell me this plan of yours."

I walk over and take a seat on the floor in front of him with my legs crossed. "First, I want to give them raises. Not much, but something to show they're appreciated. Second, we place a waitstaff manager at each location and they work with the staff on what hours they are able to work. No more eighty-hour work weeks. New work attire that they are comfortable wearing. The managers can check in with me weekly, and we can reevaluate things as needed."

"That's it?"

"I think so. For now, anyways."

"Done," Cal deadpans.

"Really?"

He leans forward in the chair, forearms resting on his legs. "Yeah. Welcome to the Blake Hotels and Resorts team."

I laugh. "You're serious? You're okay with me taking the lead with the waitstaff, without even knowing my credentials?"

"I'm serious. Whatever makes you happy, babe. I'm here to please." Cal pulls my hand until I'm on his lap in the chair. "Now, enough about work. Let's discuss our new home. If we open the resort, our private property will be gated. I'm thinking four or five bedrooms, three baths. And I happen to know an interior designer who will do a stellar job with the inside." He smirks, referring to me.

My eyes light up with excitement. "I get to design the inside?"

"Well, yeah. It's your house."

Part of me still feels guilty for changing all the plans we

made. "You're sure this is okay? We can sit on it for a while before jumping in."

"I don't sit on things. It's settled. We're building a house and opening the Cori Cove resort to the public." He bops my nose before kissing me softly.

My arms envelop his neck in a hug. "How did I get so lucky?"

"Luck has nothing to do with it. It was always fate."

CAL ENDED up bringing breakfast to bed. An entire tray of carbs—bagels, muffins, croissants, donuts. He's currently in the shower while I go over an employee list for all the clubs at each resort. I don't see Cherry's name anywhere on the list, and I assume it's because that's not her real name. After a bit of research, I find out that her legal name is Sara Hopkins.

I'm excited to start making the changes necessary to keep the waitstaff happy. I'm even more excited to start looking at designs and layouts for our new house. Cal insists that it will be move-in ready by summer, but unless he has round-the-clock workers, I don't see how that will happen. I'm leaving all the construction to him while I stick to countertops and paint colors.

On top of a new house and managing staff, I've also got a wedding to plan. Life is going to be busy as hell, but in the best way possible.

I take another bite of my blueberry muffin, dropping crumbs on the open folder on my lap. I sweep them away and chew my food, but my stomach begins to unsettle. Suddenly, blueberries don't taste so good. In a knee-jerk reaction, I shove the folder off me, the papers scattering on the bed. I jump up and haul ass to the bathroom. Cal is in the shower and steam fills the room. Ignoring him peeking out the side of the shower curtain, I drop to my knees in front of the toilet.

"Hey, what's wrong?" he asks, right before I throw up.

All of my breakfast comes out in one hurl.

"Shit, babe. You okay?"

I didn't even notice when he got out of the shower. He's standing behind me, dripping wet and rubbing my back while the shower still runs. "Maybe we should've stuck to omelets."

I smile through the nausea. "Maybe." Grabbing a hand towel off the vanity beside me, I wipe my mouth and clench it in my hand, still feeling like my stomach needs to be emptied even more.

I sit down on the bathroom floor, feeling the water from Cal's wet body soak through my pajama pants. "I'm okay," I finally say to him.

"I'll get you some water." He goes to leave, but I grab his ankle. "It's okay. I'm good. Promise."

I flush the toilet and get off the floor.

"All right. Why don't you get in the shower with me? It might make you feel better."

I nod. That sounds nice. "Let me brush my teeth real quick and I'll join you."

Sliding the curtain back open, Cal gets in the shower as I grab my toothbrush and slop on some toothpaste.

It's so strange. I felt awful, and now it's like I was never sick. It had to have been the muffin.

Peeling my clothes off, layer by layer drops to the floor. I poke my head in the opening of the shower curtain, watching Cal as he suds up his body. God, he's so sexy, and he's all mine.

Just watching him sends my body into a frenzy of need. Tingles shoot down my chest, going straight to my sex.

I went from vomiting to wanting to fuck in less than five minutes. My hormones must really be out of whack.

Hormones. That's what Cal said I was taking in place of birth control a couple months ago. I didn't even think of that. Maybe that's why I'm feeling so strange lately.

I jerk the curtain closed when the possibility of being pregnant hits me full force.

No. I can't be.

Sure, Cal and I spent an entire week at a hotel doing nothing but reacquainting ourselves with each other's bodies, but we've only just reunited. It's too soon.

Cal pops his head out, the black tips of his hair glistening from the water. He's got a little scruff on his face from not shaving for a few days and he looks hot as hell. "Are you coming or what?"

I pull open the curtain the rest of the way and get inside. Cal wastes no time pulling my body against his. "Feeling better?"

I look up at him, blinking away the drops of water coating my lashes. "Oddly, yes."

"Hmm. Hopefully it's not a stomach bug."

I could tell him that there's a possibility I'm pregnant, or, I can waive suspicion and take a test before I even mention anything. I'm sure I'm just overthinking this. I threw up one time and my period isn't even that late. I'm not even exactly sure what day I should have started, but I'm almost positive it was only a couple days.

Maybe I could call the pharmacy on the main island and order a test. I'm sure I could get Jeffery to deliver it. I'd just have to make sure he knows it's a secret. I'd have to use the word surprise to get him to oblige—no one wants to go against the infamous Mr. Ellis, by keeping secrets from him.

"Yeah," I say. "I hope not. The last thing I want to do is be bedridden with the flu, when we just got here."

Cal chuckles. "Well, we've basically bedridden ourselves for the last week and a half, so I'm not sure it would make much difference."

My hands rest on Cal's shoulders while his set on my waist. "That is true."

His face nuzzles into the crook of my neck, and he begins laying wet kisses down my collarbone. "Since you're feeling better..."

I bite my bottom lip, liking the way he thinks.

CHAPTER THIRTY

DROPS OF WATER pelt my skin as her hands glide up and down my arms. My mouth trails kisses down her neck, to her collarbone, then to her chest. My legs bend at the knee as I cup her breasts, sucking her pink bud in my mouth.

Bella takes my erect cock in her smooth hand, stroking it up and down as the water coats her hand.

I moan around her nipple. "See what you do to me, baby."

Both of her breasts fill my hands as I massage them. Thank God she's feeling better. I had every intention of fucking her once I got out of the shower, but now that she's here with me, I think I'll fuck her right here and now.

Unless… "You wanna get out of here? Have a little fun with Amara?" I know she hates the snakes, especially Amara, but there's something about making her squirm that turns me on. In fact, I think she likes the thrill as much as I do. I know Amara would never hurt her or I wouldn't dare bring her out.

"Not a chance." Her hand moves faster, sliding up and down my cock, thumb grazing my head before resuming to stroke my full length.

I'm so hungry for her. I want to devour every inch of her body. Kissing my way up her inner thigh while my tongue does laps around her clit.

Then I'll bend her over while her hands press to the wall of the shower, jerk her by the hair and fuck her from behind.

Fuck. I need her so badly.

But, first, I need to get my girl off.

My hand sweeps the crease of her leg beneath her knee, bending and lifting until her foot is sitting on the ledge of the shower. With her legs spread for me, I drop to my knees. Bella runs her fingers through my soaked hair, tugging and pulling before slamming my face into her cunt.

She's a feisty thing with zero patience when it comes to her desires. It's the innocent ones who harbor all the sexual fantasies. I plan to fulfill them all, one day at a time. If she wants me to fuck her in the club, behind a one-way glass, while she watches others go at it, I'll do it for her. I'm onto her fascination with voyeurism and I'm all for it if that's what she wants. As long as I'm the only one to touch her.

With two fingers spread against her sex, my tongue slides up and down between her folds. Stopping at her clit, I dart my tongue out in a rapid motion, and her body quivers, hands tugging tighter at my hair.

My cock twitches in delight as she cries out in pleasure.

I slide two fingers inside her, feeling the warmth and tightness of her pussy. I add in another finger, going knuckle-deep until I reach her G-spot.

Her legs spread wider as she rolls her hips, forcing my face against her. "Faster, Cal."

My fingers delve deeper, curling, and pressing, then pulling in a repetitive motion. I suck the water off her clit, grazing my teeth against her sensitive nub.

"Oh, God." She howls and rides my face like it's her own

personal toy. She can use me and she can abuse me. I don't care as long as it makes her feel good.

"Come for me, baby. Come around my fingers and let me taste your orgasm."

My words hit a nerve inside her. Her walls contract, cries become high-pitched, and her nails drag down the shower wall while her other hand pulls the hair on my head.

Wetness pools around her pussy and I sweep my tongue around her sex, licking her clean and tasting the sweetness of her orgasm.

When she releases my hair and drops her foot to the shower floor, I stand up, working the kink in my leg.

Bella begins stroking my cock again, lust-filled eyes locked on mine. I kiss her lips, sliding my tongue inside her mouth, giving her a taste of herself. "See how good you taste?"

Her response is a hum against my tongue. In a swift motion, I spin her around. Her hands hit the wall of the shower, and I lift her leg again, letting it rest on the ledge. My cock enters her pussy, like it's home and it knows exactly where to go.

Squeezing her hips, I fill her up from behind. Our bodies fit perfectly together, and I could stare at this ass all day. I slap a hand to her left cheek, pinching the skin and watching as it fills the gaps between my fingers. "All mine."

Bella moans, her hands sliding up and down the slippery shower wall. "This won't take long, baby."

I'm on the verge of combustion, so I slow down, letting the anticipation build. A second later, I'm fucking her again. Her brown hair rests against her back, and I sweep it to the side, pressing kisses on her spine.

"So fucking beautiful." She's like a dream I never want to wake up from.

My pace quickens, and I can't hold it anymore. My entire

body is zapped with electricity as I release inside her.

Bella drops her hands and straightens her back, and I slowly pull out. When she turns around, I embrace her and kiss her lips. "I could get used to these morning showers after breakfast."

She smiles against my mouth while our hearts beat rapidly against one another. "I think that can be arranged."

BELLA INSISTS she's feeling better, so she's been working hard on the changes to the clubs all day. I was able to make a few business phone calls and set up an appointment with a builder as well as get the process moving with my new attorney on getting my name changed. After speaking with my business advisor, we've decided to hold off on changing the company name until I'm officially Callum Blake. I told him in that case, I'd prefer to wait until after the wedding, so all the announcements can come at once.

I'm in my study, when I see Bella scurry past the open door and down the hall, I push my chair back, get up, then go out in the hall. "Babe, where ya going?"

Bella stops, turns around with her hands folded in front of her and a perplexed look on her face. I know that look. She's up to something. I quickly eat the space between us, meeting her at the elevator doors. My head tilts, examining her. "Why do you look like you're plotting a murder?"

She swats at me playfully. "You're crazy. Or paranoid. Maybe both."

"All three. But I know that look. Where are you running off to looking sexy as hell in that jumpsuit?"

It's true. She's drop-dead gorgeous in her all-black, long-sleeved jumpsuit with a pair of matching black flats on her feet.

"I had a package delivered from the main island." She holds up a hand, averting me from asking questions. "It's a surprise, so don't ask."

I zip my fingers across my lips. "I won't say a word. It's cold out there, though. Would you like me to have the guard bring it up?"

She shakes her head no. "My boots and coat are downstairs. I'll be fine." She kisses my lips, then taps the elevator button.

"Meet me in my study in twenty minutes and we'll go get lunch."

Her eyebrows waggle. "It's a date, Mr. Blake." Her smile widens. "I like the sound of that."

"I do, too, Mrs. Blake."

I wait until the elevator doors close before taking my phone out of my pocket and dialing Anders. "Hey. Bella is on her way down there to fetch a delivery. Keep an eye on things."

"You got it."

I end the call and put my phone back in my pocket as I walk back down the hall to my study. She's got something up her sleeve. Says it's a surprise, and I didn't have the nerve to tell her I hate surprises. They make me anxious, and I don't like that feeling.

Back in my study, I go over to the wall-sized window behind my desk and look out with my hands stuffed in my pants pockets. I can't see her from this view. I begin pacing the floor, thinking about what she could be up to.

A surprise that involved a delivery from the main island? Could be something for a new position with the company. Maybe something for the new house that isn't even in the first phase of building. Wouldn't surprise me if she's already purchasing decor. Sounds exactly like something she'd do.

I could always contact her bank and see where the purchase came from.

What the hell am I thinking? I can't do that. *Let the girl have her surprise, Cal.*

It seems I have some work to do on myself, if I plan on being a good husband. Old habits die hard and all that shit. Might take some time before I stop peering over her shoulder, out of fear that she's going to run off or get taken away from me. Baby steps. That's all I can do.

I sit down, then stand back up, opening then closing my laptop. I pace the length of the room three times and check the time twice. And now a third time. It's been twenty minutes, and she's still not here.

I grab my jacket off the hook by the door and go to leave when I meet Bella face to face. "Oh hey. I was just coming to look for you. You're late."

She cranes her neck, looking at me with a crease on her forehead. "Yeah, by two minutes." Her hands run down the sleeve of my jacket. "You really need to chill out."

I blow out a heavy breath through my nose. "I'm chill."

"Come on, you. Let's go eat." Her fingers intertwine with mine, and we head down to the yacht. It'll be nice to get out of here and get some fresh air. We've both been cooped up for a while. Cori Cove is the perfect location, but winters can be a real drag.

Once we're off the elevator on the ground level, I pry, trying to figure out what she's hiding. "Did you get your package?"

"Mmhmm."

I nod in response as we approach the main doors. "Was it in good condition? I mean, if there was any damage, I can make a call."

"Cal," she drawls with a giggle behind her audible breaths, "you're not going to let this go, are you?"

"Nope."

Bella releases my hand and scours the area. "Darn it! I think I left my boots upstairs."

There's at least a foot of snow out there and her feet will be icicles if she walks outside in those shoes. I step in front of her, slouch down, and say, "Hop on."

A second later, she's jumping on my back with her legs wrapped around my torso. "It feels like it's been forever since you've given me a piggyback ride."

"It has been. At least twelve years." I didn't do it often, but there were a few times I'd give Bella piggyback rides just for fun. One time, we had a piggyback race with some of the other kids in the house. We won, of course.

I step out the door and carry her through the snow, and once we're on the dock, I let her fall to her feet.

We walk hand in hand to the cabin of the yacht. A fire is lit in the electric fireplace, the table set with our hot meal already waiting in platters.

Bella shivers, so I grab a throw blanket from the closet next to the sofa and wrap it around her shoulders before pulling out her chair for her.

"This is perfect, Cal. You really do think of everything, even when it's just a simple lunch."

"It's all for you. I plan to spend our entire lives giving you everything you deserve."

She reaches for my hand over the table, her smooth fingers grazing my scarred knuckles. "You once told me that you wanted to buy me all the dresses in the world to prove they don't hold my beauty. And now it's my turn to tell you that all the objects in the world do not hold my love for you. I only want you, Cal. Rich. Poor. It's you and me, forever."

I'm not sure how I will ever convince myself that I'm worthy of this girl, but right now, I'm definitely not. I have so much to make up for.

Bella lets go of my hand and digs her hand down into the cup of her bra. I laugh at the expression on her face. "What are you doing?" She pulls something out and slides it across the table. "What is this?" I pick it up and...I'm speechless. I know exactly what this is. I might live a life of solitude, but I know what these two lines mean. "Seriously?"

"Looks like it's you, me, and a baby, forever."

I jump up so fast that my chair tips over as I round the table and embrace her. My mind is going a million miles a minute. *Is this real? Is she pranking me? We're having a baby? I'm going to be a dad? Fuck. I'm going to be a dad.*

I pull back and look at her, frozen in place. "When? How? Is this what you had delivered?"

Her head nods up and down. "I suspected it when I got sick this morning, then I remembered the fertility pills I took. My body has been out of whack, so I did a little research and the effects of those pills can last through a couple cycles. I didn't think it was true, but I ordered a test just to find out. And...well, it's true."

I'm stunned. Trying to put together the right words, but I've got nothing.

Bella looks longingly into my eyes and there's a sliver of worry. "You're not disappointed, are you?"

"What? Hell no, I'm not disappointed. We're having a baby, baby." I've never been more excited for anything in my entire life. This is what I've always wanted. Bella—a family with her.

Then it hits me. "We have to tell your parents, and they fucking hate me."

"Hey," she lays a hand on my cheek, "you and me."

She's right. It's us against the world, and Bella and this baby are my entire world.

My lips press to hers. "Forever and always."

"Until kingdom come."

CHAPTER THIRTY-ONE

FIVE MONTHS LATER

Bella

MOM IS SHUFFLING AROUND like a mad woman as we all pitch in and help set up for the Fourth of July picnic in the park. "You can just set that on the picnic table, sweetie," she says, referring to the large bowl of mixed fruit I'm holding. "Wrong table, Dave. Food goes on this one," she barks at Dad, who's carrying a plate of hot dogs.

Dad walks behind me to set the hot dogs down beside the fruit bowl. He leans close and whispers in my ear, "It's just a few hours. We can get through this if we stick together."

I laugh, knowing that we will get through it because we have every year since I joined this family. "It's all about team-work," I tell him.

I'm wiping down an empty picnic table when I catch Cal out of the corner of my eye. He's playing catch with Benji, Mark's new girlfriend's son. I smile at the sight. It won't be long, and he'll be playing catch with our little guy.

He glances in my direction, catching my stare. His back straightens, and he winks, right before the ball smacks him in the stomach. Cal curls over, exaggerating, while Benji laughs hysterically. "Did you see that, Mark. I hit that guy with the ball."

Mark looks over his shoulder at Benji, who now has the ball back. "Aww, I missed it, bud. Why don't ya do it again so I can see?"

I swat Mark with the rag in my hand. "Be nice."

"Hey, I'm here. He's here. No one's killed anyone yet. I think it's a good start."

Dropping the rag on the counter, I place a hand on my growing bump. "Please just try."

Mark throws his hands out. "This is me trying."

"Okay. Please try harder. You've both made some mistakes. Some much bigger than others. I've forgiven you for a lot of shit, now please just forgive him."

"Forgive him for almost getting us both killed through his game of manipulation? Or forgive him for luring you into his darkness and putting a ring on your finger while knocking you up, so you're stuck forever?"

"I'm not stuck, Mark. I've loved Cal since I was a little girl, and if you can't see that, then you can turn your head and pretend we don't exist, for all care."

Maybe it's my hormones, or maybe it's because I'm being rational for once. My parents and Cal have made amends, and they've agreed to welcome him into the family with loving arms. In fact, he and my dad are talking right now.

Shit. They're talking. I toss the rag at Mark and hurry over to them, hoping I'm not too late before one of them puts a foot in their mouth and a brawl begins at our annual family picnic.

I step beside Cal, listening in on the conversation.

"Stocks are predicted to skyrocket within the next couple months. Now's a good time to hit the ground running."

I breathe a sigh of relief. Just a boring conversation about stocks.

"Hey, hun," Dad says, poking a finger at my arm. "I see you managed to escape your crazed mom."

I look over and see her piling plates, napkins, and cutlery in Mark's arms. He glances in my direction and scowls. "Yeah. I think she's got help for the time being."

"Listen, you two," Dad begins while my pulse quickens. *Here we go.* "We're really happy for you guys. Cal, I know we got off to a rocky start, but I can see the way you look at my little girl. I trust that she's in good hands."

My heart doubles in size. "Thanks, Dad. I am in good hands. Cal's the love of my life."

Dad extends a hand to Cal. "Welcome to the family, Callum."

I look up at Cal, who is just standing there, staring at my dad's hand like it's contaminated. I give him a nudge, and he snaps out of his slumber, then finally shakes my dad's hand. "Thank you, sir."

"Well, I better go check in with the old ball and chain. I'll hear about it later if I don't."

Cal and I both laugh as my dad walks away. Once we're alone, I turn to face him and take both of his hands in mine. "You okay?"

He stares past me as if he's deep in thought, then finally says, "He welcomed me into your family."

I squeeze his hands and give him a reassuring look. "This *is* your family now, Cal."

"Ironic, isn't it? Thirteen years ago, we were preparing to get adopted into this family together, and now we're both part of it."

"It's not ironic." I kiss his lips. "It's fate."

We're interrupted when Mark joins our side. I take a step back, still holding Cal's hands. Mark needs to see that this is real. That I am marrying Cal and spending the rest of my life with him. Even if I have to shove our relationship down his throat, he will see that I choose Cal. Today, tomorrow, and forever.

Mark rubs his hands together, glancing back and forth from me to Cal. "All right. I'm not good with this shit, so here goes." He inhales deeply. "Bella, I know we haven't always been close, but you're my sister, and I love you. Cal, I know we have a rocky past and we both did some stupid shit, but I love my sister. Therefore, I'm willing to let bygones be bygones, if you're cool with that."

Well, damn. I didn't think he had it in him. I know Mark loves me and the reason he's been so cold toward Cal is because he wants to protect me. It's his own fucked-up way of being a good brother.

I look at Cal, who seems hesitant. But I'm hopeful he'll swallow his pride and put the past where it belongs.

When he drops my hand and offers it to Mark, I let out, yet another, sigh of relief. "Works for me."

Mark shakes his hand, then resumes helping Mom and Nina, his girlfriend, with the canopy.

It's a step in the right direction and I'm so grateful that Mark came over here. I know it wasn't easy for either of them.

"I'm proud of you," I tell Cal. He brushes it off like it's no big deal, but it is a big deal *to me*. Cal and Mark are actually a lot alike. Stubborn as hell, protective, and terrible baseball catchers.

"Anything for you, babe," he finally says, laying one on my lips. His hands cup my belly, fingers grazing gently, when I suddenly feel the baby kick. His eyes widen and he looks at me. "Tell me that wasn't just your breakfast from this morning."

I laugh. "That wasn't my breakfast. That was our baby boy. He must know Daddy is touching his mommy."

"Well," Cal nuzzles up to me, "he better get used to it because I plan on touching Mommy a lot."

I look down at my stomach. "You hear that, Jaxon Peter Blake, Daddy's making promises he better keep." I look back up at Cal. "Because I can't get enough of you, Mr. Blake."

His lips press to my forehead, holding their place. "Good. Because you've got me for the rest of your life, soon-to-be Mrs. Blake."

EPILOGUE

NINE MONTHS LATER

"HOLY SHIT. I didn't think it was possible to be this nervous." I'm talking to myself, adjusting my bow tie in the mirror of my bedroom. When you plan a wedding, you learn a lot about yourself. Like how many friends you *don't* have. Bella wanted to have a huge bridal party. Unfortunately, I'm a lone wolf, so I couldn't match her six bridesmaids. We settled on a maid of honor—she chose Cherry—and a best man—mine being Mark.

Mark and I aren't exactly friends, but when you lack relationships with other humans, it's damn near impossible to find someone to stand next to you on your big day. Doesn't matter anyways. I don't need anyone but Bella. It's been proven to me time and time again that friendships aren't all they're cracked out to be. Everyone I've encountered in life has betrayed me in one way or another—all except Bella. And Peter, but he's not with us any longer.

I'll stay in my bubble on my island. Occasionally venturing out for business or whisking Bella and Jaxon away on a family vacation. Then there's the obligatory family visits on holidays. I'll likely just drink my way through those, so I don't have to remember any of it.

Life is good.

Dave, Bella's dad, pokes his head in the open door. "They're ready for ya."

I take in a deep breath; one he must have heard because he's now walking toward me. "You all right, son?"

Son? I turn and look at him, a quizzical expression on my face. No one's ever called me that. Sure, I've been called a son of a bitch countless times, but no one's ever referred to me as *son.* I'm not really sure how to react to the title.

"Ugh. Yeah." I turn back to the mirror, fluffing the tips of my black hair. "I'm fine. Why do you ask?"

"Ya know, I remember the day I got married." I can see him in the reflection of the mirror standing behind me. He's gazing up at the ceiling, as if it's playing memories of his wedding day. "Best day of my life and the worst day of my life at the same time. If you think that's impossible," he looks down, a glint of humor in his words, "you're wrong."

I humor him as I continue to straighten my tie. "Oh yeah? How so?"

Dave places a hand on my shoulder; it's an odd feeling, and to be honest, it makes me feel uncomfortable. I'm not a fan of human touch unless it's coming from Bella. "You get to marry your best friend." He checks me with a smile. "But you also get her crazy family." My lips tug up in a smile as Dave continues, "Bella told me all about what happened before we adopted her and Mark. If you took Mark's place, well...then you probably wouldn't be marrying my daughter. Things always work out the way they're meant to." He pats my shoulder and leaves the room.

All these years, I've blamed Trent and Mark. So many nights of what-ifs and what-could-have-beens invaded my mind to the point of insanity. I spent my life plotting revenge against them, and Bella. I wanted to make them pay, while making her mine, whether she wanted me or not. Never once did I consider the outcome had I been adopted. She would have been my sister. Bella and I were never meant to be siblings; we were meant for so much more.

Chills skate down my entire body as the realization hits me—it has been fate all along.

"Ready, man?" Mark asks, poking his head in the door.

I really need to get used to other people being around. For a man who likes his privacy, it's definitely different.

I step away from the mirror, almost positive my tie is still crooked after messing with it for twenty damn minutes. "Yeah. All set."

"Wait until you see her. She's stunning."

My palms begin sweating profusely. Pretty sure this tie is trying to choke me. I loosen it a tad, then rub my hands together. "I'm sure she is." We leave the room and walk to the elevator.

I'm not good with words. Now I'm expected to stand in front of a crowd and speak from my heart, and I'm not so sure I can do it. If I had my way, we'd elope. No guests, just us. But Bella has always dreamed of a big wedding with a gown and family in attendance. We compromised on a small wedding with close friends and family in the courtyard here at Cori Cove.

"Hey. I'm not sure I ever told you…congrats, on the little man. Jaxon is adorable."

"Yeah. He's a keeper."

The day Jaxon was born was one of the best of my life. It'll be hard to beat, but today might be a close second. Bella decided on a home birth. It was just me, her, and the midwife. Everything was perfect and the minute I laid eyes on my baby boy, I couldn't imagine life without him. Bella did so good and I now have a new appreciation for women, particularly her. She's simply amazing.

We step into the elevator and the tension is thick as we make our way down. I should say something. Mark's been trying, and it's time I give a little on my end.

"I appreciate you standing up with me. I know we're not exactly friends."

"You're right, we're not." I can't tell if that's sarcasm or seriousness in his tone. "We're brothers now." He cracks a smile, and I do the same.

"Yeah. Yeah. I guess we are."

Walking out the back door, it's like my nerves have suddenly settled. It's a perfect day on the island. The sun is shining, it's not hot, but not cold. The flowers have bloomed, the trees have grown over. The entire area is decorated in white gardenias. The fountain is running and it's the only sound present, aside from the small chatter of guests. Bella wanted to invite all the staff. Aside from them, it's just her family. She reached out to Bibs, an old friend from The Webster House, but she wasn't able to attend. It's a shame; it would have been nice to see Bibs all grown up. We did make plans to meet up in the city someday soon.

I hear Jaxon fussing with Linda, his grandma, so I put my hands out to take him for a minute before the ceremony begins.

"I thought we talked about this, buddy. You can't fuss on Mama's big day." He looks up at me with a cheeky grin, his two bottom teeth sticking up. "Can I count on you today?" He giggles and I kiss his forehead. "I thought so."

I hand him back to Linda, and she begins bouncing him again as he fusses for me. "You better get up front. She's coming," Linda says.

I glance over my shoulder, thinking I'll catch a glimpse, but Bella is nowhere in sight.

Mark and I make our way to the front, where Cherry is standing in a mint green gown with a bouquet of white gardenias.

With my hand held in front of me, I steal a glance at Peter's urn on a stand next to a vase of flowers. I thought it was insane, but Bella insisted he be here.

I take a deep breath as the music begins. We decided on the traditional wedding march because Bella said that's what she'd imagined when she pictured her future wedding.

I'm staring straight ahead when she steps out of the back doors of the castle. I can't even explain what overcomes me when I see her. Like Mark said, she's stunning. It's possible my heart has stopped beating altogether.

She takes slow, graceful steps toward me. Walking into our future together.

Her green eyes are wide and beautiful and outlined with makeup. Her brown hair is all up in some fancy updo with a see-through lace veil hanging over her face. An all-white dress that hugs tight to her frame and flows out into a train at the bottom. It's simple, yet elegant. Floral embroidery covers the full length, and that top. Fuck, that top. It dips down in a V, exposing her full cleavage.

With one arm wrapped around Dave's, she clenches the bouquet that matches Cherry's, and I can tell she's a ball of nerves.

I need her to hurry and get to me, so I can calm her. I want to take her hands and squeeze them, letting her know I'm always here when she's nervous or scared.

Just a few more steps. She's almost here. My heart begins racing, ready to do this. To make her my wife and begin our lives together.

She's here. And she takes my breath away.

"Hi," she whispers. Cherry steps out and takes her

bouquet. I can't help but smile at her nervousness, it's cute as hell.

The officiant begins by asking, "Who gives this woman to be married today?"

"I do," Dave says before kissing Bella's cheek.

He steps back, then takes a seat in the front next to Linda, who is holding a bouncy Jaxon.

I reach out and take Bella's hand, walking her in front of the officiant. She's trembling, so I place my other hand overtop our clasped ones.

Our eyes lock as we seek stability in each other. My legs feel like they could give out at any moment.

The officiant rambles off some shit that I don't even hear as I'm lost in her eyes. It's not until she squeezes my hand and nods toward the officiant that I realize it's my turn to speak.

"As I said, the bride and groom have decided to write their own vows. You may begin, Callum."

Shit. I had it all memorized. Replayed it in my head a thousand times, and now I'm drawing a complete blank.

I stutter, choke, and nothing comes out.

Mark leans over and whispers, "Just speak from the heart, man"

Speak from the heart. Okay. I can do this.

"Bella," I begin, still not sure what I'm going to say, "you came into my life when I least expected you. I was sure that I was meant to spend all my years alone. I'm not talking about the day you arrived here at Cori Cove. I'm going way back to The Webster House." I glance over my shoulder to where Mark stands, though I don't catch sight of him. Then I return my eyes to my bride. "You were my best friend. On the days I didn't get to see you, because I was in trouble, I counted the hours until I could be near you again. When you left, you took a piece of my heart with you, but I always knew, deep down, that we'd be together again. Whether it was orchestrated or simply fate. Regardless, we found our way. You complete me, Bella. You are the beauty I see in the world, the light in the darkness. You are the air I breathe. I promise to spend my entire life showing you how much I love you."

Tears fall from the corners of her eyes, and I can feel the sting in my own as they threaten to break free. I swallow hard, feeling a lump in my throat. I'm not sure what it is, but it's an odd sensation.

"Bella, you may begin."

"I wrote everything down, but of course, I lost it. That's me. Always misplacing things and ending up in places I don't belong." *She's not lying.* "So I'm winging this and I hope I get it right." Her throat clears. "When I was a little girl, I used to dream of my wedding day. I envisioned everything I wanted. I watched myself walk down the aisle to marry the love of my life. I have a confession," she smiles, "it was you I saw. When I was a kid, I pictured fourteen-year-old Cal. When I was a teenager, I tried to imagine what you looked like, and it was still you. There is no one in the entire world I would rather have as my husband and the father to my children. You love me in a way that makes me feel worthy. The safety of your arms is my favorite place to be. I love you more than all the castles, islands, and empires, Cal. It was always you."

I pull her to my chest, not sure if it's allowed, but hell if I care. I make my own rules. Bella begins sobbing softly against me, and I just hold her through it, even though I know they're happy tears. My heart squeezes, and at the same time, Jaxon squeals. We both laugh and look over at him.

Bella extends her hands to her mom, asking for our son.

Linda gets up and brings him over and we finish the wedding with the three of us becoming one happy family.

"You may kiss the bride."

And I do. I lift her veil, and I kiss her beautiful lips, over and over and over again.

"I'm pleased to introduce to you, Mr. and Mrs. Callum Blake."

We raise our held hands while everyone claps.

I did it. I got the girl.

The end.

If you liked this duet, check out the Bastards of Boulder Cove Series!

A dark academy, secret society, why-choose!

ALSO BY RACHEL LEIGH

Bastards of Boulder Cove

Book One: Savage Games

Book Two: Vicious Lies

Book Three: Twisted Secrets

Wicked Boys of BCU (Coming March 2023)

Book One: We Will Reign

Book Two: You Will Bow

Book Three: They Will Fall

Redwood Rebels Series

Book One: Striker

Book Two: Heathen

Book Three: Vandal

Book Four: Reaper

Redwood High Series

Book One: Like Gravity

Book Two: Like You

Book Three: Like Hate

Fallen Kingdom Duet

His Hollow Heart & Her Broken Pieces

Black Heart Duet

Four & Five

Standalones

Guarded

Ruthless Rookie

Devil Heir

All The Little Things

Claim your FREE copy of Her Undoing!

ABOUT THE AUTHOR

Rachel Leigh is a USA Today bestselling author of new adult and contemporary romance with a twist. You can expect bad boys, strong heroines, and an HEA.

Rachel lives in leggings, overuses emojis, and survives on books and coffee. Writing is her passion. Her goal is to take readers on an adventure with her words, while showing them that even on the darkest days, love conquers all.

Join the fun in Rachel's Facebook Readers Group: Rachel's Ramblers

Made in the USA
Las Vegas, NV
23 August 2023